STRANGER THINGS HAVE HAPPENED

A Novel

Kasie West

SATURDAY BOOKS
NEW YORK

This is a work of fiction. All of the characters, organizations, and events portrayed in this novel are either products of the author's imagination or are used fictitiously.

First published in the United States by Saturday Books,
an imprint of St. Martin's Publishing Group

EU Representative: Macmillan Publishers Ireland Ltd, 1st Floor, The Liffey Trust Centre, 117–126 Sheriff Street Upper, Dublin 1, D01 YC43

www.saturdaybooks.com

Title page art: oranges © AnnaSivak/Getty Images

Library of Congress Cataloging-in-Publication Data

Names: West, Kasie author
Title: Stranger things have happened : a novel / Kasie West.
Description: First edition. | New York : Saturday Books, 2026.
Identifiers: LCCN 2025033963 | ISBN 9781250349163 trade paperback | ISBN 9781250349170 ebook
Subjects: LCGFT: Romance fiction | Novels | Fiction
Classification: LCC PS3623.E84478 S77 2026
LC record available at https://lccn.loc.gov/2025033963

First Edition: 2026

10 9 8 7 6 5 4 3 2 1

PRAISE FOR *WE MET LIKE THIS*

"West's adult debut is everything—vulnerable, spicy, funny, and squeal-out-loud romantic."

—*Kirkus Reviews* (starred review)

"YA author West's (*Better Than Revenge*) adult debut gives second-chance romance and opposites-attract tropes a new twist. This engaging, witty, unputdownable romance is a must for all collections." —*Library Journal* (starred review)

"YA author West makes her adult debut with an endearing rom-com about the pitfalls of modern dating . . . West has a gift for witty dialogue and successfully mines the horrors of dating app conversations for humor." —*Publishers Weekly*

"A fun and delightful romance from a beloved author."

—*Culturess*

"This smart, sexy read proves Kasie West and modern romance are a perfect match." —Emily Wibberley and Austin Siegemund-Broka, authors of *The Roughest Draft*

"*We Met Like This* is a delightful take on the world of dating apps that will have you rooting for the heartfelt characters from the first chapter." —Betty Cayouette, author of *Tell Me How You Really Feel* and creator of Betty's Book List

ALSO BY KASIE WEST

We Met Like This

To Michelle Wolfson, my agent, cheerleader, and friend

STRANGER THINGS HAVE HAPPENED

CHAPTER 1

"Are you breaking up with me?" My voice was laced with incredulity. Not anger or sadness or heartache. Just pure shock, disbelief. I stopped in the middle of the sidewalk and spun a full circle, sure I'd find him standing by his car with a wide smile on his face, ready to tell me it was just a joke.

Nate wasn't there. Instead, his voice in my ear said, "Yes, Sutton, I am."

"Over the phone? You couldn't drive here and say this to my face?" That sounded like a threat. I hadn't meant for it to, but he was supposed to be here. I hadn't seen him in two weeks. We were going to go on a date, relax, laugh. I needed to laugh. I had gotten us a hotel room, called in a caretaker for my mom.

"Now you're going to tell me how I'm allowed to break up with you?" Nate asked.

I bristled. "I'm not telling you how to break up with me. It's just common sense."

"You're more than four hours away. This had to be a phone call."

Apparently, I, and our two-year relationship, weren't worth a four-hour drive. "Was there anything else you wanted to say, or does a phone call five minutes before you were supposed to be here cover it?"

"I should've known this would be how you'd handle it."

"How's that?"

"Like you're conducting a business meeting, going over an agenda. Very lackluster."

My entire body tensed at the word he deliberately used. It was a quote from the food critic in the *Los Angeles Times* about my recently opened restaurant. I had the longer version memorized: *Good food, well run, but lackluster atmosphere and dining experience*. I feared that was as much a description of me as it was of my restaurant. Review of Sutton Scott by any boyfriend she had ever dated: *Good heart, organized, but boring as hell.* Lackluster in my restaurant was fixable. In myself, probably a lost cause.

But Nate was the one who was breaking up with me, so why did he have to deliver such a low blow? "Now who's the one trying to dictate how this should play out?" I asked.

"I never dictated anything in our relationship, Sutton."

"I guess that's why you're breaking up with me."

"I'm breaking up with you because I am number four in your life. After your business, after your mother who doesn't even want you there, after your apartment."

It was a nice apartment. I wasn't going to leave it to move into a bigger place with him after only two years. I had the best rent in the city *and* a brick fireplace.

"Are you really telling me you didn't see this coming?" he asked.

I really hadn't. Had I not been eleven months into opening

a restaurant with my best friend that I was now trying to help run from three hundred miles away. Had I not been taking care of my mother who, after a major car accident, had both a serious concussion and a shattered tibia but who still insisted she didn't want me here. Maybe then, I might have seen some signs. But I figured the distance between us was a result of our busy schedules . . . and the literal distance between us. It obviously wasn't.

A couple brushed by me on the sidewalk, hand in hand.

"Are we done here?" I asked.

"Done," he said, and without another word, the phone went dead.

I was twenty steps from the front door of the fancy steakhouse where we were supposed to meet, but my legs felt like rubber, standing there in my high heels. I had gone all out for him: put on a slinky black dress, slicked my long waves into a high pony, painted on lipstick, shaved everything . . . twice!

My eyes stung, but I bit the inside of my cheeks, not allowing any emotion to rise to the surface.

The closest door to me was a cowboy-themed bar. I didn't care about themes at the moment. I stepped inside, needing a drink. Fast.

A neon decoration of a man tipping his wide-brimmed hat over and over glowed on the far wall as I headed to the long bar. I took the closest empty seat, a low-backed barstool, beside two guys who seemed too preppy for the surroundings—both in pastel polos and too-tight jeans. The bartender, a woman wearing a leather vest and a studded belt, approached me right away. Maybe she sensed the urgency in my expression, or maybe nobody else needed her at the moment.

"You look like you should be next door" was how she greeted me, her eyes traveling over my attire.

"I should be," I said, but didn't elaborate.

"What can I get you?"

"Something strong," I said.

Her eyebrows popped up. She pulled a shot glass from beneath the counter and filled it with vodka. I downed it, cringing at the burn before nodding for another.

She obliged. "That bad, huh?"

"Not a great day."

"You're not from around here, are you?" she asked, filling my glass again.

"Actually," I said with an ironic laugh. "I grew up here. Five miles east. My mom still lives here. I came back . . ." I stopped myself. My mom didn't need her business spread around. She didn't need everyone to know she'd gotten in a serious accident two weeks ago that resulted in surgery, persistent concussion symptoms, and an unknown recovery time. Hell, maybe the whole town already knew. They probably did. And yet still, I finished with "To see her." I downed my second shot.

"Enjoy your visit," she said, raising the bottle to pour me another.

I held up my hand. "How about a beer? Do you have anything local?"

She nodded and left to fill that order.

"You said no then?" asked one of the preppy guys next to me. Not to me. To the other guy. They were both very attractive. The one closest to me in a boy-next-door way, with soft brown curls and a friendly demeanor. The other had thick, dark hair, perfectly clear olive skin, and full lips. He wasn't the boy next door. He was very . . . pretty. But in a villain sort of way.

"I said, why would I go to therapy if there's nothing wrong with me?" Maybe he wasn't as *boy next door* as he looked.

I almost snorted. That vodka was going to my head quicker than I anticipated. I probably should've eaten something first. I couldn't remember when or what I'd eaten today. A granola bar? Ten hours ago?

Maybe I did snort because Mr. I'm Perfect Therefore Don't Need Therapy gave me a sideways glance. I lowered my head, staring into my empty shot glass.

"Exactly," Villain Pretty Boy said.

"Let me guess, you're a pro therapy person," Mr. Perfect said.

It took me several beats to realize he was talking to me. Had I snorted again?

"What? Not my business," I said.

"No, please, you're obviously listening."

"I just think everyone can benefit from therapy is all."

He sighed. "You see, that's my problem. If you think *everyone* needs it, then it's not exactly a remedy for anything, is it?"

"I didn't say everyone *needed* it. I said everyone could benefit from it."

"That's how they get you. They create this narrative that the world would be better with therapy. It's a gimmick, a scam."

"Who is *they*?" I asked, turning on my barstool to face him more fully, just as the bartender slid a glass full of amber liquid in front of me, the white foam on top nearly sloshing over the edge.

"The therapists," he answered.

"Obviously," Villain Pretty Boy said. There was a teasing gleam in his eye, and I couldn't tell if it was because he was humoring his friend or because he, too, found the idea of therapy laughable.

"Who wants you to go to therapy?" I asked. "Your mom?"

This time Villain Pretty Boy outright laughed.

Mr. Perfect scowled. "No, my fiancée. Couples therapy, before we get married."

"And this is too hard of an ask for you?" I said, my voice full of sarcasm. If this guy couldn't accomplish this straightforward request, what other things would he attempt to avoid in their marriage? She needed to run. Or maybe that was my recent breakup speaking. I *was* feeling extra bitter right now.

"I could do it," he said. "Humor her. But the way a marriage starts is going to dictate the entirety of it."

"So you *do* get the point then," I said.

He tilted his head in confusion when, over his right shoulder, I saw a woman walking toward me, a smile on her face. Not just any woman—Tara McKinley, my best friend from high school. Like I'd mentioned to the bartender, I grew up here. And Tara and me were inseparable back then. She was pretty much my saving grace through a lot of shit. We'd both moved away after graduation and had kept in sporadic contact, but I hadn't talked to her in months.

"Oh my god," she said in both surprise and joy as she reached me. She was wearing jeans and a fitted graphic tee. Her blond hair was big and wavy. I stood and we came together in a hug. "You're here."

"*You're* here," I said.

"I moved back," she responded, still holding on to my arms as we talked.

"You did? When?"

"Like a year and a half ago."

"Really? I didn't realize." Okay, maybe it had been longer than a few months since I'd talked to her. I felt guilty that I didn't even know she had moved. That I was so wrapped up in my own things.

"I know. You've been busy with your restaurant, and I've been busy with the move and settling in. Sorry, I should've told you."

Great, now I felt doubly guilty. She'd kept up with my life in the last eighteen months. Probably saw all the online posts about the grand opening.

"No, I should've asked. I'm glad to see you."

"You too. Are you here for your mom?"

"You heard?" Of course she had. It was a pretty small town. There was probably a meal train started on Facebook.

"I did. Is she okay?"

"She will be."

Her eyes traveled over my face and outfit. "Have you been in Los Angeles so long you forgot how to dress for a Clovis bar?"

"Long story," I said. It really wasn't a long story. *My boyfriend dumped me five minutes ago.* It was actually quite a short story. Regardless, I didn't want to tell it.

"Sit down. We obviously have a lot to catch up on," I said, turning toward my empty stool and pointing to the one next to it. I had some making up to do after not talking to her for so long.

"I'm actually here with my fiancé." As if in slow motion, her hand reached out to Mr. Perfect. Behind him, Villain Pretty Boy had an openly smug smile on his face, seeming to enjoy the turn of events.

"Oh," I said. My stomach gave a flip-flop, the alcohol not sitting well.

"This is Michael," she said, her arm proudly around his shoulder.

"Right, good to meet you," I said.

"Confess," Michael said. "You planted her here." He nodded toward me.

"What do you mean?" Tara took the seat I'd previously occupied and patted the one next to her.

I really should've just left. My mood wasn't improving. Not even with the appearance of one of my favorite people. Why was I sitting down? Maybe because what waited for me at home was a grumpy mother, a caretaker I'd already paid the whole night for, and thoughts of how I'd been dumped in the coldest manner possible.

"She didn't plant me here," I said. "Our opinions about therapy are the right ones and therefore the same."

Tara let out a loud sigh. "This? Again? I thought we had this settled."

"We don't. I have people on my side too." He patted Villain Pretty Boy on the back.

"Your *brother*? Of course he's on your side," Tara said.

They were brothers? Not surprising.

"I made an appointment for Monday," she said.

"With the therapist you've already been seeing? No way, we need neutral ground."

"Why do you think this is going to be some sort of ambush? I haven't been complaining about you. She's just going to give us tools to start our marriage right."

"See. Scam," Michael said.

I took a sip of my beer, already forgetting my stomach was too empty to add another helping of alcohol. My head was starting to feel a little spinny.

"It's not a scam," Tara said. "Therapy has helped me so much. Going together will only bring us closer, help us learn how to fulfill our specific needs."

"Please," he said with a groan. "I bet two strangers could go to couples therapy and she'd give the same generic advice. She probably wouldn't even know they were strangers."

"Not true," Tara said.

I shook my head, silently backing her up. The bartender came over to check on us, and I asked, "Do you have peanuts?"

"Seems like you need popcorn," she replied under her breath, giving a quick nod toward Tara and her fiancé. With those words she left, without supplying either of the aforementioned snacks. I took another drink.

"How much you want to bet?" Michael asked.

"What?" Tara responded.

"Two strangers, a neutral therapist, couples therapy."

"Oh, wow," I said with a laugh. He was really getting creative in his avoidance. What ghosts did this man not want flying out of his closet?

"It's not a bad idea," Villain Pretty Boy agreed, giving me an eyebrow raise as if we were somehow enemies and he'd just won this round.

"It's a terrible idea," I said, fulfilling my side of the roles he'd put us in.

"What are the parameters of the bet?" Tara asked, seeming to give in to this completely inane suggestion.

"Four sessions?" Michael said. "If the therapist doesn't know they're strangers, or at the very least, not in a relationship, after four sessions, I win and therefore don't have to go to therapy."

"And if she figures it out?" Tara asked.

"Then we'll go, like you want."

She clapped her hands as if this wasn't the most unhinged idea on the planet. Like this was somehow romantic and chivalrous.

God bless the unsuspecting therapist who gets roped into this mess. Let her know in session one she's dealing with foolishness.

I chuckled at my internal thoughts. I was tipsy. I needed to stop drinking, I thought, as I took another gulp.

"Now we just need a couple of strangers." Tara's eyes swung to me just as her fiancé slapped Villain Pretty Boy on the back.

"Not it," he said.

"Leave me out of this," I concurred. Even newly minted enemies could agree once in a while.

"You both had pretty strong opinions. How about backing them up?" Michael said.

I laughed. "I have nothing to prove."

Tara's shoulders fell as though for a moment she had hope and now it was gone. Guilt wiggled in my chest, a memory from high school trying to take root there. I pushed it down.

"I'll pay for the sessions, of course," Michael said, leaning forward and looking around Tara to me. "Think of it as the therapy you believe in so much, but for free."

I shook my head. "Nope. I won't even be in town for four weeks." That was a lie. The fact that my mom could hardly sit up without becoming dizzy, could barely eat on her own right now, let alone drive herself to physical therapy and doctors' appointments, was an indicator that I'd be here at least four more weeks. Probably more.

"They know we're right," Villain Pretty Boy said. "We don't need proof."

Could two shots of vodka and a half . . . oh, a *full* glass of beer cause drunkenness? It was the only reason I could explain why that smug little gleam in Pretty Boy's eyes was getting to me, making me want to accept this bet and prove them both wrong in one session. Or maybe the reason I was hesitating was because of the look on Tara's face. The disappointment. It had been years since I'd seen that look, but I remembered it well. I hated letting her down again after how much she'd been there for me over the years.

And shit, with my breakup and my business and my mom, maybe free therapy *could* push off some of the anxiety I knew was building in my chest that I had been ignoring so well. Plus, would someone *lackluster* volunteer for something so out of the box?

"Fine," I said. "I'm in if you are." I unleashed a smug smile of my own on Villain Pretty Boy and watched his fall.

CHAPTER 2

I groaned as the sunlight shone red through my closed eyelids. I hadn't pulled the blackout curtains all the way shut the night before. Yes, I'd stayed in the hotel. It had been too late to cancel when Nate broke up with me. It was going to cost me the same whether I stayed in the room or not. And honestly, I needed the break, with or without Nate.

I squinted my eyes open, memories of the night before causing me to groan again. Had I agreed to go to therapy with a complete stranger? A smug one at that.

After I called his bluff, he'd shrugged, like he agreed to these things on most weekends, and said, "Care for a secondary bet? Between the two of us?"

"What did you have in mind?" I asked.

"If I'm right"—he gave me a once-over, like he could read me just by looking at me—"you have to . . ."

"Make her do karaoke or a poetry slam," Tara said. "She hates doing fun, embarrassing things in front of a crowd."

I whipped my head toward Tara and her betrayal. After

all, I'd agreed to this mostly for her. She gave me a sheepish smile and a shrug. I swallowed down my feelings, realizing she was probably hanging on to things from high school as well. Things I thought we'd put in the past.

"Not surprised you like to maintain all the control," he said, and hot anger poured through me.

"If I win, you have to shave your head, Pretty Boy," I snapped.

Michael let out a burst of laughter. "She has your number."

His eyes went to his empty glass. He looked inside as if he was studying the patterns in the dried foam along its sides. Then he met my eyes, held out his hand, and said, "Deal. By the way, I'm—"

"A stranger," I interrupted, not touching his outstretched hand. "We're supposed to be strangers. I should leave before we learn any more fun facts about each other." Now that humiliation was on the line, I needed to make sure I won.

He retracted his hand, holding it up instead, his smug smile back on his face as if I'd just cemented his one and only opinion of me to this point—that I was a control freak.

I wasn't. I was organized and structured and task oriented. Without those things there was little to no productivity.

"You obviously won't be strangers for all four sessions," Michael said, challenging my logic.

"I'm counting on *one* session," I said.

"Yes!" Tara said, like we'd already won. Hopefully the therapist was a good one.

I shrugged, then pulled some cash out of my purse, put it on the bar, and walked away. My stumble on the way to the door reminded me how much I'd drunk.

"I'll text you a time and location," Tara called after me while I was pulling up a rideshare app on my phone.

Now, lying in the hotel bed, completely sober, I wondered again how I had been talked into such a horrible idea. I didn't have time for this game. I was running a business and taking care of my mom and getting broken up with. I needed to cancel. I was going to cancel.

I pushed my palms against my eyes and sat up. My phone buzzed from the nightstand next to me, and I wondered which of the three life events I'd just laid out awaited me on its screen.

Raya. My business partner at Luminesce, our bar/restaurant.

Will you send me the delivery schedule for this week?

I'd already sent her the delivery schedule.

I know you already sent me the delivery schedule but I dropped my phone in the fryer last night, yes the fryer is fine, no my phone is not.

I should've been shocked that Raya's phone had somehow ended up in the fryer. I wasn't. She had probably been holding it in the same hand she was also using to hold the fry basket.

I hope customers didn't get phone fries, I texted back. Because honestly, I could see her thinking the food was somehow unaffected by the presence of a phone melting in the hot oil.

Of course they didn't, Sutton! We shut that fryer down for the night, had it thoroughly cleaned and it will be up and running again tonight. I can do *some* things without you.

It wasn't that I didn't think she could . . . okay, I mean, nobody did it exactly the right way, but out of all the somebodies in the world, she was the only one I would ever open a business with, so there was that.

We'd met in college in an entrepreneur development class. We'd actually opened a fake restaurant for our final project.

Laid out the plan so thoroughly that at the end of the semester, we'd decided that one day we were going to make it a reality. And we did.

Raya was so good at the main thing I wasn't: marketing. She attended parties and frequented events and passed out flyers to get the word out. She made a social media page and posted almost daily . . . well, three times a week. I was the one scheduling deliveries and ordering food and alcohol and organizing the waitstaff and doing all the things that made the business actually function. And I was still doing those things, even from three hundred miles away. She just had to make sure she was at the back door for said deliveries.

I sent both the delivery schedule and the staff schedule for the week again.

She responded with a Thank you!

Btw, Nate and I broke up last night.

My phone immediately started ringing, her name scrolling across the screen.

"I'm fine" was how I answered, sliding off the bed.

"What the hell?" she said. "Why?"

"Why am I fine? I don't know, because I can't think about it right now. It helps that I haven't seen him in two weeks. It softened the blow a little." At least that's the reason I was telling myself this didn't hurt as much as I thought it should've.

"No, why did you break up? What did he do? Did he cheat? I will kill him."

I swallowed. "No, he didn't." At least I didn't think he had. "We've just grown apart."

"I always hated him anyway," she said.

"No, you didn't." I straightened the comforter on the bed, pulling on each corner to smooth out the wrinkles.

"You're right, I didn't . . . and I can't if he's still going to talk to the meat guy for me on Tuesday. Tell me he's still going to take care of the meat."

I squeezed my eyes shut. I'd forgotten about that. "Yes, it's taken care of. You don't have to worry about it."

She took a deep breath. "Thank god. After that, I'll start hating him."

I walked to my overnight bag and pulled out my outfit, laying it over the chair. I should've pulled it out the night before, like I typically did, and hung it, but I hadn't been thinking clearly last night. "You don't have to hate him."

"Too bad, I will."

I gave a breathy laugh. "Fine."

"I have to go," she said. "This place doesn't run itself."

No, it didn't. I had about a dozen calls to make and a dozen more bills to pay to make sure it continued to run.

We ended the call, and I stared at the lit screen of my phone, wishing I didn't have to reach out to Nate. His parents ran a diner in North Hollywood, had for thirty years, so he had knowledge and contacts. Both of which I rarely called on. I had never wanted him to think I was using him. Raya and I were strong, capable women, after all, but damn, he'd negotiated a good price on filets that I didn't want to miss out on.

Can I have your meat contact? I texted.

Is this some backhanded way of asking for a dick pic?

I'll take one of those, too, if you're offering.

There's something seriously wrong with you, he texted, but he sent me the name and phone number anyway, along with the quote he'd gotten.

There *was* something seriously wrong with me because I felt nothing at his words. All I felt was numb. Cold.

Thanks, I responded.

He left me on read.

I felt nothing about that either.

CHAPTER 3

"Mom!" I called, opening the door. "I'm home." I'd heard the television while my keys were in the lock, so I knew she was awake. It was nine o'clock in the morning, so that wasn't always the case. This had been the longest I'd stayed at my childhood home since I left for college ten years ago. I still called Mom every Wednesday evening and visited for a long weekend once a quarter, but I'd been here for two weeks now. It felt like twenty.

"No need to shout," Mom said from where she lay on the couch, her feet propped up with pillows, her rented wheelchair close by. "I have a headache."

Maybe it is from the sheer volume of the television, I thought, but didn't say out loud. I picked up the remote from the coffee table and clicked it down several notches.

"Well, now I can't hear it," she said.

"Didn't the doctor say to limit your screen time?"

"What would you have me do then, Sutton, stare at a wall? I can't work, I can't read, I can't scroll on my phone." Mom was one of the administrators of the local school district. She obviously wasn't going back to work anytime soon. She'd been working there for over twenty years. She'd built up some time off.

"You're right. I get it," I said. "How was your night?"

"Terrible," she said.

"I'm sorry. When's the last time you took some pain medicine?"

"Ask that woman you brought in."

"Right," I said. Where was she? Wherever she was, she was probably done with my mom.

I headed for the kitchen, which was empty, and then to the back of the house, past the room I was staying in, my childhood room, and then on to my mom's room. Lucy was folding a clean basket of towels.

"Hi," I said. "You don't need to do laundry."

"I had time. You're early," she responded. "I thought checkout wasn't until eleven."

"I was up," I said. "How did it go?"

"Great," she said. "Your mom is a sweetheart."

I laughed, but when she didn't join me, I stopped and nodded slowly. I was glad, but that hadn't been my experience over the last two weeks. Either she was lying or Mom saved her special attitude for me. It could've gone either way. "Did you fill out the medication schedule I left?"

"I did. It's in the kitchen. We were right on time for all doses. Her next one is in two hours."

"Thank you," I said. "Perfect."

"You have me for three more hours. What else can I do?"

"That's okay. You can leave. I bet you're exhausted. I don't know if I could do an overnight shift." I'd worked many late nights at the restaurant but never any all-nighters.

She lifted the stack of towels, and I directed her to the linen closet in the hall. "Call me anytime," she said.

"Thanks again." I walked her to the door, where she collected her bag of medical supplies and personal belongings and left.

"I can take care of myself," Mom said as soon as the door was shut.

"I know," I said, because it was pointless fighting her. But really, she couldn't. Aside from her concussion, which brought on bouts of dizziness and nausea, she'd had a big surgery that left most of her right leg in a cast. She also had a laceration across her abdomen, caused by the seat belt, that was closed with upward of thirty stitches and one across her forehead from the steering wheel. Her left arm was splinted. She'd spent a week in the hospital, in and out of consciousness, and now she was acting like she was perfectly fine. I didn't understand how she could say she could take care of herself when I'd been lowering her onto a toilet since she'd come home.

"You didn't wash your hair today?" Mom asked, giving me a once-over.

I had washed everything else the night before in the shower, scrubbing until I was red and blotchy. But she was right, I hadn't felt like blow-drying my hair, and it was still stiff with product. I'd pulled it out of the ponytail, creating a poufy monstrosity. "I didn't."

"You need to. It looks crusty. And your face looks swollen. Did you drink too much last night?"

"Not at all," I lied, because I didn't want her to think she was right. "Are you hungry?"

"That woman fed me."

"Her name is Lucy."

"If she's not coming back, why do I need to know her name?"

My mom hadn't always been so . . . bitchy. Sure, she was hard on me growing up, expected a lot. But she hadn't turned grumpy with me until my dad left when I was thirteen to go tour with a symphony in Europe. She hadn't said it out loud before (surprisingly), but I got the feeling she thought that was somehow my fault. She may have been right.

He never wanted to be a father. He was a brilliant violinist and I was a surprise. Cramping everyone's lifestyle. I was twenty-eight now. My mom could've joined him many times over at this point. But she hadn't. They had never gotten a divorce. They just existed separately. Both still said they were married, even though his visits home dwindled to nothing over the years.

I didn't call him after the accident, but Mom had. He seemed concerned. He seemed sad. He didn't come home.

I picked up a plate from the coffee table and carried it to the sink, where I rinsed it and loaded it into the dishwasher. I sprayed and wiped down the counters, then made myself a cup of coffee, heavy on the creamer.

"I need to make some phone calls for work, Mom," I said. "Just ring the bell if you need anything." I'd gotten her a bell. One of the many mistakes I had made since being here. She abused it.

"Turn my show back up," she said as I headed for the hall.

Instead, I doubled back and handed her the remote. She was cranking up the volume before I'd even made it five steps.

Like I did on the daily, I'd already talked to Raya when I was at the hotel, but now was a more appropriate hour for other calls. My first one was to a server who I was hoping could cover for another server who'd called in sick. It took me three calls before I found someone. The morning didn't get any better as I dealt with a vendor that didn't have our order and my mom's ever-ringing bell requests. The most recent one was to close the blinds, but not all the way, because she wanted some light. I swear I twisted the adjusting stick one millimeter to the right and one millimeter to the left a dozen times before she was satisfied.

That afternoon, just when it felt like things had settled, I got the worst text of all.

Would tomorrow at four work?

It was Tara. Asking about the therapy appointment. I could get out of this so easily. Just one text. *No* was a full sentence. *No, I was drunk last night, I'm not going to do this* was an even fuller sentence. I typed the words into the text bar. Her disappointed face from the night before made me hesitate.

"Sutton!" Mom's voice, along with three sharp shakes of the bell, sounded down the hall. "Sutton! I need to go to the bathroom."

I took in a deep breath.

"Sutton! I need to go now!"

I deleted the words I had just typed and instead wrote, Yes, tomorrow works.

CHAPTER 4

"You're late," Pretty Boy said as I entered the waiting room of a small therapy practice. The plaque on the door only had two names: SARA FRANKLIN, MARRIAGE AND FAMILY THERAPIST, and ROBERT LLOYD, MARRIAGE AND FAMILY THERAPIST. I wondered which one was ours. The office looked like a regular house from the outside, but inside, the living room had been turned into a reception area with a long desk at the back and chairs along each side wall. My fake fiancé sat in one of those chairs. He was the only one there. I wondered if the receptionist was off for the day. At four PM, we were probably the last appointment.

I hated being late, and the fact that he called me out on it was even worse. I looked at my smartwatch. "Five minutes." I hadn't wanted to come at all. My mom had a rough morning. Had spilled an entire carton of orange juice onto herself and the couch and the floor and probably the wall—I needed to check the wall later. It had taken me forever to clean up.

His eyes traveled down my outfit selection for the day:

a pair of jeans, a tucked-in band T-shirt, and a loose blazer. Much different from my cocktail dress from the night we met. But I'd still pulled my hair into a tight ponytail. I hadn't had time to wash it, yet again, today.

"I'm beginning to think this isn't important to you at all," he said, feigning irritation. I could tell by the glint in his eyes that it was just an act though.

Before I could respond, a door opened and a young woman walked out. *Young* was the right word. She might have even been younger than me. She looked about twenty-five. I wondered if this was part of Michael's strategy: Pick the most inexperienced therapist in the area so she definitely wouldn't be able to tell she was sitting with two strangers.

"Hello," she said with a friendly smile. "I'm Doctor Franklin. Nice to meet both of you." She extended her hand.

Was she even married? How could she give advice to people getting married?

"I'm Elijah," Pretty Boy said, shaking her outstretched hand.

Elijah. Huh. He didn't look like an Elijah. Or maybe he did. I hadn't looked at him for very long. I wondered if people called him Eli. He definitely didn't look like an Eli.

Dr. Franklin turned her gaze on me, and I realized I hadn't said anything. "Hi, I'm Sutton."

"Sutton, my little button," Elijah said, wrapping his arm around my waist and pulling me against his side.

"It's great to meet both of you," Dr. Franklin said. "Follow me."

When her back was turned, I peeled Elijah's hand from my waist and mouthed, "No touching" to him.

He gave me a nod like he understood. I hoped he did because

I wasn't in the mood for some stranger's paws on me for the next hour, no matter how much he probably thought his touch was a gift to women.

In the room, which had obviously been a bedroom in this office's previous life, was a small desk, a small couch, and a chair. I wondered if she chose the size of her couch to force couples to sit close, because that was what we had to do when we both sat down. Our thighs and hips and shoulders touched. So much for needing some space.

She took the chair across from us and turned back the cover of her notebook. She reached over to the desk and plucked a pen from a jar sitting on the corner. "You've signed up for my premarital sessions," she said, and wrote something at the top of a clean notebook page. I hoped it said something like *Two people who look like they've only met once before in their entire lives. They seemed surprised to learn each other's names.*

"We did," Elijah said. "Thought we needed to start this thing off on the right foot. Get the important tools needed for success."

"This *thing*?" I asked.

He smiled at me. "Our endless future, dear."

Dr. Franklin nodded. "And you agree, Sutton? That's your goal here as well? To start your marriage on the right foot?"

"Sure," I said.

"These sessions are a little different from my normal sessions. They're designed to work on communication and connection." She paused and her eyes were on me when she said, "What's going on? You seem tense."

A bubble of hope rose in my chest. She was observant. This was a good sign.

"She's always tense," Elijah said.

"I'm not," I said, because that wasn't true.

"Well, as long as I've known her. She needs to learn to relax. Let things go."

"Do you have a hard time letting things go?" Dr. Franklin asked. "Relaxing?"

"I can relax in the right circumstances," I said. "But my life is hectic right now."

"With wedding planning?" she asked.

I took a breath. "Right. Yes."

"And how is that going?" she asked Elijah.

He raised his hands. "I can't help. She likes to do most things on her own. Just this morning, I said, 'Babe, let me help you pick out some flowers. You shouldn't have to do everything.' And she said, 'No, I have a vision and you don't live in my head.'"

I could feel the frown on my face, all my muscles pulled downward.

"Is that not how it happened?" Dr. Franklin asked me.

"Not at all." Because it didn't actually happen. "But he thinks he can just swing in last minute and give an opinion about flowers? Those have been planned forever. His last-minute opinions are more stressful than if he'd been helping out all along."

"She never asks for help," Elijah said.

My head swung in his direction and our eyes locked. I hoped mine said, *Cut the bullshit and stop making things up*.

His seemed to say, *This is fun*.

"Is that true?" Dr. Franklin asked. "Do you never ask for help?"

I asked for help. When I needed it and when I felt like someone else could handle a situation better than I could—

which wasn't as often as I would've liked. But she wasn't asking about my real life. She was asking if I ever asked the stranger next to me for help. "He has a hard time listening and an even harder time reading body language."

"I'm very good at reading body language," he said, almost under his breath, his voice low and husky. "Very good."

Our eyes met; his were teasing, mine were probably full of fire. I wondered if these smarmy lines usually worked for him.

"It sounds like maybe you two have different styles of communication."

"Yes," he said. "I use words and she uses looks."

"He uses sarcasm and I use common sense."

"Can you give me an example where he used sarcasm?"

Two could play at this game. "Yes, this morning when I was cleaning up an orange juice spill, instead of just helping me, like a person with observational skills would, he said, 'Do you want some bacon with that OJ?'"

"That wasn't sarcasm, I was actually making bacon." His thigh was pushing against mine, and I wanted to stand up and walk out of this room. This wasn't going to be free therapy. This was free irritation, a free raising of my blood pressure. How was this going to help me at all? It wasn't. My thought that it might give me tools to ease some tension in my current situation was shortsighted. And this experience definitely didn't make me more fun and spontaneous, another one of the reasons I had said yes to begin with. This was just going to be scheduled stress.

"Do you feel like that might've been the wrong time to ask about the bacon?" Dr. Franklin said.

"I do," he agreed. "This is why we're here. To work on blending our communication styles. Because we're both very passionate people. *Very* passionate, if you know what I mean."

I nearly choked on air but managed to get away with a short cough.

"I can tell," Dr. Franklin said.

"Can you?" Elijah asked. I could hear the smugness in his voice. He thought he was winning.

"What are some other strengths in your relationship?" Dr. Franklin asked. "Aside from passion."

"Yes, button, what do you think our strengths are?" Elijah asked.

My strength right now was that I was resisting the urge to smack him. It was taking all of my willpower. But beyond that, my mind was blank. Had we been in a real relationship, I sensed we wouldn't have lasted more than two dates. He thought everything was a joke. I could tell by the way he hadn't stopped smiling since I walked in the door. But not a genuine smile. A mocking smile. A smile that said, *Go ahead, speak so I can make fun of you in my head.* A smile and attitude born from a life of extreme privilege. I wondered just how much was in the trust fund I was sure he had.

When I still hadn't answered the question, he said, "I'll start. I think we balance each other out. She helps us focus on the bigger picture with her plans and her structure, and I help us focus on the here and now."

"Would you agree?" Dr. Franklin asked me.

"Sure," I said, because what else was I supposed to say? Elijah had an image of me in his head, and the sad thing was, it wasn't far from the truth.

"You don't have to agree just because I asked," she said.

"No, it's a good answer." Apparently, I was that predictable.

"Do you have anything to add? Any other strengths?"

"He's a loyal friend," I said, thinking about how he was doing this for his brother, even though the longer I sat here, the more I wondered why either of us was doing this. She had to know this was all a sham. She would know by the end of the session. I just had to make it to the end of the session.

I hadn't looked at him when I said those words, but I felt him shift in the seat beside me.

"Friendship is an important part of a marriage. If you two already have that bond down, you're on a great path."

I almost laughed but didn't.

"Like I said, this won't be a typical session. I would like to do an exercise with you," she said, then stood and walked to the corner of the room, where she retrieved a thick yoga mat. She laid it on the ground in front of the couch. "If you could sit facing each other, cross-legged on this mat, please."

"Um, what?" Elijah asked. It was the first bit of panic I had heard in his voice, and that brought me a little bit of satisfaction. It was short-lived though, because I realized I, too, had to do this.

Dr. Franklin smiled. "It's just a small exercise. Five minutes."

"I'm a little sore," I said. "From a workout I did yesterday. Floor sits sound terrible right now."

"No problem, you can stay on the couch. It might not be as comfortable, but that's fine," she said. "Just turn and face each other."

If I refused again, would she start to suspect we were strangers? Or maybe if we were actually forced to look at each other for any length of time, she'd realize we were strangers based on our uncomfortable body language. Yes, I decided that was more likely and took my place cross-legged on the mat.

"You changed your mind?" she asked.

"It will be good for me to stretch," I said, popping my eyebrows in Elijah's direction.

"Right," he said, joining me on the floor. Our knees touched.

"Now," Dr. Franklin said, "when is the last time you had uninterrupted eye contact?"

"It's been forever," Elijah said with a smirk.

"I recommend five minutes every day. It doesn't seem like a lot . . ."

It actually seemed like an eternity.

"But it goes a long way in strengthening your connection. I'll start the timer now."

"Oh, we're doing this now?" I asked.

"Yes, now."

We locked eyes. His were a honey brown with a ring of green around the pupil. I wondered what mine looked like now. Mine were a gray-blue hue, probably more gray in this light. I'd put on minimal makeup today. But I knew my lashes were coated in black mascara.

The door opened and I turned to see Dr. Franklin leaving the room. "Where are you going?" I asked.

"Uninterrupted," she said. "I'll be back in five." She closed the door behind her.

So much for her observing our awkward body language. "Is this her way of getting a paid break?" I asked under my breath in case she could somehow hear us.

He smiled. "It's pretty clever."

"We probably don't have to keep staring at each other," I said, but did, in fact, keep staring.

"What if that mirror is two-way?" he asked quietly.

"True," I conceded with a quick glance at the large mirror on the far wall. Maybe that was her way to see how healthy a relationship truly was. Would it be ethical to watch us without our knowledge? I wasn't sure.

His lashes were long, a deep chocolate brown. He had really clear olive skin too. He'd earned my original nickname of Villain Pretty Boy. Because there was a devilish spark in his eyes and a sharp upturn to his grin. "Do people call you Eli?" I wondered aloud.

"Mostly," he said. "Do people call you button?"

"Never," I said and hoped my look said that he shouldn't either.

It must've, because he laughed. When it was genuine, he actually had a very nice smile. Not so conniving. I felt myself slouching into the floor and straightened up, putting my hands on my lower back to support myself for a moment. I really was sore from the orange juice cleanup that morning. It had required a lot of squatting.

"Your back hurt?" he asked. Maybe he was good at reading body language after all.

"No, I . . . yeah," I said.

"We don't have to keep sitting here. We're not in a time-out."

It felt like we were. And we both obviously thought we had to do exactly as she told us, because our eyes were still locked in place. She might've been on to something with this eye contact thing. I could see how being forced to connect for a few minutes every day might re-center a couple. Not us, but a hypothetical couple. It was making me feel . . . what, I wasn't sure. But something stirred in my chest and loosened in my shoulders.

"Are we being hypnotized?"

I smiled. "To do what?"

"Whatever she wants us to," he said in a spooky voice. "Her little army of marketers."

"How *did* Michael get her name?" I played along.

"I need to find out." His eyes shot down to my shirt. "Do you like the Strokes or is it a statement piece?"

"Yes, I like them, but if you ask me to name three songs to prove myself, you will become my enemy."

"Am I not already your enemy?"

"Fair point."

"And I don't know three songs," he said.

"You don't know the Strokes?"

"I've heard of them, but they are not on my playlist."

The door opened to my right, breaking our eye contact. I stood and stretched as Dr. Franklin walked in.

"How was that?" she asked, as if our world had just been altered forever.

I sat back on the couch and Elijah joined me.

"It was hypnotizing," he said with a smile in his voice.

"What are other things you do to strengthen your connection?" she asked, settling into her chair, her pen still hovering over her notebook. I willed it to write, *These people are very much strangers. They wouldn't be able to pick each other out of a lineup of similar-looking people.* That last part probably wasn't true.

I wondered what she'd have to say to count as a win for Tara. Michael had said that even deducing we weren't in a relationship would count. Had she really not deduced that yet?

"She loves to give me back rubs," Elijah was saying. "They're my favorite."

"What?" I asked, turning to him.

"She asked what we do to strengthen our connection," he said. "You give me back rubs."

"And what do you do for her in return?" Dr. Franklin asked.

Elijah said, "We should probably keep that to ourselves. But believe me, she likes it."

Dr. Franklin actually blushed, and even though I'd told him not to touch me, I reached over and squeezed his leg in a death grip. He squirmed.

"Well," she said, "for this week, your homework is five minutes every day of uninterrupted eye contact. No screens, no phone calls, no . . . uh, touching. Just eye contact."

I nodded. That wasn't happening.

"And I'll see you guys same day, same time next week?"

"Sounds good," Elijah said.

Another week was not happening. We were done. I needed to talk to Tara.

Elijah stood and I followed. Dr. Franklin shook each of our hands and walked us to the door and then the lobby.

When we walked outside, Elijah said, "I'm so winning this bet."

CHAPTER 5

"What?" I asked, even though I'd heard him perfectly.

"She doesn't know," he said, his smug smirk in place.

"That's because you're lying," I said, walking toward my car.

"Lying?"

"Yeah, making stuff up. She's not a lie detector." I unlocked my car with my key fob, but since he'd followed me, I paused before opening the door and faced him.

"What was I supposed to do? We're strangers."

"Answer her questions honestly."

"How could I honestly tell her what our strengths are? We don't know each other."

"It wasn't the strength question as much as the actual stories you made up." I changed my voice to a low-pitched impersonation of him as I said, "I asked her if I could help her with flowers and she said no. She never asks for help. She gives me back rubs, and I return the favor with a solid pounding."

He choked out a surprised laugh. "I did *not* say that last one."

"You implied it."

Tires squealed on the main street and a car honked loudly, drawing our attention. Back to me, Elijah said, "Well, it's on the table if you'd like to offer a back rub."

"I would *not*," I said.

He shrugged. "Just letting you know."

"Let me know less, please," I said.

He released a low chuckle. "So what do you propose for session two if lying is not allowed?"

There wouldn't be a second session, but Tara could tell him that, so I said, "The truth. Or as close to the truth as we can manage."

"How?" he asked.

"Get creative."

"Okay, fine. I accept your challenge. But if we're going to be truthful with our new therapist, then we need to do the homework she assigns."

I tucked the key fob I'd been clutching back into my purse. "You want to stare into my eyes every day for five minutes for the next week?"

"She's going to ask us if we did it," he said.

"And I'll tell her the truth. I'll say no, we didn't get a chance."

"How about we say that on the days we were together, we did?"

"Look at that, you *can* be creative with the truth."

He smiled. "I still think I'm going to win."

I opened my car door. "I wonder how you'll look bald."

"I wonder what song you'll pick for karaoke," he said.

I shut my door and pressed the ignition button. I was more annoyed that Tara thought I wouldn't do karaoke than I was at the idea of doing it. Just because there were things I'd had to miss out on in high school because of home drama didn't mean I couldn't put myself out there. I'd do it. I could have fun. So what if I couldn't sing? So what if everyone would be staring at me and judging me and wanting me off the stage? I could have fun.

I checked my phone, which showed four missed calls, then backed out of my parking spot. At the first stoplight I came to, I pulled up the first voicemail and listened.

"Hey Sutton, it's Bailey. I know you ordered two cases of limes, but there was a distribution problem this week and I can only send one. Sorry! Hopefully we'll sort it out for next week."

I clicked through to the next message, which was from Raya. "Don't let Mac tell you I was late for delivery this morning. He was five minutes early, I was five minutes late. Which is basically on time. If he wasn't early, he wouldn't have cared."

I rolled my eyes and eased off the line as the light turned green. The next message played. "It's Mac. Talk to Raya. I can't wait around in the mornings. It gets me off schedule. Don't make me drop you."

"A bit dramatic, Mac," I mumbled, flipping on my blinker.

The last message was from my mom. "What's for dinner? Are you bringing anything home?"

I'd gone grocery shopping that morning, but I didn't feel like cooking. Today, I would stop by Mom's favorite fast-food restaurant—Cane's.

I got us each a box with three chicken fingers and fries and drove home.

"Hey, Mom."

"I took my meds," she said.

"You what?" I asked, coming into the living room to see her sitting up on the couch, a feat that was very hard for her to accomplish alone with stitches in her stomach and one arm in a sling. "It's not time for your meds."

"My leg hurts."

"Mom, you weren't supposed to take your pills for another two hours. I told you that. It's on the schedule."

"It's fine," she said.

I contemplated whether to call the doctor, but she seemed fine. It had been four hours since her last dose. I made a note to move her pills to a high shelf in the kitchen.

"I brought you Cane's." I set the bag on the coffee table in front of her and reached for the television tray on the side of the couch. My eyes collided with the framed family picture she kept on the end table from when I was ten or so. My dad had a smile on his face as my arms were tightly wrapped around his middle, a wide smile on my own face. My mom stood on my other side, her hand resting on my shoulder, her eyes soft and her lips upturned. I wondered why she kept the picture there in a place where she had to see it so much. I was tempted to tuck it into the drawer. Or throw it across the room. Either option would work for me. I resisted the urge.

"Cane's?" she said. "I can't have Cane's. The doctor said I need to avoid greasy foods."

The doctor also told you how often to take your pain meds and not to watch television, but you don't find those important. I didn't say that out loud. It wouldn't be helpful.

"I thought you went shopping this morning," she said.

"I did," I responded. "I'll make you some chicken stir-fry."

"That's better," she said.

I moved the bag of Cane's to the kitchen. It would still be

my dinner. I could save her box for the next day. I marked the pain meds onto the schedule that she had taken out of turn and moved the pills to a high shelf. Then I picked at the Cane's as I seared a chicken breast and washed rice and cut up vegetables. I wasn't the chef for our restaurant, but I had spent a fair amount of time in the kitchen with prep and development and I missed it. I missed being in my own city, with my own space, and my really nice apartment, and a job that I felt competent in.

"Is something burning?" Mom asked from the other room.

Nothing was burning. "No!" I called back.

"The bits on the bottom of the pan are probably burning. Turn down the heat and just stir them a little. Add some more oil too."

"I got it, Mom," I said. "Thanks."

When the food was done, I plated it and brought it to her in the living room with a glass of water, setting it on the tray I'd positioned earlier.

"Can you get me the salt?"

"You haven't even tasted it," I said.

"I just know I like salt."

"Will you just taste it first?"

She did. She carefully selected a piece of chicken, a bit of broccoli, and a scoop of rice to sample. She chewed her first bite and nodded slowly. "Very nice, honey. Good job."

"Thanks."

"I'd still like some salt."

I sighed. "I'll get the shaker."

CHAPTER 6

"Can you show the bartenders how to maximize lime garnishes? We're a case short this week," I said in my morning phone call with Raya the following day.

"How do you maximize lime garnishes?" Raya asked.

"Cut them into thinner pieces."

"Right. You could've just said it like that."

"I could've. How is everything going?" The view out the window in my bedroom was the neighbor's fence, light brown and water stained. I really did miss the view from my apartment. I was on the fourth floor, city-facing.

"Everything is fine. We're doing well. I have things under control."

I didn't want to tell her that her illusion of control was because I was dealing with all the fires from here. "I've been thinking about that review."

"Stop thinking of that review," she said.

"I can't help it," I said. "We need to work on the inside of the restaurant. Give it more atmosphere."

"Like what?" she asked. "We already have all the tables and linens and artwork picked out and in place. What else is there?"

"I don't know," I said. "I need to figure it out."

"Or, you could stop worrying so much. It was one review. Any restaurant takes a minute to get on its feet. We are handling things. There's nothing you can do about the inside of our restaurant for now. It will keep, Sutton."

"You're right. Thank you. I appreciate all you're doing. I'm not sure how much longer I'll be here. My mom is still recovering."

"Take all the time you need. I totally understand. And remember, I have a honeymoon happening this summer, so this is helping me feel better about taking time away for that."

"You never needed to feel guilty about that," I said, ticking two items—discuss lime shortage, brainstorm ideas for the inside of the restaurant—off the to-do list in my daily calendar next to me before closing it.

"And you don't need to feel guilty about this."

I rubbed the bridge of my nose between my eyes. "You're right. Okay."

"Nate came through with the meat, I see," she said.

"That sounded wrong."

She laughed.

"He gave me his contact, yes," I said.

"But we still hate him?" she asked, her subtle way of asking me if we'd made up.

We had not made up. We would never make up. He broke up with me in the coldest way possible. I didn't do second chances. "We do."

"Okay, done."

My phone buzzed with a text. "I better go. My mom is probably asking for fresh fruit and a cappuccino."

"She's been a difficult patient?"

She's always difficult, I wanted to say. *But now she's difficult and in pain.* "She's been fine," I said instead, because that's what I did: I protected my mom from outside opinions. I was the only one who got to judge her.

My phone buzzed next to my ear again, and I pulled it away to see if the text that came through was something I needed to talk to Raya about. It wasn't. It was from Tara. How did the first therapy session go? Did she guess that you were strangers? Please say she guessed.

"I think that's it," I said, back to Raya. "Unless there's anything you need to talk about."

"No, I don't think so."

"Tell Selma hi for me." Selma was her fiancée.

"Sutton says hey," Raya said.

I heard a soft voice in the background.

"She says hi back and that she hopes your mom feels better soon."

"Me too," I said. "Talk to you later."

"Okay," she said. "Bye."

My phone buzzed again as I was hanging up. Tara. Again.

Can I take you to brunch right now? So you can tell me everything.

I'd just helped my mom settle down for a nap in her room. Her meds made her sleepy, and she'd probably be out for three hours. And even if she wasn't, I'd put her cell phone next to her in bed, so she could call me if she woke up and I wasn't there. Like she always did.

I really needed to talk to Tara face-to-face if I was going to cancel this nonsense with the therapist. And I was.

Yes, send me an address and I'll meet you there now.

• • •

I wasn't exactly a hugger, but Tara was, so I returned one as we met in front of the Kountry Kitchen in Old Town.

"I think I was a little tipsy the other night when everything went down," she said. "But have I said thank you?"

"You have," I assured her. "A lot." Which was making it hard to tell her that I couldn't do another session.

"Good, because seriously, thank you for doing this. I know it's weird."

"Just a little," I said, sarcasm heavy in my voice. "Do you guys do stuff like this a lot?"

"Make strangers go to therapy?" she asked.

"Or something comparable."

"Michael is a prankster, but no, this is a new level. But if it's how I'm going to get him in front of a professional, it's worth it." She laughed as she said it and turned toward the door.

I closed my eyes and took a deep breath. Then followed her inside.

It wasn't very busy and we were seated right away. After the waitress took our drink orders (I stuck with water instead of the mimosa Tara ordered so I wouldn't agree to testing the priest and wedding planner next), I opened the menu.

"It's not that I think Michael needs a therapist," Tara said suddenly, bringing my eyes up from where I was trying to decide between an omelet and French toast. "I mean, I think everyone could benefit from talking through their past and having tools for their present. It's more about me, really. It will give me peace of mind to know we have our communication dialed in before taking the leap. You know?"

"Are you worried about your communication?" I asked.

"Not more than anyone about to get married should be." She shrugged. "My therapist says it's normal."

"I'm sure it is," I said.

"Are you in a relationship?" she asked.

"Not at the moment," I said.

"Remember Clint? From high school?"

"How could I not?" He was my high school boyfriend. I broke up with him because he was constantly copying all the answers off me for our homework assignments. I was worried the teacher was going to eventually realize our answers were exactly the same and I'd be dragged down with him. "Wait, do you still talk to him? Does he still live around here?" I may have visited my mom quarterly for the last ten years, but Tara was the only other person I had visited here before she too moved away. I had my schedule and it worked perfectly. Introducing other people to it might have changed that.

"No, I don't think so. I was just thinking about him and how much everyone loved him. He was so fun and cute. I was beyond jealous when he asked you out."

"You were?"

"I'm obviously over it now."

I laughed. "I hope so because he wasn't that great."

"What are you getting?" she asked, nodding toward the menu.

"An omelet," I said. "What about you?"

"Pancakes with strawberries." She closed the menu and leaned her elbows on the table. "So? How did the session go?"

"It went fine. I thought she was catching on at first, could tell that we didn't really know each other, but then Elijah started lying and making up stories about us," I said.

She leaned back against the padded booth and crossed her arms. "Of course he did."

"If she didn't realize after one session, I'm not sure she will in four."

"You don't think so?"

"I don't."

Tara's eyes dropped to the table.

I reached across and grabbed her hands. "You shouldn't have to do this to prove he's a good guy. He's not Bobby." Bobby was *her* high school boyfriend and a huge jerk. Had cheated on her twice, even after she'd forgiven him the first time. It felt like she'd been dating nothing but Bobbys ever since. I hoped she wasn't dating another one now. "Right?"

"No, of course not."

I shifted back in my seat, releasing her hands. "Then I think we need to call it. No need to play this game. Trust your heart."

"You don't want to do this for me?" she asked.

I swallowed down the lump that immediately formed in my throat. The memory of her standing on my front porch jumped to the front of my mind. She was dressed in a mid-length black dress, gripping a folder holding piano sheet music. She was supposed to perform that day. I was supposed to go with her and help her turn the pages while she played, but mostly for moral support. She'd been nervous. Behind me, my mom was in the middle of angry cleaning. She'd insisted I help. She was unreasonable when she got like that.

I'd texted Tara that I couldn't make it. Then she'd shown

up on my porch, telling me she couldn't go through with it. It was her parents' dream, not hers. I'd blamed it on Bobby back then, her quitting piano. After all, she had just caught him cheating for a second time a few weeks before. But it was at least partially my fault for not being there for her that day when she'd been there for me so many times. Guilt overwhelmed me now.

"This will help you feel better?" I asked.

She nodded emphatically. "Will you give it one more session? If there is any chance it will work at all, if it will get him to do therapy with me, it would mean the world to me."

I drew in a deep breath. "Is Elijah the kind of guy to honor a pact?"

"What?" she asked, confused.

"We made a pact about not lying in the next session, so maybe that will help."

She smiled. "I picked the right woman for the job."

I held in a groan. One more session. I'd do one more session for her.

The waitress came by and took our orders. When she left, I said, "So is he? The kind of guy to honor a pact?"

"If Eli said he wouldn't lie, he won't," she said.

"Good."

"But maybe we need a backup plan as well," Tara said, thinking. "How can we get her to know you two are strangers without outright telling her?" Her eyes shot to the door over my shoulder. "Oh no."

"What?" I asked, looking too.

"It's like they know we're talking about them."

Elijah and Michael walked in, side by side, scanning the room. I rolled my eyes. Clovis was a small town, but not this small. "Did they know we were going to be here together?" I asked.

"Yes," she said. "They probably don't want us scheming. Also, they work up the street."

"They work together?" I asked.

"Yes," she said, but before she could say more, Michael was leaning over and placing a soft kiss on her lips.

"Hey, babe," he said.

Tara slid down the bench like she was going to welcome them into our brunch. I gave her a look that said, *If you want to win this bet, I need to spend as little time as possible with this man.*

In high school, she was so good at reading my looks. But now she was unpracticed because she just gave me a confused face back. I sighed when Elijah gestured for me to scoot over, but I inched down the bench anyway.

"Good morning, fake fiancée," he said.

"It *was*," I replied.

He laughed.

"Sutton was just giving me a report on the therapy session."

"One down, three to go, baby," Elijah said, and he and his brother high-fived over the table.

I watched Michael closely, the way he brushed a piece of hair off Tara's forehead, how he smiled while she talked. He seemed sweet and attentive. I wondered if it was Tara's past that was making her nervous or if there were red flags she was worried about.

The waitress came back. "Do you two want to order something?"

"They aren't stay—" I started to say.

"Do you serve burgers this early?" Elijah asked over the top of me.

"I want one of your breakfast skillets," Michael said.

Okay, apparently, they *were* staying. I must've sighed again because Elijah gave me a sideways glance. "Try not to be too welcoming," he said. "You might hurt yourself."

I gave him a forced smile. The less I said, the less he'd know.

CHAPTER 7

I was doing well with my saying-less plan but was having a hard time listening less. And listening meant I was learning things about Elijah Russo. Things like the fact his last name was Russo. That he and his brother ran a boxing gym, which surprised me. They didn't dress like they worked at a boxing gym. I wasn't sure how people who ran a boxing gym dressed (lived-in hoodies and mesh shorts?), but it definitely didn't involve loafers. He and Michael had a sister who lived in Washington. Apparently, she moved there after graduating. They grew up here . . . well, north of here, in a big house on the bluffs. Or at least that's what I gathered from how they were talking—the parties they threw, their pool, their land.

But even when Elijah wasn't speaking, I was learning things about him. Eating a meal with someone tended to provide insights into their preferences and opinions. Like the fact that he didn't like tomatoes and thought french fries were overrated. I almost chimed in with an emphatic counterargument to the french fry position but held my tongue. I also left the mushrooms on my omelet, even though I had strong feelings about those as well, so he couldn't learn things about me.

Was I treating this game like a test I couldn't fail? Maybe. But not only would I not fail, I would ace it.

"Can I . . . ?" I turned toward Elijah, hoping he'd get the hint that I needed to stand up but was stuck against the wall in our booth seat.

"Can you what? Add something to the conversation? Yes, you can. Do you have a big family?"

"No comment," I said.

Tara laughed, understanding my strategy. Maybe our connection from high school wasn't completely stale.

"I need to go to the bathroom," I said.

Elijah shook his head but slid down the seat to let me out. He even gave me a hand up. And because I really did have to go to the bathroom, I went. After using the restroom, I washed my hands and then checked my phone to make sure my mom hadn't called or texted. She hadn't.

I stepped out into the dim back hall of the restaurant, and Elijah was waiting there. At first, I thought he was waiting for the bathroom, which was a single, all-gender one. But he didn't step through the door I held open.

"I'm here for our homework," he said.

I released my hold on the door, and it slowly closed behind me. "What?"

"Our homework. Five minutes of uninterrupted eye contact on the days we see each other." He leaned his shoulder against an open wall and gestured to the space beside him for me to do the same. "It is a day and we are seeing each other."

My eyes went out to the restaurant. It wasn't exceptionally crowded, but it wasn't empty. The hall we stood in was tucked away, a path only for those who needed to use the restroom, but still, it felt too exposed. "Here?"

"Unless you'd like to go sit in a car or take me home." He said that last bit in his husky voice.

"I would not," I said.

"Then pull up a wall, baby," he said.

"Don't call me baby," I said, mimicking his lean.

We faced each other, our eyes colliding as instructed by Dr. Franklin. My heart galloped at the intensity of his stare.

"Timer," I said, averting my gaze and fumbling for my phone.

"We wouldn't want to go a second too long."

"Exactly," I said.

I started the countdown and then recommitted to my lean and met his stare again.

"You like 'button' better than 'baby'?"

"I like neither."

"Sutton," he said slowly. "What does that mean?"

"My dad was British," I said, forgetting for a moment that I was supposed to keep my life to myself.

"Was?"

"Is. My dad *is* British."

"Do I sense dad issues?"

I narrowed my eyes at him. "No, you don't."

He didn't say anything, just stared, like he knew I was lying. He had some stubble on his face today, which took away some of his polished, shiny edges. It should've made him less approachable, more gruff or something, but it did the opposite. It actually softened him.

He had a single thin scar through his right eyebrow, almost unnoticeable. I wondered how he got it. I would not ask. I was committed to knowing as little as possible about this very pretty man.

"You have a nice nose," he said.

"Don't," I replied, bristling. It wasn't that I didn't have a nice nose. It was something I liked about myself. It was just that compliments came with expectations. He was trying to pry information out of me. He was a grown frat boy, well versed in charming a woman, I was sure. And his only goal was to charm me into giving up facts about myself.

"Don't what? Don't give you a compliment? I'm standing here staring at you. I can't help but notice things. Like your gorgeous eyes and your glowing skin and your perfect lips."

My brows drew closer together with each compliment until I could feel the scowl on my face.

He just laughed. "You'd think I was insulting you."

"Just don't," I said.

"I'm getting to know you better and better by the second. I can see how this exercise could strengthen a relationship."

"It's like she knows what she's doing. Maybe your brother and Tara would benefit from some of these skills." If I could convince Elijah to convince his brother to go to therapy already, he and I could stop going.

"Maybe," he said.

"Then why fight this so hard? Why this stupid bet?"

"Because I support my brother," he said.

"Even when he makes questionable decisions?"

He rubbed at his shoulder while adjusting his position against the wall. "I've learned that people can't be told they're making questionable decisions. They have to figure it out on their own. But in the meantime, I support him."

"So you *do* think he's making a stupid decision."

"In this case, I understand his side. Their relationship is fine. Why nitpick a good thing?"

"*Strengthen* is the word you used earlier."

"You hanging on my every word?" He rubbed at his shoulder again. He had nice shoulders. Broad but lean. I wondered if his shoulder was bothering him. Was it sore? Why was it sore? No, I didn't care.

"I have listening skills, yes," I said.

"They have to figure out their own relationship," he said.

"And yet here we are, right in the middle of it."

He blinked, maybe realizing I was right. But then his teasing eyes, the ones he wore most of the time, I was learning, were back. "Are you saying *we've* made a stupid decision?"

"Phenomenally stupid."

He let out a surprised laugh. "But you're going to see it through."

"One more session," I said. Because I cared about Tara. Because I could show up for her despite the times I hadn't in the past. "Because Tara is right, Elijah."

"Why do you say my name like that?"

"Like what?"

"Like an expletive."

It was my turn to give a surprised laugh. "I didn't realize I was."

"You are."

"I'll work on it," I said.

"You have no intention of working on it, do you?"

"I'll start by curbing the use of your name."

"Try Eli," he said. "Maybe one less syllable will help."

I laughed again just as my phone started vibrating in my hand. The smile slid off my face as an image of my mom leapt into my mind, helpless in her bed. I quickly raised my phone to answer it when I saw it was just the timer going off.

I clicked the Stop button and held the phone in his direction.

"Looks like the best part of your day is over," he said.

A voice behind us said, "Have you knocked? Is someone actually in there?"

I turned to see a middle-aged woman standing there. She pointed to the closed bathroom door.

"Oh," I said. "We're not waiting in line. It's free."

"You could've said so," she grumbled, walking past us.

"How long had she been there?" I asked Elijah. He'd been the one facing the restaurant in our exercise.

"I have no idea," he said. "I didn't see her."

I lowered my brow. "Really?"

"I only have eyes for you, apparently," he said with a wink.

I groaned at the terrible joke and spun around to walk back to the table. Elijah just chuckled and followed after me.

"Did you have a quickie in the bathroom?" Michael asked when we were back.

"Ew," I said. "Definitely not."

"Ew?" Elijah asked as we sat down.

"A public bathroom?" I said. "Yes, a million *ew*s."

"So you weren't repulsed by the thought of my brother in said bathroom?" Michael asked.

"I was *ew*ing the bathroom, but I will extend the *ew* to your brother."

Michael laughed and Elijah bumped his shoulder into mine as if I'd been teasing.

"You've never done it in a public bathroom?" Tara asked.

"No, and I don't want to know if you have," I said.

She and Michael met each other's eyes and then sputtered out a laugh.

"What about an airplane bathroom?" Elijah asked, his brows furrowed as if this was a serious question. One that would give him all the insights into me and my life and my personality.

"An airplane bathroom?" I asked. "Those things are tiny. And public. Not only public, but you can't just walk away from the people who saw you go in. Who know what you did." I studied his expression. Had he done it in an airplane bathroom? That actually told me a lot about him. That he didn't care about others' time or needs, that he didn't follow rules, that he was driven by impulses or status or bragging rights. Like I'd thought: a frat boy.

"What's your aversion to public places?" he asked.

"Mainly the germs," I said, "but also the public part."

Elijah slowly leaned closer to me and under his breath said, "You've never felt the urgency of needing someone immediately?" He didn't touch me with the question, but heat seemed to radiate from his body to mine and goose bumps formed down my bare arms.

"Never," I assured him, which was the truth. "No feeling is urgent enough to risk a staph infection. Or getting put on the no-fly list." I took a bite of my omelet, mainly to avoid his stare.

My mouth immediately heated up, and Michael started laughing. I grabbed my water and downed half of it. "You don't mess with people's food," I said. "Not cool."

"I don't know what you're talking about," he said.

Elijah chuckled beside me, and I knew then that I'd failed today. I'd revealed too much.

CHAPTER 8

I quit.

That was the text I woke up to a couple of days later. It was from my very best server, Presley, and it had me springing out of bed faster than anything had in a while.

Can we talk? I texted her back.

My phone immediately vibrated with a call. Since I'd literally just woken up, my voice was sleep-deep and rough when I answered, "Hello."

"I can't anymore," Presley said. "It's too unorganized. Not enough servers at night and last-minute changes to the schedule. Raya lets anyone switch whenever they want and then people forget what they switched to because nobody writes it down."

"If I fix it, will you stay?" I asked.

She sighed. "I don't know, Sutton, it's a lot. I'm feeling overwhelmed."

"Would you like to be in charge of the schedule? For a

two-dollar-an-hour raise?" I shouldn't have offered the raise without talking to Raya first, but desperate times and all that.

"Truthfully, no. I have school. That's why I'm up so early today, and I don't have time for that. But I will stay for two weeks, and if the schedule gets sorted in those two weeks, I'll stay longer."

"Okay, I'll fix it. I'll make sure everyone knows they can only change through the online app," I said. "It has to be officially recorded."

"Thank you," she responded. "I personally think you need to hire at least one more server, probably two."

"Done," I said. Then I spent the day online reading through résumés and putting phone interviews on the calendar. I could whittle it down to a few good candidates and then have Raya conduct some in-person interviews to get a better feel for their personalities. I'd fix this.

• • •

"Mom, you have to hold on to my neck or I can't transfer you." We'd done this every time I had to move her from wherever she was to the wheelchair. And then from the wheelchair to the toilet or bath or bed. And every time, she didn't want to hold on to me. I was sure it was her pride. She didn't truly want my help at all. She wanted to do this all on her own. Like she'd been doing all her life until now, she liked to remind me. But she literally couldn't walk, and one of her arms was immobilized and she was still battling dizzy spells. She couldn't do this on her own, but that didn't stop her from pretending.

"That nurse you hired last week was better at this," Mom said.

"I'm sure she was."

"She knew what she was doing."

I placed her hand around my neck. "Just hold on, okay?"

This time she held on and I was able to shift her to sitting. She cried out in pain.

"I'm sorry," I said. "I know it must hurt."

"You don't know," she said. "You've never been in this situation."

"Are you ready?" I asked, because fighting with my mom was pointless most of the time. Without waiting for her answer, I helped her move her good foot into position to support some of her weight as I used all my strength, plus a lot of leverage, to maneuver her into the wheelchair. I was going to be toned after my stint here.

"See, I'm not helpless," she said.

"You're not," I responded. I was trying to be understanding. I would hate it if someone had to take me to the toilet too. "We have a physical therapy appointment tomorrow." I wheeled her down the narrow hall, trying to avoid bumping into the walls.

"Physical therapy? On what?"

"On you, Mom," I said.

"Neither of my injured limbs can move yet."

"And they want to fix that," I said.

"It seems too early," she grumbled.

"You can tell the doctor that," I said.

"Maybe I will," she said.

• • •

I lay in bed that night staring at my phone. Nate's name was pulled up on the screen, and the Call button was staring back at me. That little outline of a phone telling me that if I pushed on it, I could talk to someone. Someone who until last week cared about me. I could vent about my day. I needed to vent. I knew that's all I needed and that wanting to call Nate now was selfish. Nate wasn't good at handling vents anyway, I reminded myself. He'd just try to solve my problems. He'd tell me to hire a full-time nurse for my mom, even though I didn't have the money for that. Our restaurant wasn't losing money, but it wasn't making much either. We were definitely still in the building phase. The fragile stage.

Nate would tell me to call my dad and ask for money. I hadn't even done that when we were starting our business. Raya's parents had come through in the end for the full amount we needed, thankfully. Because I knew my dad: He could've been sitting on a dragon's hoard of wealth and he'd still claim poverty. And he'd do it in the most smooth-talking way possible so that by the end of the conversation, I'd be tempted to send *him* money. That's who he was.

I put my phone down before my body pushed the Call button, and Nate appeared on my phone without my mind agreeing to it. I rolled onto my side. My brain immediately took over, thinking of all the things I needed to do the next day and the things I'd done wrong in the last few weeks.

And then a set of hazel eyes flashed through my mind. I cursed Dr. Franklin for the five-minute stare-offs she'd assigned us. I wouldn't know his eyes so well if I hadn't stared at them for a total of ten minutes in the last week. That was a long time to look at someone's eyes. I needed to avoid them from now on if I could, because having them invade my thoughts at midnight was not something I was fond of.

I closed my eyes and tried to think of anything else.

CHAPTER 9

The physical therapist was young and handsome, and I was grateful for it because it put my mom on her best behavior. Everyone wanted to impress a young, handsome doctor, including her. Right now, she was laughing at a joke he told that wasn't all that funny. Something about a two-legged dog. Was he comparing my mom to a dog?

"Sutton," he said, pulling me out of my head.

"Yes?"

"I'll have her for an hour. You can stay, of course, but you can also walk the grounds or run some errands, or I don't know, read in your car."

"Sutton's not really a reader. She only does things she puts on her little list," Mom said.

I lowered my brow but bit my tongue. "I'll be back in an hour," I said.

"I'll take care of her."

That sounded like a threat, which made me smile on my way out the door.

It was nearly lunchtime and I hadn't eaten all morning. I headed for the cafeteria. Some people stuck their noses up at hospital food, but this particular hospital was actually known for its above-average offerings and its below-average prices.

The line to order wasn't long, and as I was walking toward it, I saw Tara at one of the tables in her scrubs. I knew she was a nurse, of course. I hadn't realized this was her hospital.

Her eyes lit up when she saw me. "Sutton, what are you doing here?" The second she asked it, before I could even answer, she said, "Oh, your mom. How is she?"

I pointed up, indicating the floor above us. "She's in physical therapy as we speak."

"That's a good sign."

"Is it?"

"Means she's on the mend, right?"

"Yes," I said.

"Are you eating here?" she asked.

"Figured I'd grab something."

"The soup today is amazing. Come sit with me when you're through the line. I have forty-five minutes left on my lunch."

I got a bowl of soup and half a turkey sandwich and then rejoined her at the table.

"Remember when we came here for a double date in high school?" she asked.

"Yes, actually, I do. I was just thinking about that. Were our taste buds less discerning then or is the food actually good?" I set my tray on the table and sat down across from her.

"It's good," she said. "Not as good as we thought it was in high school. But better than hospital food has any right to be. And cheap!"

I nodded at a wedding magazine open in front of her. "How

is wedding planning going? How much longer do you have anyway?"

"Six months," she said. "We get married in six months. It feels so close and yet so far away."

"Are you the first one of our high school friends to get married?" I asked. At twenty-eight, she could've been the last for all I knew. I really hadn't kept in contact with anyone aside from what I saw on social media, which didn't always give me the up-to-date news of people's lives, especially when I didn't check it regularly. Tara had moved away too, but I had a feeling she'd kept up with everyone better than I had. Plus, she'd been back for over a year and worked in a hospital. I was sure she'd heard tons of gossip disguised as genuine concern.

"No, Fiona married Mitchell right out of high school. I'm surprised you didn't hear. I'm sure she sent you an invite."

"My mom's not big on forwarding my mail. But she may have opened it and told me about it." I didn't remember. I probably would've disregarded something that would've brought me back to town outside of my scheduled visiting times. I had been in school and working. I didn't have a lot of free time back then. I didn't have a lot of free time now.

"They have three kids now," she said.

"Three? Wow."

"They have a ten-year head start on us," she said. "It's not even that shocking."

I unwrapped my sandwich. "I guess you're right."

"I can't wait to start having babies," she said.

"Yeah? You still want six?" I asked. That's what she used to say in high school. I was surprised I remembered it. Maybe because, as an only child, that number had always seemed shocking to me.

"I think I'm down to a reasonable four," she said. "What about you? Have you come close to marriage in the last ten years?"

"No, I haven't. Just got out of a two-year relationship." I took a bite of my sandwich.

"I'm sorry," she said. Tara was easy to be with. I had almost forgotten. She was light and fun and did a good job of getting my mind off things.

"It's okay, we were incompatible," I said.

"That leaves you free for Elijah."

I laughed, but when I realized she was serious, I cleared my throat and said, "We are even more incompatible. Besides, we're supposed to be strangers, right?"

"That's true," she said. "But good luck not falling for him. He's very charming."

I laughed again. "I think I'm safe." Frat boys weren't my type and I was sure type A, emotionless, lackluster women were far from his type as well.

"Do you want to check out a venue with me after I get off today? Michael can't go."

"You haven't picked your venue?"

"We have, I just need to find the spot on the property for the ceremony."

"What time?" I asked. "I'm here for another hour and then have to give my mom meds at three."

"I get off at four," she said.

"That could work." I needed to visit more venues to see what they did to create atmosphere and personality. Maybe I could implement some things in my restaurant.

• • •

"This is a great coat closet," Elijah called from where he stood by the main building, thirty feet away. "For coats. Nothing else but storing coats should take place in this closet."

The lady, Rebecca, who was giving us the tour of the venue, gave him a confused look. "The wedding is in September. There will be no coats."

"Oh, yes, you're right. I guess it's open for other things then." He threw a smirk my way.

I didn't humor him with a reaction. When Michael couldn't come, he'd sent his brother as a replacement, probably not realizing Tara had found her own replacement. Either Tara hadn't known he was coming or she was a really good actress because, when we'd pulled into the parking lot and saw him standing there, she'd seemed genuinely surprised. Had I not driven over with her, I would've found an excuse to leave by now. We'd already been here twenty minutes, and this was not the first *look at this place where adventurous people who aren't uptight can have sex* comment Elijah had made.

The venue was gorgeous: gazebos and man-made rock waterfalls and flower gardens and even a small lake. There were so many good spots that Tara was having a hard time picking a place for the ceremony. Both Elijah and I had given our opinions when asked. I'd picked the dock by the lake, he'd picked the rock garden. But those opinions didn't seem to help her choose.

So now we were in the pavilion, where the reception would take place, going over details about food and décor. It had a large stone fireplace at one end and a walkway to the main building and kitchen at the other end. And apparently a coat closet.

We needed more plants in our restaurant, I decided, as I stood by one of the large pillars holding up the pavilion, and stared out at vast amounts of green. Our restaurant had an outdoor patio and we had a large tree and some plants, but not nearly enough. I wondered how hard it would be to drape greenery in the overhanging beams of our patio. It could use a water feature too.

"Tara," Elijah said. "I'm stealing your friend for five minutes. We have some homework to do." He took me by the hand and started leading me away.

"Not in the coat closet," I said to Rebecca, who I could tell now, by the expression on her face, wasn't oblivious to all the less-than-subtle comments Elijah had been making. "We're not even together."

"You needed to make that clear?" he asked.

"Very much," I said.

When it was obvious that I was following him without coercion, he dropped my hand. I wasn't sure where he was leading us until he stopped at the waterfall spot we'd seen earlier. The one we'd all decided was a little too distracting for a ceremony. Water poured over a large slab of smooth rock, coating its face and landing in a narrow horizontal opening at the bottom, where it then traveled around a square sitting area. It was very pretty but also a bit echoey and demanded attention. No bride wanted to compete with that—well, Tara didn't and I didn't blame her.

Elijah swung his leg over one of the chairs, straddling the back, then nodded to the chair positioned behind his.

I sat.

"I didn't think I'd see you today," he said. "But rules are rules, and it's convenient for me that you're the rule-following type."

He draped his arms over the back of the chair. I crossed my legs.

It was one of the first warm days since I'd arrived, and the birds were enjoying this fact. They chirped in the tree branches above.

"Did Dr. Franklin tell us we couldn't talk during these staring sessions?" he asked.

"No, she told us we couldn't touch," I said.

"Right, she knows us so well."

I raised my eyebrows. "I mean, she's not far off on your side."

"You think I'm having a hard time not touching you, button?"

I leaned forward, our eyes still connected, and said quietly, "Don't worry, I don't feel special. I think you have a hard time not touching everyone." With those words, I reestablished the distance, pressing my back into the chair.

"Oh, but you are special," he said with a smile full of sarcasm. "Coming back to your childhood home after some kind of setback. On a healing journey or something. Oh, wait, that's not special, that's pretty standard."

I nearly laughed out loud at how wrong he was. But I didn't. I wanted him to think all the wrong things. The more wrong things he thought, the easier it would be for the therapist to tell that he didn't know me at all. "Healing is important," I said.

"That's why you promote therapy?"

"I mean, I'm not running its marketing campaign or anything, but yes, I think therapy is important," I said.

"If you lose this bet, are you going to change your mind?"

"When you lose, are you changing yours?"

He smirked. "I'm not going to lose."

"You're not accustomed to losing, are you? Been handed

everything you wanted your whole life but think you know something about struggle so decided to run a gym where you teach people how to punch because that's the way you've always solved any minor inconvenience you've faced."

"You know me," he said.

I must've hit a nerve because, for the first time, his snarky smile was gone. His jaw jumped as he clenched it. He was wearing scruff on his face again today, and once again, I noted how well it suited him. It softened the sharp edges of his jaw, both darkened and lightened his face in a way. It intensified the color and depth of his eyes. His nose was strong, just crossing over into large, but again, suiting the shape and size of his face. Why was I studying his face so much?

The waterfall over his shoulder was going strong. I wondered if it ran all the time or if Rebecca turned it on for this appointment.

"If you look away, we have to start the timer over," he said.

My eyes snapped back to his. "Wait, who's timing this? Did you start a timer?"

"I forgot," he said.

"Shit," I responded. "I think it's been five." I stood.

"I think it's been three," he said.

"I guess we'll never know." I smiled over my shoulder as I walked away.

When I was almost back to Tara, I heard a loud, high-pitched scream. I ran the rest of the way, only to learn that Michael had jumped out of a bush or something, scaring her. Apparently, he didn't need to miss today at all, he just thought it would be funny to surprise her. I couldn't decide by the look on her face if she found this surprise funny or annoying.

I'd ask her later.

CHAPTER 10

"I thought the physical therapist said you could use this arm now," I said, wrapping a towel around her body because my first attempt to move her from the shower stool to her wheelchair was a series of slippery fumbles.

"He said that I could try more, but it still hurts."

I just wanted her to help brace herself. She was like a floppy fish, offering little to no help in my attempts.

"I hate this chair. And I hate that you're in here invading my privacy."

"Mom, I'm not looking, I'm just helping. Once you start using your arm and you're less dizzy, maybe I won't need to be in here. I don't want you to fall." I had spent the morning doing phone interviews for the server position. They hadn't gone well. And this wasn't a good follow-up activity to help lift my mood.

"You don't have a great bedside manner. It's a good thing you didn't become a nurse, like Tara. She's a sweetheart."

"She is," I said. "And yes, I'm glad I'm not a nurse." If this caretaking gig proved anything to me, it was that. I finally got a good grip with the towel, and I moved her to the chair.

She settled in. "You're going to blow-dry my hair too? I'm cold."

"Yes, I am. Do you want to get dressed first?"

"Of course I want to get dressed first."

"Okay, let's go."

The house wasn't made for a wheelchair, and that was never more apparent than when trying to squeeze her chair out of the bathroom. Every time it nicked one side or the other of the doorframe, and every time she complained about the paint job she was going to have to take on when I was gone.

In her room, I dug through her drawers for the things we needed and proceeded to wrestle her into her clothes. At least that's how it felt, like a wrestling match. Like she was fighting the process instead of making it easier. It was worse than clothing a squirmy baby.

As I kneeled on the floor in front of her, pulling a sock onto her one exposed foot, I felt a hand along my cheek. I looked up at her in surprise.

"You're a pretty girl," she said.

"Thanks, Mom." A compliment from my mom was rare, and I felt my cheeks heat a bit from it.

"But that color looks terrible on you," she said.

I looked down at the burnt orange T-shirt I was wearing. "Noted."

"I used to be young and pretty."

"You still are," I said. My mom was a striking woman. At sixty-one, she had white hair that she kept shoulder length and icy blue eyes. Her skin was soft like rose petals, and she smelled like rose petals too.

"Cherish your looks, you won't always have them."

"But we'll always have our winning personalities," I said, mostly as a joke because I was feeling far from charitable lately, and my mom, well, she was a grump. But that wasn't new.

"I should call your father," she muttered, almost to herself. "Tell him what's going on."

I wondered how often she called my dad. When I had lived here, it had been at least once a month. Sometimes he'd call as well, but not as often. "You should."

I pushed her to the vanity in her room and retrieved the blow dryer from the basket on the floor.

When I finished drying her hair, my phone was buzzing on the counter in the bathroom where I had left it. I could hear it from where I stood. My heart nearly stopped in my chest when I saw the name scrolling on the screen: Nate.

I answered it quickly. "Hi, hello," I said, sounding breathless.

"Hey," he said. "When will you be home?"

My heart thudded heavily in my chest. I wasn't sure why. I'd already established that Nate wasn't getting any second chances. Not after how he broke up with me. I only needed to be shown a red flag once. "Uh . . . why?" I asked.

"Don't worry, I don't want to get back together or anything. I just left some stuff in your apartment that I need. Can I use my key and let myself in?"

The feelings seeing his name on my phone had elicited, whatever feelings those were, drove off a cliff and crashed into the rocks at the bottom where they belonged. "Oh, yeah, of course."

"Thanks." He paused. "How are things? With your mom?"

I glanced over my shoulder. She was messing with her hair

in the mirror of her vanity. I walked out of the bathroom, out of her room, then into my room. "Okay . . . hard."

"Is she not doing well? Complications?"

"No, she is. It's just hard to be back, I guess."

"For sure. I don't know that I want to hang out in my childhood bedroom for very long either. I bet you miss your memory foam mattress and your five-star hotel sheets."

Because he thought all I cared about were my belongings. "Yeah . . . how are you?"

"Good. Got back on the dating apps. I forgot how atrocious those things are. But hey, I need to run. Oh, did the meat guy work out?"

"Yes," I said.

"Good," he responded. "Bye."

"Bye."

I set my phone down and braced myself on the dresser. I didn't miss Nate. I didn't. I missed being home. I missed things being easy . . . or easier. I missed having a person to do life with. Even if that person told me that it seemed like I was doing life alone and not including him. I really was. I could do life alone.

I did not miss Nate. At least that's what I was trying to convince myself.

CHAPTER 11

Wait, why had I made us vow to be truthful in this therapy session? I hadn't thought through the consequences of that. The main one being, *I* had to be truthful.

"What do you think your parents did well in their relationship that you can take to yours, and what do you think they did poorly?" That was the question Dr. Franklin had asked. The one that had me frozen, trying to think of a creatively truthful answer that didn't give away everything.

Elijah went first, like he often did when I stayed silent. "My parents talked about everything. Even if it was at loud volumes, they talked things through. And when they fought, they always let us see them make up too. That's what they did well."

"That's important," Dr. Franklin said. "Both healthy disagreements and productive makeups. What about on the flip side? What weakness did you learn from?"

He was thoughtful, like he had to rack his brain for that answer. Like they didn't have any weaknesses at all. "Maybe that they never seemed to learn from their arguments. They had the same ones over and over again. Neither of them changed."

"And in your relationship now," Dr. Franklin asked, looking at me, "has he broken that cycle? Does he learn from past arguments, attempt to change?"

I didn't mean to, but I let out a single laugh. "We seem to fight about the same thing." These therapy sessions. The only thing we disagreed on because it was the only thing in our relationship.

"Seriously?" he said.

I tried to hold in my smile and gave him an innocent look. "Seriously."

"You don't agree?" Dr. Franklin asked him.

We were still looking at each other and his eyes narrowed a bit. "I guess I do," he admitted.

"Recognition is the first step," she said. "What about you, Sutton? Were your parents good at arguments? At making up? At changing?"

"No, my parents separated when I was thirteen."

"They're divorced then?" she asked.

"Mostly."

She gave me lowered brows, but I barreled forward so I didn't have to explain that. "But they were good at supporting each other's dreams." I wanted to laugh at how well my mom had supported my dad leaving to play in a symphony across the world. She supported him so well that she never made him come back.

"And the two of you?" She gestured between us. "Are you two good at supporting each other's dreams?"

"She doesn't care for my career," Elijah said. "She thinks it's just about people punching each other."

I let out a huff of air. "I support your career."

"This is the first I'm hearing this." His teasing eyes told me this was in retaliation for my creative truth earlier.

"Why do you think she doesn't support your career?" Dr. Franklin asked.

"Because she's never even come to see the place. Never wanted to try boxing. Even for thirty minutes."

He was such a punk.

"Is that true?" Dr. Franklin asked.

"Yes," I said. "But I can support from afar."

"What about you? Do you feel supported?" she asked me.

Maybe it was the conversation I'd had with Nate the day before or how hard it had been to help my mother out of the shower, but the word "No" came out of my mouth without much thought. I quickly tried to backtrack. "I mean, he's trying." Because that was true too. He was trying to learn things about me. But not in order to support me. To win this stupid bet.

"Where do you feel undersupported?"

"Mainly with my mom," I said, because I had a feeling Tara had told Elijah about her. About why I was here, although I was now remembering that he had spouted off something about coming home with my tail between my legs to find myself. "I'm taking care of her right now. She got in an accident." My voice caught on those words, and I tried to play it off with a cough.

"I'm sorry to hear that," Dr. Franklin said.

And it was more than obvious that this was the first time Elijah was hearing it because he gave me wide eyes but then softened them for our audience and took my hand in his. Yanking it away might've given Dr. Franklin the clue she needed, but the gesture surprised me so much that I went still. I let his thumb move slowly over my knuckles in a soothing pattern. I even held on.

"How did last week's homework go? Did you do it?"

"On the days we saw each other," I said, because that's what we had already decided we were going to say.

She tilted her head slightly. "Do you not live together?"

"We don't," I said.

"She's taking care of her mom right now," he said, using my revelation against me as a way to solidify our couplehood.

I took my hand back, irritated. His arm went to the back of the couch behind me.

"Maybe that's why you're both feeling a bit unsupported right now, because you don't see each other every day."

That, or we're strangers, I wanted to say. *That could have something to do with it. Why haven't you figured this out yet?*

"Did you feel like the eye contact assignment brought you closer together?" she asked.

"Much," Elijah said. He started pulling on the ends of my hair, and a shiver went through me. "I've never felt closer to her."

"And you, Sutton?"

"He's not hard to stare at," I said, because that was the truth.

Dr. Franklin gave a little chuckle like she completely agreed. "Okay, homework for this week," she said. "I want some show of support. Sutton, one boxing session. Eli, some help with Mom this week."

"Oh, no, that's unnecessary," I said, tension spreading across my shoulders.

"Which part?" she asked.

All of it, I wanted to scream. But most importantly, "The Mom part. She's very particular about who helps her." She didn't even want *my* help.

"Do you and Sutton's mom not get along?" This question was directed at Elijah, and I turned to him with raised eyebrows to see how he was going to creatively truth his way out of this one.

"I'm unaware of any problems," he said.

I nodded slowly. That was good. So good that Dr. Franklin turned to me. "Are there any problems between Eli and your mom?"

"Nope," I said, because that was true. "None."

She clapped her hands together once like that was the end of the discussion. "Okay then. I can't wait to hear the report next week."

There wasn't going to be a next week here. I'd told Tara I'd give her one more session and that was it. I'd hoped Dr. Franklin would figure it out this time. She was supposed to have figured this out. She was supposed to realize we didn't belong in an engaged couples' program. But unfortunately, that didn't seem to be the case.

The thought of Elijah and Michael winning this bet irritated me. I didn't want to let them win. But there was no way Elijah would become more involved in my life because of this. There was no way he was going to help me with my mom.

Dr. Franklin stood and walked us out.

"Yeah, I know," I said in the parking lot, heading toward my car, because I could feel the held-in gloat radiating off Elijah. "She didn't figure it out."

"I even told the truth today."

"Maybe with your mouth, but not with your body," I said.

A half smile came onto his face. "Excuse me?"

"Holding my hand, leaning against me, pulling the ends of my hair. Your mouth was truthful but your body was lying."

"You're saying I shouldn't touch you?"

"That's exactly what I'm saying." I reached my car, then turned to him. "Oh, and I'm done. Tell Michael he won."

"Wait, what? You're giving up? Just like that?"

"I'm accepting the truth." Tara would be disappointed, but I could see the writing on the wall. This particular activity wasn't going to help her. I'd try to think of another way to help her convince Michael to go.

Elijah narrowed his eyes and tilted his head like he was trying to figure something out. Figure *me* out. "Does this have to do with the homework assignment this week?" he asked.

I flinched. "No, not at all." I opened the car door.

"Sutton, wait."

I sighed, pausing. "What?"

"I thought you said no lying."

I pointed to the building. "No lying to her."

"So you *are* lying to me then. You don't want to do the homework? Do you have something against boxing?"

I blew air out of my mouth. "Boxing? This has nothing to do with boxing."

"You'll box?"

"I'll box."

"Okay, I'll have Tara send you the address." He turned and headed to his car.

"No, wait, I didn't mean—"

"See you soon!"

I grunted and climbed into my car, pulling the door shut. I sat there without starting the engine for several minutes. Elijah drove away and I looked over at Dr. Franklin's office. I was so tempted to march back inside and clue her in. Wouldn't it be better for everyone if I did? Elijah and I could stop talking altogether. Tara and Michael would work on their relationship before their wedding. Really, it seemed like the right thing to do.

Would Dr. Franklin play along though? Pretend that I didn't tell her? Because if she didn't, that would ruin everything. I wasn't sure how she would react. She could be angry that we lied to her. And ethically, she probably wasn't allowed to then lie to Elijah about what she knew and didn't know. Yeah, telling her wasn't an option. But being done with this whole sham was.

CHAPTER 12

"Have you ever been to a therapist, Mom?" I asked as I dished rice onto a plate.

"You think I need a therapist?"

Yes. "That's not what I said. I'm just curious."

"You know what they say about curiosity?"

"That it's the precursor to discovery?"

"No, that it's just a nice way to say nosiness."

"I've never heard that one." She'd probably made it up.

"I haven't been to a therapist," she said, for some reason deciding to answer my question after all. "Have you?"

Why hadn't I anticipated her turning that question around on me? But since I asked it, I had to answer. "No," I said. Because even though I had seen a therapist twice now, it didn't count. It turned out that couples therapy with someone you weren't really a couple with did very little for your mental health.

I arranged her plate of food on the television tray in front of her. Then I dished up a plate for myself and poured a glass of wine.

"It's rude to drink in front of someone who can't drink," Mom said. Her medication made alcohol off-limits.

"I know," I said, and sat at the table in the kitchen instead of joining her on the couch in the living room. My shoulders were stiff, and I had a kink in my neck that I tried to work out as I sat. I was sure both were from lifting my mom into her various places throughout the day.

"Can you turn the TV on?" she asked.

"I think the remote is right next to you," I said.

"It's not," she answered.

I stood and found the remote on the couch right next to her.

"Oh," she said, taking it. "You should've put it on my right side. My left arm is injured."

"I will next time."

"What are we going to do about my car?" she asked as I sat back down. She turned the television on with the question, and it was loud.

"I'm dealing with the insurance," I said. "Hopefully they'll cut you a check, and we can get you a new one."

"What?" she asked.

"Turn it down, Mom," I said.

The volume changed very little as she pointed the remote at the TV. Then she looked at me expectantly.

"The insurance will take care of it," I said.

"It's totaled. Was that man drunk?"

"*You* hit *him*," I said. On the freeway, going at least seventy. She changed into his lane without looking first. Or at least without seeing. She flipped, he flipped, they were both lucky to be alive.

"He wasn't there. Then he was."

"I know," I said, because that was the story she'd told me many times. It wasn't the story the other driver told, or the witnesses. "It was an accident. I'm glad you have good insurance."

"This rice is crunchy," she said.

I sighed. I wouldn't know. I hadn't been able to take a bite of my food yet. I did now. She was right. The rice was crunchy.

• • •

The space was like a big warehouse—all cement floors and exposed metal beams. In the center was a big boxing ring. And around the edges were lines of punching bags of various shapes and sizes. The boxing ring was empty, but several people were punching bags, and the noise echoed through the room along with voices and music.

I'd pulled my hair up into a ponytail, like I always did, and wore spandex shorts and an oversized T-shirt, which I rarely did. My shoes were too clean, showing how little I used them. At home I hadn't had time to work out much in the last year or so, what with prepping to open a restaurant and then actually opening that restaurant. I was surprised I had the foresight to bring my shoes at all, but I remembered thinking that I would probably need an outlet here, like running. I did need an outlet. That's why I'd come today. Tara had sent me the address, and I'd realized that punching something might actually be good for me. Help me. Definitely more than the fake therapy sessions had.

I hadn't spotted Elijah yet in my scan of the room. He wasn't at the punching bags. He and his preppy polo shirts and loafers were nowhere to be seen. He had told me ten, right? I checked my watch, it was five minutes until ten.

"Sutton," a jovial voice said from behind me. I turned to see

Michael walking in the glass front door, Tara trailing behind him. "What are you doing here?"

"Something you two should be doing," I said.

He tilted his head. "Boxing?"

"Working out?" Tara asked.

"No, therapy homework."

He laughed, then with that same laughter in his voice said, "She still hasn't figured it out? I'm so shocked."

I narrowed my eyes at his sarcasm. Now was when I was supposed to tell them I was finished. That I didn't want to do this anymore. Why did his smug look and Tara's lowered-eyed reaction make me say, "We still have two more sessions," instead?

Tara smiled at me. "Yes, we do. Don't count us out yet."

He shrugged like he didn't think two weeks was going to make any difference. I waited to feel terrible that I had recommitted to this thing. It wasn't like me to go back and forth like this, but I didn't feel bad. It felt good that I was seeing this through. That *was* like me.

I looked past him. "Where is Elijah?"

"Is he not here?" He moved toward the back corner of the large room, where I could now see a door leading to a windowed office. "Eli!"

Tara fell in step beside me. "Hey, thanks for doing two more sessions. It really means a lot to me." She squeezed my hand. "I'm so glad you're here."

"I'm glad you're here," I said, because that was true. It had been nice to see her these last few weeks. Something I hadn't expected when I came back. She always had a way of making me feel lighter.

"Is this really therapy homework?" she asked.

"It is."

"The therapist told you to box?" she asked, confused.

"She told me to support Elijah in his dreams," I said.

"And he told you *this* was his dream?"

"Is it not?" I asked.

"I mean . . . I didn't think so . . . it could be, I guess."

"If Michael won't agree to therapy, maybe at the very least you can convince him to do the homework we're assigned: five minutes of uninterrupted eye contact a day and supporting each other in some way."

"Maybe I can tell him my dream is therapy."

I laughed. "Yes, do that."

Through the windows, Elijah's head poked up from behind a computer as we approached.

"Do you have any stories about Tara?" Michael asked, holding the office door open for us. "From high school?"

"Please, no," Tara said.

"I'm sure you've heard them all," I said. She was an average student who liked to have fun and party. I didn't go to many parties, where any good stories I could tell probably occurred. The stories I had about her were *not* ones I wanted to share: How she talked me through breakdowns about my dad. How she invited me to sleep over when she could tell I was struggling with my mom. How we binged television shows and made food boards to get our minds off problems. How she quit piano because I wasn't a good friend.

"You kept me grounded," Tara said.

"I did?"

She nodded.

Michael turned to Elijah. "Your fiancée is here."

"Funny," Elijah said, but then he smiled in my direction. "You actually came."

"I told you I would," I said.

"And I'm learning that you are good with follow-through."

"Stop," I said.

"You're not good with follow-through?"

"No, stop learning things."

"But I thought you were quitting," he said.

"I'm not," I spat out. "Two more sessions."

He raised his brows. "Really?"

Tara laughed. "Because she's the best friend ever." She pulled me into a side hug.

I hadn't been the best friend ever, at least not all the time and especially not lately.

Michael shuffled some papers on the desk, then held a stack in the air. "We just came by to pick up the forms for the tournament sponsors."

"Tournament?" I asked.

"Yeah, they're having a big tournament here next month. It's so much work," Tara said. "You should come."

"Yeah, maybe, if I'm still here."

"It was good to see you," she said, heading for the door.

"You too," I said, as both she and Michael left, papers in hand.

Elijah clicked a few keys on his keyboard and then brushed his hands together like he was finished with whatever he was working on. A pile of papers labeled as score sheets sat on the desk nearest to me. "You guys still score matches by hand?"

"Yes, and it's a pain in my ass. It will be ten times more painful for the tournament. Adding and crunching and grouping contestants. Don't get me started."

I almost said that an iPad for each judge and a shared Excel program would take half that pain away. Or even better, someone had probably already developed an app for this. That was very likely. But I was staying out of this. By next month, we'd be done with our therapy wager and I would most likely be gone. So instead, I said, "I will not get you started."

"So, you're not quitting, after all, huh?" That annoying little gleam was back in his eyes.

"Don't," I said. "It's for Tara and no other reason."

"Didn't think there was another reason." He came out from behind the desk. "Don't you look adorable."

"Do your compliments always sound like they should be directed at small animals or children?"

"You're in a good mood today," he said, obviously meaning the opposite. "You don't want to be here?"

I closed my eyes. I didn't want to be home, that was for sure. My mom was on one this morning. She'd spilled her juice again, and this time I'd seen her do it and it seemed purposeful. Her eyes meeting the glass seconds before the back of her hand did. I tried to tell myself that maybe she was having double vision, was dizzy, but I wasn't sure anymore.

"I won't be offended if you want to leave. I can even truthfully tell Dr. Franklin that you came and saw the place."

I took a deep breath. "No, I . . . I said I would." My eyes caught on his stack of scoring sheets again. "Unless you're busy with tournament prep. I can leave."

"No," he said. "I mean, I am, but I need a break."

Were both of us unwilling to be the one to say we didn't want to do this? Or maybe we were both unwilling to say that we really *did*. "I'm here. Let's get this over with."

"Not exactly enthusiastic participation, but participation."

I gave a breathy chuckle. "It's all I have today."

"I'll take it."

I eyed the boxing ring as we walked out of the office. "Am I going in there?"

"Only if you want to, but that's normally a session two or three thing."

"I don't want to." I didn't need to be on display for the whole gym. There were at least half a dozen people working out.

"Have you ever punched a bag before?"

"No," I said.

"Then let's get you punching things."

CHAPTER 13

Elijah led me to a large shelving unit with cubbies of gloves on display. He looked at my hands, then plucked a pair from the third cube. He handed them to me, and as I was about to pull them on, he said, "Wait, I need to wrap you first."

"Wrap me?"

"It's not as intimate as it sounds," he replied.

"Good to know."

He took a black tube of rolled cloth out of a basket, then held one of his hands, fingers splayed out in front of him, nodding for me to do the same.

I tucked one of the gloves beneath my opposite arm and held out my hand.

He unraveled the roll of cloth and began wrapping it around my hand and then between each finger. He was leaned over my hand, his floppy hair brushing my cheek, his sharp, clean scent clouding my space. His touch was gentle yet firm, his fingers brushing my palm with each pass. My stomach gave a flip and I thought, *This is more intimate than you think it is, sir.*

I quickly reminded myself that it had been a while since I'd been touched by a man in any sort of intimate way and that was the *only* reason I was having any sort of reaction to his touch.

"How does that feel?" he asked, straightening up and meeting my eyes.

My cheeks heated up as if he had heard my internal dialogue. "What?"

"Is it too tight? Too loose?" He clenched then unclenched his hand.

"Oh." I mimicked his movement. "It feels fine. Just right?"

"Is that a question?"

"Well, it's my first time," I said, quieter than I meant to, which made it come out sultry, flirtatious.

One side of his mouth raised into a half smile, and he nodded toward my other hand. I readjusted the gloves I held and presented him with my other hand. As if he really did know what had been going through my head, his movements seemed slower this time, deliberately sensual. After each pass, he squeezed my hand, as if testing his placement. But he hadn't done that on the other side. When one drag of his fingers across my palm produced a chill through my entire body, I tensed and let out a small gasp.

"Too tight?" he asked in a low voice, tucking the end under itself.

I pulled my hand away. "You're the worst."

"I have no idea what you're talking about." The smile in his eyes contradicted his statement.

I fisted, then released my hand, testing the comfort, like I had with the other side. "It's good," I said, not willing to give voice to his games.

He helped me slide on each glove, then tied them. Like I suspected everyone who had ever put on a pair of boxing gloves in all the world did, I flared my elbows and punched the ends together twice.

He stared at me, raising his eyebrows, like that wasn't the innate human reaction to putting on a pair of boxing gloves. "Okay, Hulk," he said. "Let's go." He spun around and led me to what I assumed was the most beginner punching bag in the entire gym. Or maybe all punching bags were the same. I had no clue.

"Okay, I'm just going to go over a few basic moves with you."

"Sounds good."

He stood, one foot in front of the other, hands up by his face, bouncing in place. "This is boxing stance."

"Do I have to bounce like that? Is that required?"

He smirked. "Yes."

"Punching is as much in the hips as it is in the arms. Your hips will rotate, your weight will shift depending on which hand you're punching with. I also want you to let out a breath every time you connect. Loud enough that I can hear it." He demonstrated a loud breath. "Yes?"

I nodded.

"Let's start with a jab. Hands up by your face, rotate your hips, shift weight, connect." He demonstrated each word with the accompanying action. "Now you."

I stepped up to the bag, self-conscious at first, but attempting to ignore it. I punched.

"Were you trying not to do anything I just showed you?"

"I thought I was."

He stepped in front of me, put his hands an inch beneath

my elbows without touching, and raised his eyebrows. "Am I allowed to touch you here or is that lying with my body?"

I smirked and then looked around. "Wait, is Dr. Franklin here? Are you trying to convince her we're a couple?"

His hands still hovered.

"Yes, you can touch me," I said with a sigh.

"Say it again," he said in a gravelly voice that took my breath away. I hid my reaction by play-punching him in the chest.

"Ouch," he said, pretending it hurt. "Okay, hands up." He pushed up on my elbows, directing them into position. "That's how you keep yourself from getting punched in the face when you have an opponent."

"I will never have an opponent."

"Probably not, but that doesn't mean you shouldn't learn correct form."

"Yes, sir," I said.

"Ooh, I like that title." He met my eyes with a teasing crinkle at the corners of his. "You can keep calling me that."

I rolled my eyes but then let out a laugh.

"Okay, so remember: Rotate hip, shift weight, punch, connect, breathe." He showed me again.

This time, I actually tried and when I connected, he was right, it felt different, a stronger connection with the bag.

"Good," he said. "Better. Again."

And so I did. I punched some more. He stood behind me, giving me small corrections, in the form of either words or a light touch to my elbow or hip, until he was no longer giving me corrections.

Next, he taught me something called a hook and then a cross with my dominant hand. I repeated those over and over. Then combined them. Sweat formed along my hairline and dripped down my temple. I wiped at it with the back of my forearm. It had been a while since I worked out, and it honestly felt good. He was a good teacher. Patient.

"Shoulders down, not so bunched up," he said, his hand going to my shoulder. When I didn't relax, he said, "You're tight."

"Yeah."

"Can I?" he said, again asking permission to touch me.

I nodded.

He rubbed his thumb in circles along my shoulder and neck. I sucked in some air.

"You have knots all along here. Do you lift weights?"

"Yes," I said. It wasn't a lie. I lifted my mom every day, and she was the reason my neck and shoulders were in the state they were in.

"How do *I* get a special lesson with the owner's son?" a voice over my left shoulder said, too close.

I turned to see a woman standing there in short-shorts and a sports bra. Her dark hair was slicked back into a ponytail, and her brown eyes were on Elijah, not me. She was beautiful.

"I thought you didn't do lessons," she said.

"Hey, Mercedes. I don't." For the first time since I'd met him, Elijah's confidence seemed shaken, like this gorgeous woman standing by us had knocked him off his game.

Her eyes went from Elijah to me, her expression saying, *Then what do you call this?*

"Family friend," he said. "Onetime thing."

"I'm Sutton," I said, because it was obvious he was too nervous to introduce me.

"Hi," she said, smiling, which made her even more beautiful. "Nice to meet you."

"I'm going to get a drink," I said, pointing my gloved hand toward the drinking fountain on the far wall. Giving them a few minutes alone might help. Nobody wanted to flirt with an audience.

When I reached the fountain, I tried to take off one glove, but it was tied on tight. I could pull on the end of the bow with my teeth, but that seemed unsanitary for a public glove. I didn't need that communal string in my mouth. This was obviously a team activity—putting on and taking off boxing gloves. I gave up in my attempt and pushed the long bar of the drinking fountain with the glove. It worked. As I bent over to get a drink, I wondered how often this thing was cleaned. It had been a while since I'd used a public drinking fountain. But I was thirsty. Next time, I'd bring my reusable water bottle. No, not next time. There wasn't going to be a next time. Like he'd said to Mercedes, this was a onetime thing.

I took a drink and turned to see how Elijah was faring and if I needed to give him more time, but he wasn't where I'd left him. My eyes scanned the room and found Mercedes setting up at a punching bag alone, pulling gloves she obviously brought from home out of a bag. They seemed to Velcro on, not tie. I kept looking and finally found Elijah at the wall of cubbies where we had started earlier. Maybe he was ready to take my gloves and call it a day.

I approached him, stopping in front of him and holding out my hands so he could untie the bow.

"What?" he asked. He held two square pads.

"Are we not done?" I asked.

"We can be. I thought I'd do one more exercise with you, but if you need to leave, that's fine."

"No, I just thought . . . One more exercise would be good."

"Okay, good." We walked to an open area of the gym.

"Why don't you do lessons? You're obviously good at teaching," I said.

"If I told you, you might know too much about me. And that would be dangerous, right? Now that you're back in the game."

"True," I said. "Never mind."

He laughed, then slid his hands into the straps at the back of the square pads he held.

"What are those?" I asked.

"These are for you to punch."

"I'm punching something you're holding? That seems dangerous."

"It's not," he said. "I'm going to call out punches and combos, and you do them. We can go as fast or as slow as you need."

"Slow," I said. "We need to go slow."

He met my eyes. "Whatever you need."

My stomach clenched and I nodded.

And that's how it went for the next five minutes. He called a punch, I executed, and then he called another. Our speed slowly increased until it was a steady rhythm in a predictable pattern.

"Does Mercedes make you nervous?" I asked as I kept punching.

"What?"

"Mercedes? You have a crush on her?"

"No, I don't," he said.

I wanted to say, *Yeah, right*, but I sensed that would make him defensive. *Jab, cross, hook. Double jab, cross. Jab, cross, hook.* That was our pattern. His hands seemed to meet me halfway to each punch and absorb some of the power. I wondered if his hands hurt, I was hitting as hard as I could.

"Why do you ask?" he said with a smirk. "Are you jealous?"

His question made me stutter-step, and instead of doing a double jab, I only did a single with my left and moved to the cross before he was ready. My right hand connected with his jaw.

"Oh shit," I said as he stumbled back. His foot caught on a duffel bag that seemed to appear out of nowhere on the floor, and he went down.

I rushed forward, trying to take off my gloves as I went, but they were still stuck on my hands. I used my teeth to untie one string this time, trying not to think about the germs, and then tucked that hand under my left arm and yanked. One hand was finally free, and I used it to free the other. He had landed on his ass, and he sat there for a moment, arms draped over his knees, a stunned expression on his face.

I dropped down to my knees in front of him. "Are you okay? I'm so sorry." I studied his face where I had connected. "KO?" I said quietly, really the only boxing term I knew. Knockout. At least I thought that's what it meant.

"I'm not unconscious," he said.

"Is that why you don't teach lessons?" a deep voice called from the other side of the gym.

He waved as if acknowledging the truth of the statement.

"I'm an idiot," I said. "I'm sorry."

He gave a breathy laugh. "You're not an idiot. I should've had my hands up."

He had a light pink mark on his jaw, and my fingers instinctively went to it, ever so gently tracing a line around it. "Do you have ice? We should put ice on it."

"I'm not going to put ice on it. It was a tap."

"A tap?" I said, looking around for an ice machine or a door leading to a place where one might exist. It had not been a tap. I obviously wasn't a pro, but all my weight had been behind it. I'd felt the hit, heard it.

"We don't have an ice machine," he said.

"You should really have one at a boxing gym. For injuries."

"We're too tough to care about injuries." He pushed himself to standing, then reached down to help me up.

When I was on my feet, I pointed to the front door. "I'll be right back."

"Where are you going?" he called, but I was already fast-walking away.

CHAPTER 14

"Where did you get that?" Elijah asked when I found him in the office again after my trip down the street.

"At the restaurant next door." I held up the ziplock bag full of ice. In my other hand were the black wraps I'd taken off my hands while waiting for said ice. I set them on the corner of his desk.

"You're going to give me a bad reputation," he said.

"They don't know you're human? Who do they suspect you are? Wolverine? He's the one who can heal himself super-fast, yes?"

"Yes," he said. "That's exactly what they think." He was standing at a file cabinet, putting something away.

"Sit down," I said.

"Sutton, I'm fine. I promise. I've been punched in the face before."

"You have? Why?" I remembered the thin scar going through his right eyebrow. I wondered if that was from getting punched.

"Because I work in a boxing gym."

"Fair point." I nodded to his office chair. "Will you just sit down? Please. I already have one difficult patient at home, I don't need another."

I don't know what he saw on my face—exhaustion, perhaps—but he sat down without another word.

I stepped in front of him and pressed the ice against his jaw. I should've grabbed some napkins while I was at it, but I hadn't. "Tell me if it's too cold."

"Okay." He was leaning forward, his elbows on his knees, looking at the ground. The top of his head was nearly brushing my stomach. One of his hands *was* brushing the side of my leg, resting there. His skin on mine created a heat I wasn't expecting. I stared at the back of his neck and had a strong desire to dig my fingers into his hair—something else I wasn't expecting. I swallowed.

"I could help you figure out how to put the score sheets in Excel," I blurted out. I really did feel bad about punching him. "It would do all the adding and grouping for you."

"What?" he asked.

"For the tournament. To save your ass all that pain. I'm really good at Excel."

He let out a chuckle. "You don't have to do that."

"I know, but let me know if you want me to."

He nodded. "What did you think about today?" he asked. "About hitting things. Not me, but the other things."

"Surprisingly therapeutic."

"Exactly," he said. "Who needs therapy when they have some gloves and a bag?"

"That's not what I said."

"Close enough."

"Does Tara come here to punch things?"

"Of course. You know Tara."

It did seem like her.

"She didn't think *you* would come here," he said. His voice made it seem like he won some side bet about that. I wasn't sure how I felt about it.

"Yeah, well, that was high school me."

"You're different now?"

"Yes," I said, even though I wasn't sure if I was. My mom was still dictating my schedule, after all.

"How long do I have to do this to make you feel better?" He gestured to the ice and smiled up at me.

"A little longer," I said.

"You make a good nurse," he said.

"No, I, I really don't . . ." I took a step back, bringing the ice with me. "You're probably good now." It was hard to tell. The ice had made his jaw even more red. "You'll thank me tomorrow."

"Possibly."

My hand was cold and water dripped from the bag, through my fingers and onto the floor. "I should go."

He remained seated, leaning back in the chair. "When can I do my homework?"

"What?"

"Your mom."

I shook my head. "No, never."

"So I get to look bad at our next session, and you get to look like the supportive fiancée?"

"Coming to my house. Being around my mom. That's different."

"It's not that different."

I took another step back, toward the door, water still dripping through my fingers. "It's my house."

"Technically, it's your mom's house, right? I'd like to help."

"I don't need help from you."

His eyebrows popped up. "Ouch."

"You know what I mean."

"You punched me in the face, Sutton, and I let you help me. Let me help you."

"That makes no sense. I *punched* you in the face. You've done nothing to warrant owing me a favor."

"I let you help me. That's what I did. And I'll let you help me with this spreadsheet thing. Now I owe you a favor."

"Fine," I spat out, surprising myself.

I think I surprised him too because he immediately grabbed a pen from the jar on the desk and a scrap piece of paper and said, "What's your address?" like he knew I was going to change my mind if he didn't write it down as fast as humanly possible.

I was already regretting it as I told him the address.

"Tomorrow?" he asked.

"You don't work tomorrow?"

"I have some flexibility, being the son of the owner and all that." There was a darkness to his words when he said them. A story there. I didn't know what. I didn't need to.

CHAPTER 15

"Have you been a server before?" I asked the young man on the phone.

"Not technically," he said.

"What do you mean?"

"I mean, define the word *server*."

I got the feeling he meant for that to be a rhetorical question, but I answered it anyway. "Someone who takes food orders and then delivers said food."

"I've never done that," he said. "But I have worked fast food."

That wasn't nothing. Fast food was hard. "How long did you work there?"

"Like two weeks."

"Right. Okay, well, I'll be in touch, Timothy. Thanks for your time."

He was the fourth phone interview I'd done today and the fourth one I didn't feel I could advance to the next stage. Raya would take pity on the Timothys of the world, and soon we'd have a staff full of incompetent people. I had to at least get some good candidates in front of her.

I sent Presley a quick text, asking her how she was doing. It was one week into my promised two-week fix, and although the staff was using the app consistently now for schedule changes, I was afraid not much else had changed and she was still feeling overwhelmed and dissatisfied.

The bell rang from the other room along with the words "Sutton! Refill!"

I closed my eyes, took a calming breath, and stood. I sucked in some air. I was sore. I hadn't thought I'd used every muscle in my body the day before, but apparently I had.

"Hey, Mom," I said, coming into the living room. She was lying on the couch, her leg propped up. "What do you need?"

"Water."

There was a large lidded cup with a straw and handle sitting on the coffee table that I'd filled earlier. I picked it up to refill it, only to be stopped by its weight. It was full.

"There's water in here, Mom."

"I can't lift that. It's too heavy. I need a normal glass."

Right. Because her perfectly working arm had lost all its strength apparently. I moved to the kitchen.

"Mom, remember someone is coming over today. One of my friends." I wasn't about to tell her that he was coming over to help me with her. She wouldn't like that at all. But she seemed to be relatively kind to strangers, so I had high hopes that my mom would actually treat a pretty boy like Elijah well. Be on her best behavior. Even if he did nothing else, that, in and of itself, would be a nice break.

"Is it Tara?" she asked. "She's a nurse, you know." She always said that like she was the proudest parent in the world. Like she had something to do with Tara's accomplishments.

"Yes, I know. But no, not Tara. His name is Elijah." After several quiet beats I added, "Mom, you know I *own* a restaurant, right?"

"Of course I do. That's very brave of you. Have you paid that girl's parents back yet?"

I didn't know why I ever told her we borrowed money from Raya's parents to start Luminesce. Probably because she had asked point-blank how it was possible, but I regretted it now. "We make monthly payments."

"Well, then . . ." she didn't finish the sentence, but I knew how it ended: *Then you don't own it, do you?* "I read that review about your restaurant online. I saved it on my phone."

She saved the review that called my restaurant lackluster? Why did that make my insides twist? Why did that make me want to defend myself, to tell her that was from months ago? That I was trying to figure out how to give the restaurant more character? That things had picked up? I knew how I'd sound if I opened my mouth though, so I just filled a plastic cup with water and brought it to her.

"I need to go to the bathroom," she said.

"Okay, I'll help you." As I transferred her to her wheelchair, I said, "If you start exercising this arm, the doctor said once your dizziness clears up, you can use a scooter."

"You're tired of helping me?" she asked.

Yes. "No, of course not."

"Because I didn't ask for this to happen to me."

"I know."

"And you're my only daughter. You said you wanted to be here."

"I do." I wheeled her to the bathroom, wondering if now was the time Elijah was going to show up. We hadn't talked about a specific time. We really should've exchanged numbers, but we'd yet to do that. Probably my fault since I'd been trying my hardest to keep him at arm's length. To not know him. To get out of this therapy thing altogether.

But he didn't show up while I was helping my mom in the bathroom. Or when I made her lunch or gave her a sponge bath or changed the bandages on her head and abdomen. He didn't show up when I made her dinner or helped her into some pajamas. He didn't show up as I was giving her night-time meds and muscling her into bed. And he definitely didn't show up when my mom said, almost as an afterthought, "I guess your friend never came," like she wasn't surprised at all.

It wasn't until my mom was long asleep and I had done the dishes and was straightening up the living room that I heard a soft knock on the door.

I wiped all emotion off my face—all the exhaustion, frustration, anger, disappointment—and replaced it with indifference as I opened the door.

Elijah's face was the picture of penitence, brows drawn down, big, sad eyes, disheveled hair. "I'm so sorry," he said.

I looked over my shoulder and stepped out onto the porch, pulling the door shut behind me. "It's fine," I said. "I told you I didn't need help anyway."

"You're not mad?" he asked. "I feel terrible."

"Nope, I do this every day. I don't need an extra body in the way."

"Sutton," he said. I wasn't sure if he wasn't buying my nonchalant routine or if he just felt extremely guilty; whichever the case, he kept talking. "My brother said he'd be at the gym all day today, but he had some wedding emergency. So I asked my dad if he'd come but . . . well, that didn't happen. And I don't have your number—I need your number—or I would've called you. I tried to get it from Tara, but she was on a long shift today and wasn't answering her phone. You're . . . sure you're . . . fine . . . ?"

"No big deal. I had almost forgotten you were coming."

"Right. Okay. Is there anything I can do now?"

"At ten o'clock at night?"

"Is it that late?" He pulled out his phone. "Shit. It is. I'm sorry." His eyes popped back up to mine.

My phone buzzed in my hand. It was a text from Presley. She hadn't gotten back to me earlier. **A little better, but not much. What happened to hiring more help?**

"Everything okay?" Elijah asked.

"Yes, fine. Work stuff."

"Something I can help with?"

"No," I said. *I* couldn't even do anything at the moment.

"What about food?" he asked. "I can get you food. Are you hungry at all?"

I shook my head and backed toward the door, grasping the handle behind me. "I already ate. But I'll see you at therapy, yeah?"

"I can come back tomorrow. I'll come—"

"Please," I interrupted. "Please don't . . ." *Make promises you can't keep.* I kept those last words to myself because that would give away too much. Make him realize that my throat was burning and my eyes were stinging right now. I was just tired. I didn't need a person. People had the ability to disappoint. To not follow through. Like he had proven today. I could take care of myself. Could take care of everything. I just needed sleep.

"Okay," he said.

I pasted on a smile. "Looks like I don't hit that hard after all," I said, noting his jaw was not discolored in any way. Not even the slightest bruise.

"It was probably this great nurse I had who held some ice to my face," he said.

"Or your Wolverine powers."

He smiled, the guilt finally gone from his expression, and took a step back. His eyes scanned the house around me as if this gave him another piece to the puzzle he was assembling about my life in his head. "I'll see you soon."

I nodded.

CHAPTER 16

By "soon," he meant early the next morning. I had been up for a while, but I'd just gotten my mom out of bed and was starting the coffee when, like the night before, there was a soft knock on the door. I was still in my pajamas. But like every morning, directly out of bed, I had already combed my hair and brushed my teeth.

"Who's there?" Mom asked from the couch.

"I'll check."

"It's too early for people," she said.

"Agreed." I pulled my hair into a low pony with the hair tie around my wrist and cracked open the door.

Elijah stood there with a plastic bag in his hand. "Hey."

"Hey yourself," I said.

He held out the bag. "Breakfast. You haven't eaten yet, have you?"

"I haven't."

"I got you that omelet you had at the diner last week."

He remembered my order from the diner?

"And since I didn't know what your mom likes to eat, there are several options for her. Another omelet, some French toast, an entire container of bacon." Apparently his guilt about the day before hadn't entirely left him.

"You really didn't have to do this," I said, but my stomach growled at the mention of bacon.

"I really did." He held out the bag.

I stepped one bare foot onto the porch to retrieve it. He took in my pajamas—silky black pants and a matching button-down, long-sleeved top.

"Do you always look so cute in the mornings?" he asked.

"Keep your guilt compliments to yourself," I said, but a traitorous blush crept up my face. I tried to remember the last time anyone had called me cute. When I was five years old in pigtails? I wasn't generally regarded as cute. Tall, intimidating, businesslike, sometimes stunning, when I put in the effort. But never cute.

He smiled his winning smile. I took the bag and he gave me a salute, then jogged to his car.

I closed the door and set the bag on the table, where I pulled the containers out one by one.

"You had food delivered?" Mom asked.

"Yes," I said, because I didn't want to explain that Elijah was bringing us food because he felt guilty about not coming over to help the day before. I was sure she'd have something to say about that. I was feeling too surprised . . . in a good way . . . to want my mom's commentary right now.

I plucked a piece of bacon out of its container and took a bite. "What sounds good? Eggs or French toast?"

"You know I only do coffee first thing in the morning. And a banana. I'd like a banana."

"More for me," I said, taking another bite. I poured her a mug of coffee, peeled her a banana, and took them both to her.

"I can't believe you answered the door like that," she said, nodding toward my messy ponytail.

"I have it on good authority that I look cute," I said.

She laughed like it was a joke.

I set her coffee and banana down on the TV tray before I gave in to any intrusive thoughts.

"Does this have my vanilla creamer in it?"

She has a reconstructed leg. She takes pain meds all day for it. She has to be helped onto the toilet. I would be grumpy too. I repeated these words over and over as I got her creamer.

Maybe I needed to put on some gloves and punch things again today. Good thing I happened to know someone who ran a boxing gym.

• • •

We really do need to exchange phone numbers, I thought as I climbed out of my car and headed to the gym. I'd left my mom with her phone and the remote and pillows propped up just right and told her to call me if she needed me. She was only sixty years old, she reminded me, and I was treating her like some frail old woman. I didn't remind her that she was sixty-two.

The gym was busier than the last time I was here. It was the weekend, so that made sense. My days all felt the same lately, but that didn't mean everyone else's were.

"Sutton," a deep voice said, and I turned, thinking I was going to see Elijah, but it was Michael, standing by the wall of boxing gloves, rerolling wraps.

"Hi," I said. "Elijah said I could come work out whenever."

"Of course." He nodded toward the shelves. "Help yourself."

"Thanks." I slowly walked forward, feeling way more intimidated this time than last time because I wasn't sure I could *help myself*. I didn't remember which gloves Elijah had picked out for me or if I could even get them tied up on my own.

"Eli isn't here right now," Michael said.

"That's okay," I said, even as feelings of disappointment settled onto my chest. Those feelings surprised me. "Did you get your wedding emergency under control?"

"Wedding emergency?" he asked, tossing me a rolled-up wrap.

I barely caught it, fumbling it between both hands before securing it against my chest. "Yesterday," I said.

"Yesterday was insane here, we had a last-minute qualifier for the tournament next month. Trying to drum up more interest."

"Oh." My expression must've fallen because his eyes narrowed.

Then suddenly he lifted a finger as if he remembered something. "Oh! But I had to leave because our cake lady fell through and I had to taste some new flavors from a new cake person."

"Right," I said, wondering if he made up that lie on the spot, realizing his brother had lied to me or if that was actually true. This was the guy who wanted to trick a therapist to get out of therapy, after all. He obviously had no moral compass. I looked over my shoulder to see if Elijah had shown up and was feeding him lines. He hadn't. "Cakes are serious business."

"You're telling me," he said.

I handed him back the wrap, not feeling up to boxing anymore.

"You don't want to hit a bag?" he asked. "The speed bag is fun. I can show you how."

"No, I think I'm good." I walked back toward the door.

"I'll let Eli know you came by," he said.

"No need," I said. "Tell Tara I say hi though."

"Will do."

I left the gym and headed toward my car. But instead of getting in and going home, like I had planned to do after fleeing the gym, I picked up my pace and passed my car. I settled into a steady jog. This area of Clovis was called Old Town. It was made up of family-owned restaurants, used bookstores, boutique clothing shops, small music stores, and antique shops. The storefronts looked as if they were out of an old western, with faux second-story balconies and even some posts where horses used to be tied before cars took over.

I jogged, trying to release all the tension in my neck and shoulders. I was still sore from the boxing I'd done two days ago and from the Mom lifting I did at home and from the stress of trying to find a couple of new servers. I had four more interviews this afternoon. And I needed to call the chef and make sure the kitchen was running smoothly. I didn't want any drama to sneak up on me there. In my call with Raya that morning, she hadn't mentioned any problems, but I needed to double-check.

By the time I'd circled several city blocks and was back to my car, my neck and shoulders felt just as tense as when I started the run.

"Did you work out today?" The voice startled me as I was reaching for my car's door handle, the back of my neck and hairline damp with sweat. Elijah's face still caught me off guard sometimes. He really was a beautiful man—all dark features and sharp angles.

"Um, what? No. Yes. I'm leaving."

"You okay?"

"Fine," I said.

"I had a meeting with my dad this morning."

"Okay," I said, and opened my car door. "See you for therapy." I climbed into my car, shut the door, and pressed the start button. My heart was beating fast as I watched him watching me through the front windshield.

I wanted to roll my window down and scream, "Might want to clue your brother in on the lie you decide to go with next time!" I didn't do that. I didn't care. I couldn't care. I just put my car in reverse and drove away. He, like everyone else, could just think I was boring and cold. At this point, I agreed with them.

CHAPTER 17

I couldn't believe this was our third therapy session. That I'd been here in Clovis taking care of my mom for a month now. In some ways she seemed to be doing better. She moved a little easier, when she wanted to. She seemed to be in a little less pain. But in other ways she seemed exactly the same. I still had to do everything for her, and it was never good enough. I was used to the second part of that equation.

My phone buzzed as I headed toward the office building.

What time did you say the interviews were again tomorrow? Raya's text asked.

I had told her on our morning phone call but should've written it down in a text too. One at two and one at three thirty, I quickly typed back.

And if I hire them, you'll work them into next week's schedule?

Yes, and tell Presley. She's anxious to have the help.

Presley is a whiner.

She's the best server we have. Treat her well.

I do, but between you and me, she's a whiner.

I laughed and tucked my phone away. I had seen Elijah's car already in the parking lot when I'd pulled in, but he wasn't in it. I was five minutes early, so I was surprised he had already gone inside. When I went in, he wasn't in the waiting room either. And like every session so far, neither was anyone else. No receptionist, no other patients. It was nice of Dr. Franklin to stay late for us.

I wondered if Elijah was using the bathroom when I heard voices and laughter from down the hall, in Dr. Franklin's office.

"Am I late?" I asked at the open door.

Dr. Franklin and Elijah were standing shoulder to shoulder, looking at a framed picture on her desk. She jumped at my words, putting space between herself and Elijah.

He smiled at me, then casually walked to my side. I could tell he was about to brush a hand down my arm when he stopped himself. Probably remembering me telling him not to lie with his body in front of Dr. Franklin. "You're not late. You're perfectly on time. I was early."

This was the session I needed to drop more obvious hints so Dr. Franklin could guess we weren't in a relationship. Maybe Elijah had unwittingly started the ball rolling by showing up early to flirt with the therapist.

"Have a seat," she said. "Let's get started."

We settled into the love seat and, seriously, she needed to invest in a bigger couch. This thing was too small for a couple. Our thighs and sides were smashed against each other once again. This was probably another one of her bonding exercises. Elijah moved his arm to the back of the couch, which freed up some space but felt more intimate.

Dr. Franklin shut the door, then assumed her place in the chair with her notebook. I looked at the closed door.

"How are you both? This week go well? Were you able to complete your homework?"

"Yep," I said, turning my attention back to her.

I could feel Elijah's eyes on me as if he wondered why I hadn't tattled on him. I wasn't sure either. Only that I worried if I talked about it that the genuine hurt I'd felt over him not showing up (especially after learning that it was for some made-up reason) would be impossible to hide. And these sessions weren't about genuine feelings.

"And how was it?" she asked.

"I didn't think I'd like boxing, but I did. It was a nice stress reliever."

"How did it make you feel to have her there?" she asked Elijah.

"I haven't taught someone since . . . it's been a while . . . and she was a good person to break myself back in with. She made it fun."

Did he just call me fun? "You haven't taught someone since when?" I asked, because I was trying to drop hints and because I really wanted to know.

He couldn't say something like, *You know this, Sutton*, because I did not, in fact, know this. But I could see his mind working. Hopefully Dr. Franklin could as well.

"Since I used to box," he said.

My eyes went wide. Of course, I knew he worked at the boxing gym, but I didn't know he used to actually box. He just had the one razor-thin scar through his brow, but other than that, his face did not look like it had been involved in any serious fights. "You're too pretty."

He let out a single laugh. "That's what you tell me."

"You don't want him to box?" Dr. Franklin asked me, and

Elijah gave her a look like that was the stupidest question she could've asked. But she was probably genuinely curious as well.

"I want him to do whatever he wants to do," I said, which was true.

"And what is it that you want to do?" she asked him. Again, he gave her that look.

"I run a boxing gym," he said, which didn't really answer her question.

"And that's what you want to do?" she said carefully.

The room seemed charged with tense energy. I wasn't sure what to do to defuse it. Wasn't that her job to figure out? My hand, seemingly on its own, moved to pat his chest. "I punched him in the face by accident during my visit. I don't think I'm welcome back at the gym," I teased.

"You are," he said quickly. "She is. She can come back whenever she wants."

How did this woman not know we weren't in a relationship after statements like that?

"Tell me about that feeling," she said, her gaze on me.

I was confused. "What feeling?"

"That an accident would lead to you not being welcome back."

"I was just teasing," I said.

"Were you?"

To my surprise and horror, tears stung my eyes. I was not going to unpack my childhood baggage of abandonment here. It was not the time or place. Well, maybe it was the place, but definitely not the time.

"I dropped the ball this week," Elijah said. I wasn't sure if he knew I needed saving and was returning the favor or if he was just uncomfortable in silence, but either way, I was grateful to have the attention off me.

"How?" she asked.

"I was supposed to help with her mom."

"And you didn't?"

"It turned into a really busy day, half of which I was left in charge of by myself."

"Michael really had a cake emergency?" I asked, renewed irritation at his lie coursing through me.

"He did," he said. "Right when I was about to leave."

"Okay," I said.

"You don't believe me?"

"I talked to him a couple days ago."

"Then you know."

"He said there was a last-minute qualifier."

"There was. Then a cake emergency when I was about to leave."

"You're sticking with that?"

"Why don't you believe him?" Dr. Franklin asked.

"Because I saw Michael's face when I asked him about it. He seemed to make it up on the spot to cover for him."

Elijah shifted toward me, his thigh pressing even more against mine. "Is that why you've been mad at me?"

"I haven't been mad at you," I said, even though we weren't supposed to tell lies in here.

"You were mad when you left the gym the other day. You hardly said two words to me."

"Yeah, well, you lied, so . . ."

"You have trust issues," Elijah said, obviously irritated.

"That is too broad," Dr. Franklin said. "Let's not use *always* or *never* statements."

"I didn't say *always* or *never*," Elijah said.

"But that's how it was delivered. That she has an all-encompassing issue."

"I probably do," I said. "But my issues are well earned."

Elijah laughed, his irritation melting off his face.

Dr. Franklin looked at me as though I had just derailed her attempt to support me. I had. I didn't need her to correct Elijah on my behalf over a fake relationship.

"Well earned how?" she asked.

I shouldn't have said that. "Childhood shit," I said. "Not relevant here."

"Childhood shit is always relevant," she said.

Then I was in more trouble than I realized.

"Back to the support," she said. "Eli, you didn't help her on this specific day when there was a tournament and a cake emergency." She said *cake emergency* like she didn't believe him either. I nearly laughed out loud. "Then why not a different day? The week was seven days long."

"That was the day we had agreed on," he said.

"He brought me and my mom breakfast the next day," I said, suddenly feeling defensive of him.

"Dropping breakfast at someone's house is a good start," Dr. Franklin said. "But it's important to show genuine effort."

He shifted uncomfortably. "Did my dad just channel your body to deliver that message?"

"Is your dad dead?" I asked and then immediately clamped my mouth shut.

He laughed. "You always like to joke. You know he's alive and kicking and full of *support*." He said the word *support* like he meant the exact opposite.

I smiled as if I was part of this joke and this knowledge.

Dr. Franklin leaned back in her chair, her gaze slowly and steadily shifting from Elijah to me and back again. This was it. She knew and she was going to say something and put us both out of our misery, and we could hand therapy over to the two people who actually needed it.

"Close your eyes," she said.

"What?" I asked.

"Both of you. Close your eyes."

I did as she said.

"I want you to picture yourself as a child."

This was my fault, bringing up my childhood, I was sure.

"What you looked like, how you felt back then," she continued. "Now, put your fully grown adult self, the you of now, in front of that child. What would you, with all the knowledge you have now, say to your younger self?"

My parents didn't fight when I was young. We had a quiet household. Very quiet. Unless my dad was playing the violin. Then that singular sound filled the house with sharp, haunting melodies. Sometimes they'd have friends over, and that's when my dad's loud, fun side came out. It always surprised me that he seemed like such a different person around his friends.

"Can you picture yourself?" Dr. Franklin asked. "What you looked like, what you wore, what you were doing?"

My mom dressed me well. She liked to thrift shop. It was one of her hobbies. She was really good at finding the best clothes. She had style that she extended to me.

In my imagination now, I wore a pair of burnt orange corduroy pants and a striped T-shirt. My hair was in a low ponytail, a velvety ribbon tied around it. That was back when my mom did my hair. Before my dad left. She didn't take me to parks or play places or library story times, like other parents did with their kids. But I tagged along with her to the things she wanted to do—brunch or nature walks or searching antique stores for treasures. I may have been a surprise addition to her life, but she folded me into her already-established routine like nothing had changed.

"What would you say to that child?" Dr. Franklin asked.

I remembered that first year after my dad left, things were hard. Mom retreated into herself, into her routines, but didn't include me anymore. I felt alone and scared. My dad had left, and it felt like she had left right along with him.

"You're going to be fine. You're strong and you don't need anyone." The words were out before I realized I'd said them out loud. But that was what I'd tell that scared little girl. That she turned out fine. Strong. That she would accomplish the things she set her mind to and that she didn't have to count on anyone.

"Let's unpack that," Dr. Franklin said. "Do you still feel like you don't need anyone?"

I opened my eyes, not really wanting to unpack anything. The answer was yes, of course. Because I didn't. "I want people in my life. I don't need them."

"And do you consider that a strength?" she asked.

"Not needing people?" I clarified.

"Yes."

"I think it's important to trust myself. And I do."

"Do you ask for help when you need it?"

"She doesn't ask for help. Doesn't want it," Elijah said. And after I didn't tattle on him!

"You wouldn't even let me put a pack of ice on your face

after I punched you," I said. "So you might want to turn that statement right around."

"Just telling the truth," he said. "And you put ice on my face, didn't you? I obviously let you."

"What would *you* say to your childhood self?" I asked.

"Yes, Eli," Dr. Franklin agreed. "Let's finish the exercise. Close your eyes."

He reluctantly did. We were all quiet for some time. I was surprised Elijah let it be silent for that long. He seemed uncomfortable in silence. But he was deep in his thoughts, and Dr. Franklin allowed the time to pass.

Finally, he said, "You can't make everyone happy."

"Explain," she said.

"I thought I could make everyone happy as a kid," he said, like the answer was obvious. "Bent myself in a lot of different directions, always trying to police everyone's emotions. Thinking I could change them by being overly accommodating."

"And now?" she asked.

He let out an ironic little laugh, most likely thinking about how we were sitting in this room because he was doing his brother a favor. "I probably still need that message."

Dr. Franklin turned her eyes to me. "Is he a people pleaser? And does he often choose pleasing other people over plans with you, like this week with the homework?"

"No, what? No," I sputtered out because that suddenly felt like too much, saying he should ever choose me over his real life. "He needs to choose himself."

"Does he choose less important people over you?"

"No." Nobody was less important than me in his life. "But I put my work first a lot too." And wasn't that the truth. "I get it."

His hand slid over mine and I nearly jumped from surprise.

"I'm not lying," he said in a low voice only I could hear.

After a moment, I turned my hand, palm up, and as our fingers laced together, my shoulders relaxed.

CHAPTER 18

"What do you do, Sutton?" Elijah asked as we walked out to the car after that disaster of a therapy session. I had revealed too much. Felt too much. I didn't like it. "Back home? When you're not here taking care of your mom?"

It seemed pointless not to answer his questions now. The therapist was never guessing. And we only had one session left anyway. Michael and Elijah were going to win this bet. I felt sorry for Tara, who only wanted to strengthen her relationship. "I own a restaurant in the city."

"You *own* a restaurant in Los Angeles?"

"Don't be too impressed. It's been called a lackluster, boring dining experience."

"How old are you?" he suddenly asked.

"Same age as Tara. Twenty-eight."

"And you own a restaurant," he said again. "For how long?"

"Almost a year." I stopped at my car and turned to face him.

He had a look of wonder on his face. "Are your parents loaded or something?"

I didn't know why that question felt like a kick to the gut. Maybe because I knew that, even if I'd asked, my parents wouldn't have given me money. Maybe because I knew that we *had* borrowed money from Raya's parents. It wasn't a lot, but enough to show the bank we were willing to put up collateral for the loan. We made payments on that family loan monthly, along with the payments to the bank. And that was all the help we'd gotten. The rest we'd done on our own. Something he obviously didn't think possible. "Something like that," I muttered and turned to open the car door.

"Sutton, wait."

I sighed and faced him again.

"My parents are loaded. They're the ones who started the boxing gym because I was somewhat good at boxing when I was a teenager. They built this whole thing around me, for me, and I don't even want it. But I have to stay. At least until it makes enough to pay my dad back. I can't fail at this." His face was open, vulnerable, pleading. Like I somehow had all the answers.

"Is it failing?" I asked.

"No. Unless you judge failure by how much you want to be in a place."

"That's hard," I said.

"Yeah."

"Maybe you should talk to your dad. Tell him how you feel."

His eyes shot to the ground, then back up to mine. "Easier said than done." His smile crept back onto his face. His vulnerable expression tucked behind it. "Probably not for you. You seem to have nerves of steel."

"*Cold* as steel, my ex would tell you."

"You're not cold," he said.

I let out a single laugh, wondering if he was being sarcastic.

He didn't return the laugh. He only seemed sincere. "You're not. Do you think you're cold?"

"Maybe . . . sometimes."

He widened his heart-stopping smile. "You searched out an ice pack for me, then held it on my face when I was being stubborn."

"After I punched you," I reminded him.

He took a step closer. "You were very good at comforting me. You're not cold," he said again.

I wasn't sure why those words, of all the words he could've said, were drilling into my chest, seeming to fracture the walls I had up. "Okay, well . . ." I took a step back, toward my car door.

"I'll see you tomorrow," he said.

My head whipped in his direction. "Why?"

"Because I'm helping you with your mom."

"That was last week's homework."

He shrugged. "Wrap your warm steel beams around it, because it's happening."

I rolled my eyes and he laughed. Then he was walking to his car, and I was letting him without further protest.

• • •

"What if we did karaoke every Friday?" Raya asked on the phone the next morning.

I tried not to immediately shut down that idea. Tried to seriously consider it. But I couldn't for long. "That's not really our crowd. We're bordering on high-end."

"True," she said. "What do these annoying food critics want from us?"

We'd gotten another average review overnight. This time from a popular social media critic. "We're in Los Angeles. They want an experience with their food." We had spent so much time perfecting the menu: tasting and reworking and tasting and reworking and tasting and reworking. We hadn't put as much effort into the space itself. By the time we'd ordered tables and had the beautiful bar built and picked out the perfect chairs, the money was all but gone. We'd spent the last of it on generic art, figuring the food would be enough. The food was apparently not enough. People wanted all their senses wowed.

"Let's have a brainstorming session with our waitstaff and chef and ask for ideas." *See, Dr. Franklin, I could ask for help.*

"Sounds good," Raya said.

"Good luck with the interviews later."

"What interviews?"

"The ones for—"

"Just kidding, Sutton. I remember. I'm doing a decent job over here. I can't wait for you to come back, but I'm holding it together."

"I know you are. Thank you."

We hung up and I rejoined my mom in the living room. "We have physical therapy in a couple hours," I said.

"Only one of us has physical therapy in a couple hours," she responded.

"True."

She nodded and then closed her eyes as if the nod made her dizzy.

"You okay?"

"Fine."

"Mom," I said, remembering yesterday's therapy session and how it reminded me that she used to do antique shopping and thrift shopping and all the unique finds she'd made. She had style. Maybe not so much anymore, but when she'd been interested in that. "When you go to a restaurant, what kind of atmosphere do you like?"

"Are you upset over the review?"

How did she know I'd gotten another review? "Do you have me on Google Alerts?"

"Yes, I actually do," she said. "This one wasn't as bad as the last one."

It felt just as bad because, before, we'd told ourselves it was just one opinion. We couldn't say that anymore.

"I don't know what kids like these days," she said, answering my question about atmosphere.

"But what do you like? Middle-aged people visit our restaurant a lot."

"Is the music too loud? Is it too dark?"

"I don't think so," I said.

"That's what my friends always complain about."

"But what do you like to see? You, personally."

"I don't know. The menu. I can't fix all your problems for you, Sutton."

Was she being difficult on purpose, trying to misunderstand me? Or was this just who she was?

"That's true," I said. "I'm going to shower before we have to leave. Do you need anything?"

"I'm fully capable," she said.

I kept the words *I guess I'm off bathroom duty then* to myself and left.

I wasn't planning on washing my hair today, I'd just washed it two days ago. But as the hot water poured over me, I put my head down and let the spray work on the knots that still existed along my shoulders and up my neck. I switched the spray pattern on the showerhead to the massage setting and closed my eyes as it pounded along my spine in a steady rhythm. Soon the hair at the nape of my neck was soaked, so I gave up attempting to keep it dry. I took out the claw clip and set it on the counter just outside the shower curtain, letting my hair fall around my shoulders and flatten with the hot water. Steam opened my lungs, and I put my hands on the tiled wall in front of me, leaning in as the water continued to work.

Hazel eyes flashed behind my closed lids, and a memory of Elijah rubbing the knots in my neck with his strong hands immediately sprang to mind. With it came an unexpected tightening in my stomach and lower. How would it feel to have his hands all over me? I turned to face the showerhead, the water grazing my nipples. I gasped at how sensitive they felt right now.

God, it had been a long time. Even when I was with Nate, my mind had been too caught up in work and stress to let myself relax enough to have any sort of release. I'd often help him get there, only to turn over and go to sleep. Shit, he was right to break up with me, wasn't he?

The water was hitting lower now and a little moan escaped. I reached up to unlatch the showerhead from its cradle. I fumbled in my attempt to thread the hose through the holder, and water sprayed the shower curtain, then straight up to the ceiling before I had a firm grip on the handle. I was out of breath as I held the pulsing showerhead in my hand. I stared at it for a moment, wondering if I was even still in the mood.

An image of Elijah's head close to my stomach as I held ice to his face got me right back where I needed to be. Picturing his hand brushing the side of my leg took me even further. I lowered the showerhead, braced my hand against the wall, and closed my eyes. I saw stars for a moment as the sensation sent a wave of pleasure through me. I lifted my foot to the edge of the tub, and more waves elicited a gasping breath. I was climbing slowly, my whole body tense with pleasure.

Then I heard the sharp rings of the bell from the living room, and my climb screeched to a halt. "No, no, no," I muttered, keeping the showerhead right where it was. I just needed a couple more minutes.

The bell was incessant and loud, and it sounded like it was closer than the couch. Had she fallen? Dragged herself down the hall? Was she experiencing some kind of emergency? I replaced the showerhead and turned off the water. I wrapped a towel around my body, my hair still dripping wet as I opened the door.

"Mom?" I called out. "Are you okay?"

The bell kept ringing.

I walked down the hall to find her sitting, perfectly fine, on the couch. She looked at me with a blank expression.

"What is it?" I asked.

"Someone is at the door." She pointed to the door that was literally twenty feet in front of us. I knew she couldn't have answered it without a lot of effort, but it felt like maybe she could've put some in.

"Let me throw on a robe," I said.

"They've been knocking for a while," she said. "Please just tell them to stop."

I approached the door, knowing full well who was on the other side. I had tried to forget he was coming today in case something came up again. And he'd never told me a time. I cracked it open, poked my head out, and said, "I need to get dressed. Give me a second."

"Why is your face so flushed?" he asked.

Maybe because I thought he deserved it with a question like that, or maybe because of my thoughts in the shower, whatever the case, I swung open the door. "Just come in. I'll be a minute."

His eyes traveled down my body, and now it was *his* face that was flushed. I'd surprised him. Quite frankly, I surprised myself. But his expression made it completely worth it.

"Mom, this is Elijah. Elijah, Andrea. I'll be back."

I rushed down the hall and shut myself in my room, leaning my back against the door. Across the way, the mirror above my desk reflected an image of what Elijah had just seen: my body barely covered by a towel, pink cheeks and chest, and dripping wet hair, wild and messy.

What had gotten into me?

CHAPTER 19

Fifteen minutes later, as I walked toward the living room, clothes on, hair brushed, and mostly dry, with a coat of mascara on, I heard my mom talking about how she was normally much more put together, but she'd had to rely on a subpar hairdresser for the last month. Me, she was talking about me.

"Considering you just had a serious accident," Elijah said, "you look amazing. You're a beautiful woman, Mrs. Scott."

I couldn't hear my mom's response, it was quiet. I wondered what she said to that. My mom *was* a beautiful woman. It wasn't until years after my dad had left, when I was older, that I'd wondered why she hadn't put herself out there again, found love. She'd just buried her head in work and seemed to forget about that side of life.

Mom had a stern expression on when I rounded the corner. Was she angry I had sprung a visitor on her? I hadn't warned her this time. If he was going to stand me up again, I hadn't wanted her to know.

"Hi," he said, meeting my eyes.

That tiny greeting and eye contact made my cheeks heat up again—not only from thoughts of the shower but from what he had seen minutes ago. "Hey," I said, trying to play nonchalant. "I'm going to grab some water. Mom, do you need anything?"

"I'm good," she said.

I brushed by Elijah and went to the kitchen. He followed me.

I retrieved a glass. "Can I get you some water?"

"I'm not here to be waited on. What can I do?"

"My mom has a physical therapy appointment today." I glanced over his shoulder at my mom, who was searching for something on the couch beside her. Probably the remote. I lowered my voice. "Maybe you can help me put her in the car in about thirty minutes. That would be very helpful. And then you can go back to that job you hate."

I gave him a smirk to show I was mostly teasing. I didn't want to poke at a sore spot, but Elijah liked to joke, so I was pretty sure he could handle it.

"Yeah," he said. "You probably think I'm a complete ingrate. I really am."

"You're not. You shouldn't do something you don't like." I walked the thirty steps to the living room, picked up the remote off the end table, and handed it to my mom.

She immediately turned the television on to the unnecessarily loud volume that she liked, and I returned to the kitchen without saying anything about it. "Does your dad just go around starting businesses for people without much input, or what?"

"Actually, yes. He has a very successful, large car dealership, and it was his dream that each of his kids run their own business doing something they love. My older sister has a salon he helped her start and market."

I took the glass I had retrieved earlier and filled it with ice. "What about Michael? Where is his forced career?"

"For now, he's helping with the boxing gym 'til he figures out what his passion is."

"And his passion is not boxing, I take it?"

"That would be too convenient."

"It really would," I said, using the dispenser in the refrigerator door for water.

Elijah leaned back against the counter while I drank several gulps, then refilled my glass.

"What?" I asked, because he was staring at me.

On the television, the sounds of the wheel spinning on *The Price Is Right* filled the room.

"You"—he gave a long pause, then nodded toward the front door—"are sexy as hell."

And there went my cheeks, heating up again, probably bright red. Someone must've hit the one-dollar space on the wheel because there were screams of joy on the television. I patted my pockets and realized I didn't have my cell phone. It was probably in my bedroom. I pointed toward his pocket. "You need my phone number to avoid future towel greetings."

"If a phone number is going to take those off the table, I've decided I don't need it." His words were obviously a joke because he freed his phone and handed it to me.

I entered my number, then texted myself his name so that I had his.

When I handed him back his phone, he said, "What do you think about our homework this week?"

"We don't have to do the homework this week. She hasn't guessed, Elijah. One more session and we're done and she's none the wiser. Then Michael doesn't have to do big, bad therapy. He wins." I was still trying to think of a way to help Tara convince him outside of this bet, but I hadn't thought of anything yet.

He tucked his cell back into his pocket. "Maybe he *should* do therapy. I feel like it has brought me closer to a complete stranger. Imagine if we were in love."

I swallowed. "Imagine."

He smiled.

"You should tell your brother you changed teams." I knew Elijah was the answer to change his mind.

"Maybe I will," he said. "You don't want to do the homework?"

"Aren't you doing the homework right now?" I asked.

"This is last week's," he said.

"Close enough."

"You have to tell her if we don't."

"You really are a people pleaser, aren't you? Worried about getting in trouble."

He thought about that statement, like my saying it out loud made him realize that's exactly what he was doing. "Maybe not doing the homework should actually be my homework."

The homework this week was a scratch-off date night game that I was pretty sure Dr. Franklin had invented. She had pulled one sheet out of a bundle of them. If we thought it was fun and it helped us, she'd probably offer to sell us the whole pack. We were not going to do a scratch-off date night. Especially because I knew the risk that the last thing we scratched off on the sheet would probably be some creative sex game.

This exercise was for already-established couples, after all. People she was trying to help communicate their needs in a relationship better. The last thing would probably read, *Tell each other what you like in bed and then get in bed and do those things.* Or maybe something like, *Think of a place you've never had sex. Go to that place and do the sex.*

A voice in my head said, *But that scratch-off would give you an excuse to have sex with this beautiful man.*

I shook my head. If I needed an excuse, then I knew I shouldn't. It was too complicated. He lived here and was obviously stuck here for a while paying off a loan. I didn't live here. My whole life existed somewhere else. He thought therapy was a joke, I didn't. He would have sex with me if a scratch-off told him to because he wouldn't want to disappoint our pretty therapist. I wouldn't. I would do it because my body was starting to react every time he was around, and that was a recipe for heartache. At least heartache on my side. And one-sided heartache was the worst kind.

"My mom is still in a lot of pain, which makes her kind of"—I looked once over my shoulder, although I wasn't sure why, the television was so loud that I could hardly hear the conversation we'd been having until this point, and I knew she couldn't hear us—"grumpy," I finished. What I didn't say was that even when she wasn't in pain, she was pretty grumpy. He didn't need to know all that. I protected my mom from those things.

"Is that why, when I called her beautiful, she said, *I don't need pretty words?*"

"She said that?"

He nodded.

"She's an excellent bullshit detector."

"I don't bullshit."

I laughed. "I think you're a professional bullshitter."

"Rude," he said.

I smiled. "Just have some patience with her. That's all I'm saying." That was my daily mantra.

"You don't think I'm patient? I taught you to box, didn't I?"

"Rude," I said, mimicking him. Then I used his boxing technique to playfully land a jab on his stomach.

He swatted my hand away with a smile, and as I was leading him back out to the living room, he said, "Do you really think I'm a professional bullshitter?"

"Yes, I think you say things people want to hear. And also, I think you and your brother like pranks and bets that not everyone is always privy to."

The smile that had been lighting his face slipped away. "Glad to know you think so highly of me."

I stopped behind the love seat adjacent to the long couch where my mom sat. "Mom, what do you want to wear to therapy today?"

She looked down at the pajamas I had helped her into the night before. "Not this." Then her eyes went to Elijah. "Are you staying?"

"For a bit," he said. "If that's okay."

"Why are you here?" she asked.

"To see Sutton. And to meet you," he said.

Like I said, she was an excellent bullshit detector, and at that answer, she narrowed her eyes in his direction. "Is she paying you?"

I groaned. "I'm not paying him. He's not a medical professional. He's my friend."

"Since when? Sutton only has one friend around here, and she would actually be helpful to me. Why didn't you ask Tara to come instead? I know her."

"Can I be honest with you?" Elijah said.

"It would be nice if you'd start," she said.

"I met your daughter about a month ago. We ended up on the wrong end of a bet. But I'm beginning to think that it was actually the right end because I kind of dig her."

My throat tightened. Was that true? And what did it even mean?

"*Dig* her?" Mom said, with skeptical eyes.

"Okay," I said, holding up a hand to stop Elijah from trying to get on my mom's good side. I wasn't sure claiming to like me was the flex he thought it was. And I wasn't sure my mom had a good side, but his people-pleasing nature was going to have him jumping off cliffs to find it. "He's here. He's going to help us with a few things because he is, in actuality, my friend." I approached her. "Put your arm around my neck."

I braced myself on the back of the couch as she wrapped her arm around my neck, and I used my body weight to shift her to the wheelchair. Elijah, taking a second to catch on to what was happening, rushed around to hold the wheelchair from behind as I transferred her.

Once she was in the seat, I mouthed, "Wait here" to him. He nodded.

"You want to wear sweats?" I asked Mom as I wheeled her back to her room.

"That would probably be best," she said.

I shut her door after wheeling her inside her bedroom. That's when she said, "I don't like him."

I sighed. "Why?"

"He's a smooth talker. The type to make big promises and never follow through."

"He's nice," I said, feeling the need to defend him. He really had been nice.

"He reminds me of your father."

That was the first time I'd ever heard her attribute any negative qualities to my dad. The fact that she was doing it now, in relation to a guy I'd just brought home, the first one ever, made me think it was purposeful. It rubbed me the wrong way. "You don't even know him," I said.

"I know his type."

"Okay," I said. "You should try to use the bathroom before we go."

"I hate this," she said.

"Me too," I agreed.

• • •

It took too long to get my mom ready, and now we were running late. And Elijah was probably just standing or sitting or pacing, I had no idea, in the living room, waiting. It really was pointless to have him here. He couldn't change my mom's clothes or take her to the bathroom. He just had to stand around waiting.

"Sorry," I said, when we came back out. He was looking at pictures on the wall. He turned at my words.

"It's okay," he said. "You were a cute kid. I like your corduroy pants. Not common when we were growing up."

"My mom was into vintage. She was stylish."

"Still am," she said. "When I can dress myself."

I nodded toward the front door, and Elijah got the hint and opened it.

"Keys," he said as I pushed my mom in her chair through the opening. I handed them over to him, and he locked up behind us. At the car, he kneeled next to my mom. "I'm going to help you."

"Sutton can help me," she said.

"I'm going to help you," he said again, firmer this time.

She nodded and he easily scooped her up and put her in the car.

A wave of gratitude rushed through me as I watched. Mom buckled herself, and before I could move, he was collapsing the wheelchair and carrying it to the trunk.

I rushed after him. "Sorry, thank you."

"Why are you saying sorry? And you're welcome."

I had an overwhelming desire to hug him, but I kept my hands to myself. He popped the trunk and placed the wheelchair inside. Then he was heading toward the car's back door.

"What are you doing?" I asked.

"Getting in the car."

"No. I mean, you shouldn't. You don't have to. You should go back to work."

He just smiled at me, climbed into the car, and pulled the door shut behind him.

CHAPTER 20

"I don't believe you've been doing this all by yourself," Elijah said. "No wonder you have a collection of knots along your shoulders." We were walking the path around the hospital while my mom was in therapy. It was tree-lined, with a large pond in the center. In the middle of that pond, a filtration system sprayed water into the air, like a geyser.

"It's not a big deal," I said. "It's getting better."

A family of ducks paddled across the water, weaving in and out of the cattails.

"Have you thought about hiring someone to help?" he asked. When we'd arrived at the hospital, he'd lifted my mom out of the car and into her wheelchair. I wasn't going to lie, it was nice to have someone stronger than me around.

"It's expensive," I said.

"Yeah," he said. "I bet it is."

"I hired someone that first night I met you. I was supposed to . . ."

"What?" he asked when my sentence trailed off. "What was

supposed to happen that night when you looked like a goddess?"

I gave a breathy laugh. "Stop."

"You really don't like compliments."

"I don't trust them." Maybe I was more like my mom than I realized.

"Compliments? Or me?"

"Words," I said. "Words are nothing. Easy to say. Easy to give away. They can mean very little to the person offering them."

"Or they can mean a lot."

"But it's hard to tell the difference. And one time they could mean a lot and the next very little."

"How does one prove themselves to you then?"

"Actions," I said. "What you do is much more important than what you say."

He nodded slowly. "I can agree with that. But I don't think that means that what someone says should be completely discounted."

"Words need history," I said.

"Will you come to a party with me this weekend?"

"What?" I asked, his subject change leaving me confused.

"My parents are throwing this fancy party. They do it every year. A fundraiser. This year for the community boys and girls club. And I just . . . will you come?"

"I didn't bring anything to wear to something like that," I said. We passed a flowerbed on our right of pink and purple and white flowers.

"Maybe Tara has something you can borrow? Women do that, right? Borrow things from each other?"

I laughed. "Yes, we do."

"Wait, what about that dress from the first night I met you when you were supposed to be doing something? You can't wear that?"

"Would that work?" It seemed too . . . sexy? Too slinky. I wasn't sure it was the right thing to wear to meet parents for the first time. Not that I was *meeting* his parents, I was just meeting them.

"It would work very well." A little smile was on his face, like he was imagining me in it now. "So what were you supposed to be doing that night in *that* dress?"

"Meeting my boyfriend," I said.

His head whipped in my direction. "You have a boyfriend?"

"Had. He broke up with me that night."

"Is he an idiot?"

"No, unfortunately. He's not. He made the right decision." I kicked at a rock on the path in front of us, and it went skittering across the sidewalk until it was stopped by the edge of the grass.

"Why do you say that?"

"I've been very wrapped up in my restaurant and hadn't been so wrapped up in him."

"He was needy?"

I chuckled. "In that he needed me to want him occasionally, yes. What about you? Why aren't you in a relationship . . . or are you?"

"I am not. Maybe your mom has me figured out. Women see through my pretty words."

"So you don't ever mean what you say?"

"I feel like I always mean what I say, but maybe I lack sincerity. I don't know, Sutton. My last girlfriend left me because she said I would never be ready to settle down."

"Was that true?"

He shoved his hands into the pockets of his jeans. "Maybe. I had been feeling unsettled."

"And now?"

"Well, I imagined myself as a child and gave that child a pep talk and now I'm cured."

I rolled my eyes. "Nobody is claiming it's that easy, smartass."

"What was that about then?" he asked. "The *speaking to our childhood self* exercise?"

"I think a lot of the problems we carry with us originate from childhood trauma, and she wanted us to have a good, hard look at our past."

"Did it help you?"

"She thinks I'm too independent."

"Dr. Franklin?"

"Yes. She thinks that the good thing I thought I'd learned from my childhood—self-reliance—is a weakness."

"I wouldn't take her thoughts too seriously. She doesn't even know that we're strangers."

I smiled in his direction. "We're not strangers. Our bet should've just been one session. That was the only time we were actually strangers. After that, it became muddy."

"We're muddy?" he asked with a teasing smirk.

There was a bench under a tree along the path, and he pointed to it. I thought he just wanted to sit down, but when I did, he moved behind me.

"What are you doing?" I looked up and the top of my head met his stomach.

His hands went to my shoulders, his thumbs immediately kneading at the knots there. "Helping."

"You don't have to do that," I said, but I was already putting my head down and closing my eyes, my actions not matching my words.

He let out a soft, deep laugh. "I want to."

I drew in a breath as his hands continued to move along my shoulders and neck. His touch was firm and sure. His thumbs traced lines on either side of my spine, then worked along each knot. Images of the shower that morning flooded my brain, and a tiny moan escaped before I could suppress it. My cheeks went warm again. I was glad he was standing behind me.

"Feel good?" he asked.

"Yeah," I said, trying to downplay just how good.

His touch lightened and his spread fingers ran a path from the base of my neck up into my hair. A jolt of pleasure rushed through me, settling between my legs. It really had been too long since I'd been touched, and my reaction was embarrassing.

"What time is it?" I asked, grabbing for my phone. "Has it been an hour?"

"No," he said.

I shifted, turning toward him, and his hands fell to his sides. He must've sensed that meant I was done because he walked around the bench and took a seat next to me. He stretched his legs out in front of him, crossing them at the ankles and staring out at the pond with its ducks and spouting water feature.

"So will you?" he asked.

"Will I what?"

"Come to the party with me this weekend?"

"I can't leave my mom alone for too long," I started. "But if the fact that I might have to leave at a moment's notice isn't an issue for you, then sure."

"It's not an issue. I understand," he said, scratching at the back of his neck.

"Your parents will be fine with me crashing the party?"

"It's open house style. There will be a lot of people. They won't mind at all."

"Okay." I tapped his knee with my closed fist, a weird impulsive move on my part. I'd just felt the need to touch him, and that was the best way I could think of.

He tapped my knee back, teasing me, I could tell. "Okay."

But instead of a short tap, like I had done, his closed fist stayed on my knee. I stared at it, innocently existing there, like it belonged. Then slowly, I reached out, and as I was about to place my hand on top of it, he flipped his hand, palm up, fingers splayed, waiting for me. My heart picked up speed as I rested my hand on his and he threaded our fingers together.

I wasn't sure why that single action made my eyes sting. I looked away, down the path we'd been walking, trying to regain my composure. I squeezed his hand, feeling it in mine. Soaking in the connection to another human.

"You okay?" he asked.

"I'm fine," I said, still not looking at him.

"It's okay if you're not," he said. "Your life is kind of overwhelming right now."

I shook my head as more emotion rose to the surface.

"Sutton," he said softly. "Come here." He tugged on my hand and pulled me to his chest, where I held on like the world depended on it. I rested my face in the crook of his neck and breathed him in. He smelled amazing, soap and a clean, sharp scent. His hand pulled on the ends of my hair and then ran slowly up and down my back.

"Thanks for helping with my mom today," I said.

"Of course. Tell me when her appointments are. I can be your transport guy."

"No, that's too much. Thank you, but that's . . . no."

"I changed my mind," he said.

"About what?" I asked. I probably should've sat up, but it felt good to be in his arms, to feel his voice vibrate along my cheek when he spoke. To have his hand make patterns on my back.

"I agree with the therapist. Your self-reliance is a weakness."

"I know," I said. "I'm not working on it."

He let out a low, rumbling laugh, then pulled me tighter against him.

It took me too long to hear his name being called or to register that the voice in the distance was directed at us. It wasn't until it was closer and saying my name as well that I sat up. It seemed to click for Elijah at about the same time because we both looked in the direction of the hospital.

Tara was fast-walking our way, waving. "Eli! Sutton!"

I straightened up even more, smoothing my hair and planting my feet firmly on the ground in front of me.

"I thought that was you two," she said when she reached us.

"Hi," Elijah said. "You on break?"

"I am." Her eyes went back and forth between us. "This doesn't look good for me. I'm sure the therapist is really picking up on the *no connection* thing." Her voice was laced with sarcasm.

"No, this is nothing," I said. "Just stuff with my mom."

"Oh, speaking of. Your mom is looking for you. I found her in the hall. She said you might be out here."

I jumped to my feet. "You found her in the hall? Is the time up?"

She shrugged. "I don't know. I think she's done though."

"I'll go get her." I started walking. "I'll text you later, Tara!"

"Okay!" she called after me. I didn't look back.

It wasn't until I was inside, almost to the elevator, that Elijah's teasing voice was next to me saying, "Are you afraid of Tara?"

"No. What? No."

"What are you afraid of then?"

You, I wanted to say. *This. These feelings I'm having that I don't want. It's too much right now. Too much when I'm already overwhelmed. Too much when I'm leaving as soon as my mom is better.*

The elevator doors slid open. Two people walked out, one in a white lab coat. We stepped inside the now empty elevator. I backed into the far corner, holding on to the handrails. As the door slid shut again, he walked to my corner, facing me, his hands settling onto the rails outside of mine. I looked up at his teasing eyes.

I wanted to wipe that smug, knowing look off his face. The one that made it seem like he knew exactly what I was thinking, exactly what I would or, more likely, wouldn't do. I wanted to show him that he didn't know. And maybe it was those thoughts that spurred my actions or something completely different. But I slowly moved forward until our lips were millimeters apart and said, "I'm not afraid of anything." Then my lips met his.

He sucked in a surprised breath of air, but it took less than a second for his surprise to be replaced with action. He wrapped his arms around me and pressed my back against the corner of the elevator. His tongue easily gained entrance to my mouth, eliciting a moan from me. I used my hands to pull him more tightly against me, where I could feel that I wasn't alone in my desire.

It took my brain too long to catch up to my emotions—to what we were doing, in a public elevator, in a hospital, where my mom was waiting—but it finally did. I wedged my hands between us and pushed, just as the elevator settled into place on the fourth floor. I gulped for air as he stepped back and away from me. Then he turned to face the doors, just as they slid open.

In a bad twist of fate, my mom and her wheelchair and a nurse were waiting on the other side.

CHAPTER 21

I met Elijah's eyes in the rearview mirror for the twentieth time as we pulled up to my house. And like the nineteen times before this one, he smirked, which made my stomach flutter. My stomach had never fluttered before. I didn't hate the feeling.

Mom, who sat in the passenger seat, was grumbling about an exercise the physical therapist made her do and how much it hurt her shoulder. She hadn't suspected an elevator make-out, I knew that much. We had managed to compose ourselves in time and were standing feet apart when those doors opened, but she also hadn't warmed up to Elijah at all.

I turned off the ignition and hopped out to get the wheelchair ready. But by the time it was set up and I was wheeling it around the car, Elijah was already carrying my mom up to the front door sans wheelchair.

"It's easier this way," I heard him saying.

"This is dangerous," my mom said. "You'll drop me."

"I haven't dropped a person yet. I'm very strong."

I abandoned the wheelchair and rushed around them with

the keys to unlock the front door, noting how unimpressed my mom seemed by Elijah's declaration. He was probably just adding evidence to the *smooth-talker* file she'd started on him.

"You don't seem strong," she said. "You seem like you're struggling."

"Sorry," I mouthed to him.

He just gave me a wink. "I'm not struggling at all. You are as light as a feather."

My mom grunted at the words.

I swung open the door and he carried her inside, setting her carefully on the couch. I went to collect the wheelchair.

After dropping it off inside, I walked him out, shutting the door to the house and lingering on the porch.

"I'm not used to parents not liking me," he said. "It's weird."

I laughed. "You should actually feel special, she usually likes strangers." It was me she didn't like.

He grabbed his heart. "Ouch. Was that supposed to help?"

"I know, such a hard truth."

"I'll win her over," he said.

"Good luck." I looked over my shoulder back at the door. "She needs her meds, so . . ."

"Of course," he said.

I wondered if we were going to talk about the elevator kiss. Or repeat the kiss here on the doorstep. Considering I'd just told him I had to take care of my mom, I wasn't surprised when he walked away without any physical contact.

About halfway down the path to his car, he turned around and walked backward a few steps. "I'll see you this weekend for the party at my parents'."

I nodded and he smiled, then turned and jogged the remainder of the way to his car. I went back inside. I wasn't sure what expression I had on my face, but my mom just shook her head and said, "I don't like him."

I didn't know why that bothered me so much. I'd given up trying to impress my mom years ago when I realized she was unimpressible. But for some reason, in that moment, it dug into my chest and I snapped, "He just spent half a day helping you, maybe you can find some gratitude in there somewhere."

• • •

That all happened the day before, and a good night's sleep had done nothing to improve Mom's opinion because I was greeted with, "I didn't like him," again this morning.

"Yeah, Mom, I know. Have you been thinking about that all night or something?"

"It's important to make opinions clear."

"Well, it's as clear as crystal. Thanks."

"You're angry," she said.

"I'm frustrated," I responded.

"Why?" she asked.

"Because there is no basis for your opinion about Elijah. You don't even know him."

"It's a gut feeling," she said. "I've learned to listen to those."

How have your gut feelings worked out in regard to Dad? That's what I wanted to say, but I knew that was a low blow, and even though she was into low blows, I wasn't. I was into avoidance, apparently. "How is your arm feeling today?"

"Sore," she said.

"And your head?"

"Still there," she said.

I thought that was her attempt at a joke, so I offered a stiff smile and got her coffee and a banana. Then I went to my room to make more work calls or give myself some space to cool off.

Next to my computer was the homework sheet Dr. Franklin had given Elijah and me. It was the size of a regular piece of printer paper. It was laid out like a dinner date. The phrase *hors d'oeuvre* was followed by a waxy square meant to be scratched off to reveal . . . something. I wasn't sure what. Under that were the words *appetizer*, *main course*, *palate cleanser*, *dessert*, and *nightcap*. Each had its own scratch-off box. A whole meal. Meant for soon-to-be-married couples. I was dying to know what activities Dr. Franklin wanted engaged couples to do for a perfect date night. I wasn't sure why I didn't just scratch off the boxes and find out.

I shook my head. I was getting distracted. Tara should've been doing this sheet. Maybe I should take it to her.

Speaking of Tara, I grabbed my phone and dialed her number. She picked up on the third ring. "Hello."

"Hi, do you have a minute or are you at work?"

"It's my day off. But hold on, let me go into the other room."

"Why?" Michael called after her. "Is that your other boyfriend?"

"Yes!" she called back. "Her name is Sutton, and I have scheduled a make-out session later!"

"I approve!" he said.

I rolled my eyes.

A door shut and then into the phone she said, "Sorry, okay. Hi, I do not have an audience. So? Are you calling to give me an update?"

"I think this therapist is clueless. Despite what you saw yesterday, I don't know how anyone could mistake Elijah and me for an engaged couple."

"Huh. What's her name? Maybe I can do some behind-the-scenes legwork. Drop her some cryptic message like *What if a couple you were seeing was pretending to be engaged? What would you do?* Maybe that will get her thinking about all the people she's seeing. Maybe you're her only couple."

I thought about that for a minute, but it didn't sit right. Tara had made the bet. She needed to see it through without cheating and face the outcome she'd been willing to risk. "I don't think lying is a good way to trick Michael into therapy."

"You're right. I guess I just have to accept the inevitable. Realize I love the guy and have faith in our relationship without a professional having a good, solid look at it."

"I wish Michael would willingly go. If it can strengthen the bond of strangers, imagine what it would do for an actual couple."

"Right?!"

"But I think Elijah sees how it can help now. I hope he'll convince Michael."

"That would be nice. Oh! I heard you're coming to the fundraiser this Saturday."

"Am I going to regret saying yes?"

"I mean, it's not a rock concert. It's a fundraiser. But actually, maybe that's more your scene."

I blinked, a stab of hurt in my chest. Good old boring, reliable Sutton who would much rather go to a charity event than an actual party. Or maybe this was more about how I had let her down in school. Hadn't put myself out there for her. I'd apologized ages ago, but it was obviously still lingering. I wasn't sure what else I could say about it.

Maybe I was wrong. Maybe she wasn't implying anything by her statement. Just making a joke. Jokes were meant to be laughed at. So I laughed.

CHAPTER 22

We kissed! I wanted to scream.

I was sitting in Elijah's car Saturday evening in my slinky black dress, my hair in loose beachy waves, the first time I'd worn it down in ages, my makeup on. When he'd picked me up, his eyes had traveled over me like he wanted to take me right there on the porch. I wasn't sure anyone had ever looked at me like that before.

My expression had probably been similar. He wore a fitted black suit, a button-down white shirt with thin mint-green stripes, and no tie. The color made the green in his hazel eyes pop. He'd kissed my cheek, then stepped around me to poke his head through the door and greet my mom with a wave. She gave him a cold head nod.

She wasn't happy I was going out, even though she constantly liked to tell me that she didn't need me here and that she could take care of herself. When I told her I was leaving for the evening, she reminded me she was still experiencing the symptoms of a concussion and that anything that might occur to her in my absence would be my fault.

"Mom," I'd said. "Call me if you need me, okay? I'll come. Or call 911. They'll come too." I wanted to add that I was not my father. I hadn't ever been him. I'd made sure she knew that by calling like clockwork for ten years, visiting like clockwork.

"I'm not going to call 911," she'd muttered.

"What should I do to get on your mom's good side?" he asked now, his hand draped over the top of the steering wheel, a smile on his face.

"This is hard for you, isn't it? Someone not immediately liking you."

"Yes!" he said.

I laughed. "Maybe you'll grow on her . . . in about thirty years," I said, then my words caught up with me. "I mean, not that you'll be hanging around me for thirty . . . well, if we're friends or whatever . . . you don't have to . . . but . . ." I trailed off. We *kissed!*

I'd been the one to kiss him first in that elevator, and even though he wholeheartedly kissed me back, I wondered if he'd wanted that to happen. Had *I* wanted it to happen? God, did I seriously have to overanalyze everything? It could've just been a kiss. Nothing more. Nothing less. I was leaving, after all, eventually. And he had to stay here to pay back his dad. We both knew *that*.

"Thirty years," he said as though imagining that amount of time. "Tell me you don't have your life planned for the next thirty years."

"It was just the first big number that jumped into my mind." *But* don't *you have the next thirty years of your life planned,*

Sutton? a voice in my head unhelpfully pointed out. "What about your parents? Do they like the people you bring home?"

"My parents will love you."

• • •

After parking, we went through the front door of his parents' large house, even though it seemed like most people were going through the side gate. He just opened the door without knocking. The tiled entryway was two stories high and was probably as big as my mom's living room. Straight in front of us was an extra-wide staircase leading up to the second story. He led the way through the entryway to a great room. It was full of rich wood moldings, a stone fireplace, and large windows.

"That picture is gorgeous," I said, staring at the oversized black-and-white photo of Half Dome on the wall above the fireplace. This was what the restaurant could use. Some California nature pics. Big and bold. I wondered who took the picture and how expensive art like this would be. Considering the house it was in, I was sure it was well beyond our price point. I searched the corner of the photo for the artist.

"It's Yosemite," Elijah said. "It's not hard to take a gorgeous pic of Yosemite."

"I couldn't take that picture."

"I'm sure you could. With your iPhone even."

I backhanded him playfully across the stomach. "Don't disparage artists. It's not as easy as it looks." But even while saying it, I wondered if I *could*. Yosemite wasn't far. Could I drive up and take some decent pics with my phone that I could blow up? Or would my attempt look worse than the cheap art we already had?

The living room was attached to the kitchen, and maybe I was exaggerating, but it seemed bigger than my entire apartment. Maybe I wasn't exaggerating.

"You ready?" he asked, nodding toward a wall of what I thought were floor-to-ceiling windows but must have actually been doors since he was implying we could walk through them.

"Is this where you grew up?" I asked, curious if his parents had moved here more recently or if they had lived here for a while.

"It is," he said.

"I want to see your bedroom," I said. Maybe it was a stall tactic because suddenly I was nervous to walk into a party full of rich people. Or was it his parents I was more nervous about?

"I bet you do," he said in his teasing voice.

"No, not like . . . I just want to see what you were like as a teen."

"First food and drinks, I'm starving."

"Fine," I said with a smile.

The backyard was even bigger than the house. The yard was beautifully landscaped and, right now, set up for a party—tables and chairs and bars and lights and waitstaff. Were they really going to raise more money than they spent on this party?

There were already quite a few guests—at least forty or so—eating and drinking and mingling.

Elijah scanned the area and, after a minute, pointed to a group standing by the pool. "My parents. Let me introduce you, then we can get food?"

"Sounds good." But it didn't sound good. My palms immediately became clammy and my head light. Why would I be nervous about meeting his parents? We were nothing to each other but a fake relationship. Speaking of, did his parents know about the bet? About what we were doing? "Oh shit," I said.

"What?" he asked, looking around like he'd see what caused my panic.

"I forgot your last name."

He chuckled. "Russo."

"Russo. Okay. Mr. and Mrs. Russo," I mumbled, readjusted the small clutch I'd strapped around my wrist, which contained my phone, my lip gloss, and my touch-up powder, and took a step forward. Elijah did as well, his hand finding mine.

I was surprised at first, gulping in some air, then I curled my fingers around his. "Sorry my hand is sweaty," I said under my breath.

"You really are nervous," he said.

"Maybe. A little . . . A lot."

"Don't be. You are smart, charming, and gorgeous."

"You and your pretty words," I said, but a smile crept onto my face.

His hand tightened on mine. "Don't make me show you with actions right now, we have an audience."

My chest expanded with his words, making it hard to breathe for a moment. And then we were standing in front of his parents, and I had to catch my breath and quiet my insides because I was meeting them for the first time and thoughts of kissing and more weren't helpful thoughts right now.

"Mom, Dad, this is Sutton."

"Hi, nice to meet you, Mr. and Mrs. Russo," I said.

The first thing his mom's eyes shot to were our connected hands, and it took everything in me not to drop mine. She was a beautiful woman, who looked at least ten years younger than I was sure she was. Her hair was long and a honey blond. Her skin was smooth, and her teeth were bright and white against her red lips. "Hello, Sutton." She extended her hand to me.

I let go of Elijah's hand to shake it.

Elijah's dad seemed a little more approachable. He was average height and thick around the middle. He had a full head of salt-and-pepper hair, tan skin, and dark eyes that were taking me in. "Well, hello, young lady. It's been a while since my son has brought someone home." He shook my hand with enthusiasm.

"It's a charity event, Dad."

"At our *home*," he said, and slapped Elijah on the back with a hearty laugh. This man had sold a lot of cars in his life, I just knew it.

"Dad," Elijah said. "Sutton owns a restaurant in Los Angeles." Really? He was going to open with that? Just throw it right out there. Maybe he was trying to make me more comfortable, get me onto a topic that I could talk about.

"You don't say!" Mr. Russo said. "That's impressive. What kind?"

"It's a contemporary bar and grill."

"We'll have to check it out next time we're down there," he said. "What's it called?"

"Luminesce. I started it with a friend last year."

"And how is it going?"

"There have been some growing pains, but it's hanging in there." That last review was going even more viral than the first, and we had actually noticed a dip in our sales. It was stressful, and I felt like there was nothing I could do from this far away except worry. But we *were* hanging in there.

"We have some friends who own a restaurant," Mrs. Russo said. "It's a lot of work. The first two years are make or break."

"Yeah," I said with a gulp. "They are."

"Do you enjoy it?" he asked.

"I do."

"That's the important thing," Mr. Russo said.

I raised my eyebrows at Elijah, hoping that just my expression would say, *See, your dad thinks you should enjoy your work.*

"We're going to get some food," Elijah said.

"Please do," his mom said. "And thanks for coming, love. It means a lot to us." She placed a hand on his cheek and kissed the other.

"Of course, Mom. Happy to be here."

"You too," she said to me with a warm smile. "Thank you for coming. I'm so glad to meet you." She surprised me with a hug.

"Thank you. You too." I hugged her back, a lump forming in my throat.

As we were walking toward the bar, Elijah grabbed my hand again. "I told you they'd love you."

"They seem like the type who love everyone." I hadn't realized the lump was still in my throat, and my voice came out squeaky.

His brows shot down. "You okay?"

I swallowed and nodded. Did he know how lucky he was to have parents who said kind things and gave soft hugs and offered words of encouragement? "I am. I'm fine. Just need a drink."

We joined a short line at the bar, and he wrapped an arm around my shoulder and pulled me against his side. How did I go from someone who tolerated physical contact to someone who craved it in just a few short weeks? What spell did this man have me under?

I put my hand against his chest. I could feel his heart beating there, hard against my palm. "Do your parents put on a lot of these?" I asked.

"No, not really. Maybe one a year." He lifted his hand in a wave. "There's Michael and Tara."

I shifted to follow his gaze. They were heading our way, Tara in a red, floor-length dress, Michael wearing a suit sans tie, like Elijah. I was beginning to feel a little underdressed.

"Oh my god," Tara said when she reached us. "We had to walk from a block away. I thought they'd have a valet again this year." She gave me a hug. "You look gorgeous."

"You too," I said.

"Is tonight the night Sutton has to pay the debts of her bet?" Michael asked. "I can pull the karaoke machine out of the storage room."

My eyes went wide as I looked around the yard. "Absolutely not. I don't really remember agreeing to that bet. It was just thrown out there. And even if I did, we still have one more session."

He laughed. "Tara said you basically conceded."

Of course Tara told him.

"We have one more session," I said.

Elijah gave a throaty chuckle beside me as if he knew, like all of us did, that one more session wasn't going to change anything. I may have known that, but there was no way I was doing karaoke in the middle of his parents' charity dinner. I didn't care what bet I did or didn't make.

Why had I been so sure a therapist would know we were strangers? Maybe our chemistry had been undeniable from the start. Because we did have it—chemistry. It simmered there under the surface whenever he was around. I could feel it now, warming my insides as his hand brushed my arm, as his voice tickled my ear.

"Yes, Michael. We have one more session," Elijah teased.

"You're lucky you don't have to shave your head, Pretty Boy," I said.

He gave a barking laugh as if he'd forgotten that side of the bet. It had probably left his mind after that very first session a month ago. "*You're* lucky," he said, wrapping his arms around me and pulling me back against his chest.

Tara looked between us and shook her head with a smile. "This is the weirdest thing ever."

"What is?" Elijah asked.

"The two of you hitting it off. I would've never thought. You're the complete opposite of one another."

"I don't think we're all that different," Elijah said.

She popped her brows up as if to say that we weren't that far past strangers, if that's what he thought. My stomach churned. Maybe he didn't know me that well.

We were at the front of the line for drinks now, and we all put in our order, collected our drinks, and moved to a pub table. A man walked by with a tray full of bruschetta, and we each grabbed one. Michael grabbed three.

"How is your mom?" Tara asked.

"Slowly progressing," I said.

"Concussions are terrible," she said. "And her leg and lacerations, that has to make mobility a challenge."

I nodded.

"You take her to the bathroom and shower and everything?" she asked.

I wasn't sure why I didn't want to answer that question except that I was a private person, always protected my mom.

But maybe private was a nice way to say closed off, and closed off was a different way to say hyper-independent and that Dr. Franklin was right—it was a weakness. So I said, "Yes."

"You shower her?" Michael asked. "That's gotta be awkward."

"I mostly just help her in and out of the shower, help her wash her hair. She can still do a lot. I try not to make it embarrassing for her."

Elijah's hand went to my lower back. "You're good with her. She's lucky you're here."

"Are you an only child?" Michael asked.

"I am."

"Too bad you don't have siblings to help."

"Yeah."

"And your dad?" he asked.

"In London."

"What's he doing there?"

"He's in a symphony. He plays violin."

"That's cool," he said.

"He's still there?" Tara asked, eyes wide.

I nodded.

"He just up and left like fifteen years ago," she said as an explanation to the guys. "Your mom was always so stoic about it. I don't think I could be." She looked at Michael. "I would murder you."

He held up his hands in surrender. "I don't know how to play the violin, so you don't need to worry."

She laughed like we weren't talking about one of the most traumatic moments of my life. "I used to play the piano. A long time ago."

"You did?" he asked.

"I wasn't any good," she said.

"You were good," I assured her, the guilt rising to the surface again. She had been, even if it was more for her parents than for herself.

"It was great to see your mom at the hospital the other day," Tara said. "She's so nice. She always tells me how proud she is of me. I need to come by and spend more than a few minutes with her."

I bit the insides of my cheeks and nodded. "Yeah, you should."

"Her mom is nice to you?" Elijah asked. "She hates me."

"Smart woman," Michael said with a laugh.

"She probably hates men because her husband screwed her over," Tara said, laughing as well.

My phone buzzed in my purse, and I was so grateful for the interruption that I took in a relieved breath. I freed my phone, saw the word *Mom* scrolling across the screen, and turned the phone to Elijah. He nodded and I excused myself to the house.

CHAPTER 23

"Hey, Mom, everything okay?" I stepped back through the doors Elijah and I had exited through earlier and into the kitchen.

"Did you buy bananas?" she asked.

"Are we out? I can pick some up on my way home."

"Okay," she said.

"Is that all? Are you doing okay?"

"I wish I could drive."

"I know you do."

"You could get me a motorized wheelchair. That would make it to the corner mart."

"You're not supposed to be operating anything motorized with your concussion."

"It's a wheelchair, Sutton."

"I'll drive you wherever you need to go."

"Obviously not," she said, and then the line went dead. I rubbed at my arms while I stared at the large picture of Half Dome above the fireplace again.

I held my phone up to my mouth. "Hey Siri, what kind of loan would it take to finance a long-term caretaker for an ungrateful mother?"

It was a joke but Siri answered back, "I have pulled up several long-term care facilities on the web."

"If only," I muttered.

"It's a beautiful picture, isn't it?"

I let out a small yelp and whirled around. Elijah's mother stood in the kitchen behind me. For how long, I wasn't sure. She opened a drawer and pulled out a corkscrew, holding it in the air to show me she'd accomplished the mission that must have brought her into the house.

"Um . . ." It took me a moment to process her comment. "Oh! Yes, the photograph is amazing. I haven't been to Yosemite since I was a kid."

"Elijah is very talented."

"Elijah?" Again, my brain was slow to process what she was saying. "Wait, did he take this?" I pointed to the picture.

"He did. He has an artistic eye. Did he show you his room?"

"He didn't."

She smiled a sneaky smile, then looked outside as if making sure she had time. "Do you want to see it?"

"Absolutely."

She led me up the stairs to the second floor and then to the end of the hall.

"He doesn't live here anymore, but I haven't wanted to change his room because it's so beautiful." She paused at the door as if giving me a moment to anticipate the reveal, then she opened it.

The first thing that caught my eye was the large beach scene taking up the entire wall. But not just a photo of the beach, a scene made up of hundreds of photos. When I stepped closer, I could see each picture featured the color required for its position in the overall image. A light brown dog as a piece of the sand. A blue sweater, the water. All different. I couldn't imagine the hundreds of hours this must've taken.

"Why doesn't he do this for work?" I wasn't sure if she'd heard me. I'd said it so quietly.

"He tried," his mom said, proving she *had* heard me. "Nature photography is a hard thing to make money in. Especially with the rise of AI art. People just tell the internet what they want and it provides. Why would they pay?"

Maybe that was true, but it felt like a sin that Elijah was stuck in a boxing gym all day when he had this ability. If he liked the boxing gym that would be one thing, but he didn't. "Wait, did he actually have a photography business?"

"Before the gym he—"

"How did I know this was happening?" a deep voice said from the doorway, cutting off whatever his mom was about to say.

I turned with a smirk to see Elijah leaning against the frame of the door. "You're a psychic now?" I asked.

"My mom was supposed to be getting a corkscrew, and you were in the house. I put two and two together."

His mom held up the corkscrew. "I got it. I was sidetracked."

"She's hard to say no to, isn't she?" he asked his mom, nodding toward me.

My mouth opened, ready to protest, when his mom said, "I offered to show her the room when she was admiring your Yosemite photo over the mantel. She did not ask."

He narrowed his eyes at me like he wasn't sure he believed that.

She squeezed my hand, then headed for the door. "I have a corkscrew to deliver or the wine-starved people are going to protest."

"Yes," Elijah said, pulling her into a hug as she passed and kissing her on top of the head. "You do. No more bragging about my rusty hobbies."

"I will never stop bragging," she said, and left us there alone.

After a few beats of silence, I said, "She offered, I did not put up a fight."

He nodded, studying my face. "You okay? Tara wasn't exactly thinking before she spoke out there."

"It's whatever," I said. "She was being truthful."

"I'm sorry," he said.

"You don't need to be sorry. You didn't do anything."

His gaze traveled to the beach scene. "It was my photography final my senior year in high school."

"It had to be incredibly time consuming. I hope you got one thousand percent on it."

He smiled. "Close."

"What happened with this? With photography? Your mom said . . ." I trailed off because his mom hadn't said much, but I hoped he would fill in the blanks.

"This was the first business my dad invested in for me. But unlike my sister and her passion project, mine crashed and burned along with his investment. Which is why I'm now working at *his* choice." He nodded toward the door. "Speaking of, he was impressed with yours. That's a good sign. He knows what works for a business and what doesn't."

"Does he?" I asked.

"He's very successful."

I nodded; I couldn't argue that point. But that didn't mean he knew everything about everything. I hated that Elijah was giving up on a dream because he thought he had failed at it. Because his dad had told him that his time was up on trying to make it work. That Elijah figured his dad must know best and listened. And now he felt indebted to him for two separate investments. He probably felt like he was at the bottom of a deep hole.

"I should hire you to bring some character to our restaurant," I said.

"It's lacking character?"

"In a big way." Two million people big. Or at least that's how many had seen the viral review. And so many of them had left mean comments.

"You couldn't afford me," he said with a smile.

"I probably couldn't."

He stepped to my side, inspecting the photos more closely. "It's been a while since I've picked up a camera." He smelled really good. Like cedar and soap.

My body shifted toward his, my shoulder pressing into his arm. "It's probably like riding a bike."

"In what way?" he asked, turning a serious expression on me.

"You don't know that saying?"

"What saying?"

"You know, 'it's like riding a bike.' Meaning, once you've learned how to ride a bike, your body doesn't forget how to do it. So no matter how much time has passed, you pick it right back up again. Like . . ." *Sex.* My mind provided that word without any warning, and my cheeks immediately went hot.

"Like what?" he asked in a husky voice, as if he knew what I'd been thinking.

"Like photography," I said.

He let out a gravelly laugh.

"You knew what that saying meant," I said, seeing the teasing crinkle of his eyes.

"I just wanted to hear you explain it." He reached out and plucked a picture off his wall, one from the water section. It was a blue Volkswagen Beetle. He held it out for me. "Here's a start for your restaurant."

I gasped. "Do not dismantle this masterpiece." The photo had a clear, jellylike dot of adhesive on the back, and I used it to put it right back into place.

He took me by the waist, pulling me away from the wall and into his arms. "You're not the boss of me."

My back was pressed against his front, and I reached up and wrapped one arm around his neck. "If I hire you to do photography for the restaurant, then I kind of am."

"My skills aren't for hire. They only come as a perk." His mouth was pressed against my neck, and the words came out muffled. Or maybe they came out muffled because blood rushed through my ears all the way down my body, ending with a deep throbbing between my legs.

"A perk?" I asked, breathless.

"A perk of dating me."

"Are you holding your skills ransom?"

He turned me in his arms. "I have no idea what we're talking about anymore," he said. "I can't think." And with those words, my back was against the closest wall and his lips were on my neck, then tracing a pattern to the soft spot beneath my ear.

"Not on the beach," I said, trying to move us.

He chuckled and practically flung me onto the bed, my

legs draping over the edge. I gasped in both surprise and pleasure. He stepped between my knees, forcing my dress to ride up my thighs as his hands followed the same path.

My eyes fluttered closed at the sheer pleasure of his skin on mine. But when echoey laughter sounded from downstairs, I was reminded that the door was wide open and any of the many guests—or his mother!—could wander in at any moment. I pushed myself onto my elbows, his body blocking me from shifting any farther.

"There are people," I said.

"Where?" he asked, undoing the button on his jacket, then dropping to his knees. "I don't see any people." His hand pushed my dress up even more, then continued past the hem and up my inner thigh. His intense gaze was fixed on mine as his fingers came to the edge of my underwear, a lacy black pair. He traced the scalloped edge and my body reacted, lifting to meet his touch. He palmed me, and I was sure my underwear did little to hide how ready I was for him.

He let out a low hum, then placed a kiss on the inside of my left knee, then an inch higher, and another.

I wanted to enjoy this. I *was* enjoying this. But the thought of his parents, a whole party full of people, downstairs kept interrupting my ability to completely relax.

"Elijah," I said, his mouth, his tongue, now tracing the line of my underwear that his finger had earlier.

"You want me to stop?" He paused.

"No," I said, and his mouth resumed, his tongue lighting up every nerve ending on the hollow spot of my inner thigh. "I mean, yes. Now is not the right . . ."

He pulled away. Thoughts of his tongue in even more places flashed through my mind, and a spasm of pleasure went through me. I wanted to grab him by the hair and pull him right back. I didn't. I sat up and adjusted my dress back down my thighs.

He stood and rebuttoned his jacket, then held his hand out to help me off the bed.

"So we can scratch *childhood bedroom while a party is going on* off the list of places you'd have sex." He was teasing, I knew this. After our talk about airplane bathrooms and coat closets and basically anywhere in public. Okay, maybe he wasn't joking. Maybe my list of acceptable places for sex was pretty small. Maybe it was part of my personality. Maybe I didn't have the adventurous gene. I wanted stability and predictability and security. Boring.

I wasn't sure if my demeanor had changed or if my thoughts were written all over my face, but whatever the reason, his expression softened. "Hey," he said, kissing my cheek and the corner of my mouth. "I'm just teasing you."

"I kissed you in an elevator," I reminded him and myself.

He smiled. "You did. But I don't need to ravage you in a public place." He moved his lips close to my ear. "But for the record, I do want to ravage you, pretty much always."

I nodded. "I want to be ravaged."

He chuckled and started to straighten up when I smashed my lips to his in a passionate kiss. Or maybe it was a desperate one. He reciprocated, wrapping me up in his arms and exploring every inch of my mouth with his tongue. When we broke apart, I could hardly breathe.

"Go ahead of me," he said, when I moved toward the door. He tugged at the crotch of his pants. "I'm going to need a minute."

I chuckled, but as I headed downstairs, I couldn't help but

wonder what we were doing. I didn't live here. I was leaving in a matter of weeks. A month, two at the most. He knew that. I knew that. Neither of us had uprootable lives. Was that the point? This spontaneous, fun-loving, *unsettled* man saw me as someone he didn't have to commit to and just wanted to have a little fun with.

I had never wanted to have a little fun with a man in my life. I'd always dated for a purpose. Could my purpose be fun? Could my purpose be to live in the moment and then leave it all behind? Because I knew long distance wasn't for me. Not when my dad left and never looked back.

CHAPTER 24

"Am I fun?"

"What?" Raya asked. It was Monday morning. Raya was reporting to me on the weekend business. Weekends were always the busiest, but since the review, they'd been declining. She had some ideas for marketing posts, and I agreed that we needed to step up our social media game. I hoped that would help until we could figure out what to do for atmosphere. I had a feeling nothing was going to change until I got back though. I needed to get back. "Fun?"

"Yes, I can have fun, right?" The fence outside my bedroom window stared back at me.

"When?" she asked. "No, that came out wrong, I mean, like in what setting are you asking about?"

"Ever," I said, realizing that if she was having a hard time just saying *yes*, then the answer was obviously *no*. "Oh, god, I'm not, am I?"

She laughed. "Sutton, I enjoy your company. I opened a

business with you for fuck's sake. You are one of my favorite people to be around."

"None of those statements included the word *fun*."

"Is being in your childhood home for this long giving you an existential crisis?"

"Yes," I said. "You have no idea."

"I'm sorry," she said.

"I can't wait to come home."

"I can't wait for you to *be* home."

I sighed and closed my daily planner that I had been referring to for the questions I wrote down to ask her. I rubbed my eyes.

"Are you even going to ask about the new waitstaff?"

"Did I not ask?"

"You didn't."

"How are they?" She ended up hiring both the people I'd sent in for interviews.

"Amazing. Thanks for vetting the list first."

"I didn't vet the list," I said.

"I know you did, Sutton."

I laughed. "Fine, but I'm sure you would've picked the best from the pool as well."

"You're not sure, that's why you vetted the list. But that's okay, it made my life easier, so thank you."

"You're welcome. And Presley? She's happy with the additions?"

She grumbled something under her breath, then said, "She's fine. Now stop trying to make my life easier and work on making *your* life easier."

"And fun," I said.

She laughed like that was a joke. "Talk to you later. Chef just got here and I need to go over some things with him." With those words, the line went dead.

I wondered what she was going over with Chef and if I needed to be part of whatever conversation was about to happen. No, she could handle it. I trusted her.

Next to my closed planner on my desk was the scratch-off that Dr. Franklin had given me to plan a date. I had meant to give it to Tara. My hand ran over the page. "I can have fun," I muttered while searching the drawers for something to scratch off the first box with. There was nothing. I pushed myself, rolling chair and all, away from the desk, then stood.

In the kitchen, I dug through the junk drawer.

"What are you doing?" Mom asked, muting the television.

"I'm looking for a penny or a dime or any coin, really." I freed one from beneath a pen and a spool of black thread and held it in the air. "Aha!"

"What do you need a penny for?" she asked.

"To prove I'm fun," I said and headed back to my room.

• • •

Maybe I wasn't fun. Because I wasn't sure I could do what the first revealed box asked me to do. And it wasn't even that hard. *Send a suggestive text to your partner requesting a date.*

I knew this was a date sheet. I knew it was going to give me date prompts. I didn't know I'd have to send sexy texts.

I could do this, I told myself. I'd been telling myself that since I scratched the box that morning. In between helping my mom and doing household chores, I was hyping myself up. It wasn't that I'd never sent a sext. Just a few weeks ago I'd sent that text about the meat to Nate, and he'd responded by asking if I was requesting a dick pic. I'd said I would take one of those, too, if he was offering.

"That was fun," I said. Sure, it happened after the breakup and I was being more snarky than anything, knowing he wouldn't actually send a dick pic, but . . . shit, I'd never sent a sext.

How does one even ask someone on a date in a suggestive manner? "Hey, baby, you want the possibility of seeing me naked tonight after you feed me?" I sucked in my lips at the laugh that wanted to escape. Elijah would be good at suggestive texts. Dr. Franklin should've given the sheet to Elijah. I was sure that was the exact reason she'd only given one to me.

The pot I was washing in the kitchen slipped through my soapy fingers and clattered into the sink. I cringed and turned off the water to listen carefully. I had just helped my mom into bed for an afternoon nap thirty minutes ago. All was quiet from the back of the house. I turned the water back on.

"Hey sexy, I want to see your penis tonight. Clothe it in some jeans first and I'll unwrap it later." This time I did laugh. I was hopeless. I thought about asking Raya or Tara for help, but how embarrassing would that be? I'd think of the perfect way. It might take all day, but I'd think of it.

• • •

I wrote and erased a handful of texts that day, including:

I have a red, lacy bra that wants to go get dinner this week. Would you be open to showing her a good time?

You mentioned ravaging me. Can we put that on the schedule for this week?

I want to go out and then I want to stay in. Are you up for one or either of these things?

Elijah, I don't think I'm fun. But you make me want to be.

And now it was late and I was sitting in bed with a glass of wine, frustrated with myself. How could I overthink a stupid text that he was going to respond to in five seconds without analyzing at all?

I was hoping the wine would loosen up my thoughts a bit or my inhibitions, but it seemed to be doing nothing except reminding me, in detail, of the make-out session we'd had in his room the other day. His tongue on my inner thigh, his hands on my body. I closed my eyes and took another sip. Then I put my wineglass down, picked up my phone, and typed:

I thought of more places I'd like your tongue to explore. Is it available for a date this week? And if you have to come too, that's fine.

I hit send this time and immediately wanted to press unsend. I didn't. Instead, I threw my phone onto the bed like it was on fire, downed the last of my wine, and went to the bathroom to brush my teeth. It wasn't until my toothbrush was in my mouth that I remembered I'd never sent Elijah a text before. Not a single one. This would be the first one he'd ever gotten from me. How had I even saved myself in his phone? Had I put a name? I didn't remember. I'd entered my number, for sure, but a name? I must've. He was going to think this was common texting fodder for me. That I just habitually wrote sexts as my inaugural text to people.

When I came back into my room, I stared at my phone sitting innocently on my bed for a moment. I rubbed at the knots in my neck, then approached it slowly.

The text waiting for me read: Are you trying to turn me on before bed?

I smiled and typed back: If I'm turned on, you have to be too.

My phone buzzed in my hand with an incoming call, his name lit up on my screen. I took a deep breath and answered. "Hey."

"Hey, yourself," Elijah said. "Are you asking me out?"

I climbed into bed, pulling my blanket over my legs. My room looked just like it had when I'd left it almost ten years ago. A soft gray comforter, a desk, a few perfectly placed band posters on the wall. I wasn't surprised my mom hadn't changed it. She hadn't done anything to the house since Dad left. Maybe she wanted it to be exactly the same when he came back.

"I am," I said to Elijah. "Are you free a night this week?"

"I am," he said. "What did you have in mind?"

"Aside from the tongue thing?" I asked.

He chuckled. "Yes, that's a given."

I looked toward my desk and the date sheet, its other boxes still behind their scratchable surfaces. "I'll surprise you."

"Sounds good," he said.

I snuggled even more under my blanket, adjusting the pillow beneath my head. I wondered if he was in bed too. What he was wearing, what his adult room looked like.

"Can I ask why you're turned on?" he said.

A small smile flitted across my lips. "I was just thinking about what someone was doing to me in a certain bedroom during this one party."

"Less than five minutes of action and it's on your mind for days? Imagine what memories an entire night would leave you with."

"Has it not been on your mind?" I asked, my overthinking self creeping in.

"It has," he said in his husky voice. "I wanted to taste more of you."

A jolt of pleasure shot between my legs.

"Your little noises are making me want to be there."

"Did I make a noise?" I asked.

"You did. A really sexy one. Were you imagining my tongue again?"

"Yes."

"Where do you want it?"

"I don't know," I said, suddenly shy. Just like I'd never sexted, I wasn't a dirty talker either. Most sex I'd had in my life happened with little to no words exchanged.

"You know," he said.

Images of my breast in his mouth, of his face between my thighs, played like a reel through my mind. I moaned again. "I want you here now," I said.

"God, Sutton, don't tempt me."

"My bed is tiny or I'd insist you get your ass over here."

"How tiny?" he asked.

"Twin."

"Twin?" he asked incredulously.

"Weren't you the one who said you could perform in an airplane bathroom? A twin should leave you room to spare," I teased.

"Don't make me prove to you that I can definitely excel on a twin bed."

"You and your pretty words," I said.

"I'm coming."

"I was kidding," I said.

"Too late, I'm coming." And then the phone was silent.

I bit my lip and sat up. Was he really coming? Yes, I decided, this was Elijah we were talking about. A smirk found its way onto my face.

"How's this for fun?" I said to nobody.

I got up to change into some better pajamas and more thoroughly brush my teeth.

CHAPTER 25

I was waiting by the door when my phone lit up with a text.

Here

I looked over my shoulder, down the dark hall, and then unlocked the dead bolt as quietly as possible. His body was already in the doorframe before I even finished opening the door. He let out a low chuckle. "You didn't think I'd come, did you?"

"Shhh," I said with my own quiet giggle as I grabbed him by the front of his shirt and pulled him inside. He stumbled his way in because I hadn't left him enough room to make a clean entry. He grabbed me by the hips to prevent a fall, shifting around behind me as I shut and relocked the door.

His mouth was on my neck before I'd even finished the task. The only light in the room was from the porch, where a wall-mounted sconce shone through the small window at the top of the door. The house was quiet except for the humming of the refrigerator and a slow-dripping sink. I needed to get that looked at.

He didn't let go of my hips as we walked toward my bedroom, causing us both to stumble this time. I stifled a laugh with my hand. I felt like a sneaky teenager, even though I'd never done anything like this as a teenager. I reached behind me to hold one of his hands and create a bit of space to help make our walk steadier. But instead of obliging, he wrapped an arm around my waist. Bringing us closer instead. Then he was practically carrying me to my room, my back against his front.

"This one, this one," I hissed, as he almost passed my door on the right.

He pushed the door open with his forearm and then released me to shut it behind us, placing one hand high on the door and the other on the handle to close it as silently as possible. Then his eyes were on me. My room was even darker than the hall had been, with only a small nightlight on the wall creating the faintest glow, making it hard to see his expression. But I could see when he moved toward me and wrapped me up again, this time chest to chest.

"Hi," he said, his mouth against my ear.

"Hi," I returned, stretching up to wrap my arms around his neck.

His mouth met mine in a rough kiss. He tasted like minty toothpaste, like I was sure I did. His hands traveled up the sides of my silky black top. It was long sleeved, but I'd changed out my matching pants for the matching shorts before he got here. His palms brushed along the sides of my breasts and I gasped in some air.

"I believe you were going to tell me where you wanted my tongue," he said, his fingers on the buttons of my shirt, undoing each one expertly.

"Everywhere," I said as an answer, my hands searching for the button on his jeans. He wore a T-shirt as well, and as soon as he finished with my buttons, he removed his T-shirt by reaching over his head to the back of his neck. He threw it onto my desk chair while stepping out of his shoes and kicking them to the side.

My eyes had adjusted to the lack of light in the room, and I took in his toned, smooth chest as I still struggled with the button on his jeans. I couldn't remember the last time I'd unbuttoned a man's jeans. I was very much out of practice and it showed.

His hands separated each side of my now-unbuttoned shirt, his eyes traveling over my exposed breasts. He slid my shirt off my shoulders, but it was stopped by the bend of my elbows. His tongue traced a line from the edge of my bare shoulder all the way to my collarbone.

I finally unbuttoned his jeans. I could feel the evidence of his arousal against my fingertips as I slid the zipper down. He let out a growly moan. Now that my hands were no longer occupied with his jeans, I dropped them to my sides and my shirt slid to the floor. He pressed a hand to my lower back, bringing my bare chest to his.

"You are so soft and perfect," he said, his mouth finding mine again. His fingers hooked the thin waistband of my shorts, sliding them down my legs until they puddled at my feet. "I was hoping you were wearing some lacy panties again."

I didn't tell him I'd put them on right before he got here.

I tugged at the top of his jeans, trying to work them down but failing. He stepped back and assisted me in the effort, revealing a dark pair of boxer briefs. I couldn't make out their color.

His eyes went to my bed. A smile lit up his face. "I haven't seen a twin bed since I was five."

"Is it smaller or bigger than you were picturing?"

"Smaller, much smaller." He laughed, and I widened my eyes and covered his mouth with my hand.

"Sorry, sorry," he whispered through my fingers, obviously trying hard to contain another laugh.

"Have you changed your mind?" I whispered back, nodding toward the bed.

Instead of answering, he scooped me up and placed me at the foot of the bed. I inched back toward the pillow as he climbed on, his knees and hands straddling my body on the way up because there wasn't room for him to do it any other way.

When we both reached the pillow, he let one of his hips brush along mine until it rested on the bed, tight against me, giving his right hand full access to my body. And it took advantage of the access, marking a path from my thigh, along the edges of my underwear, around my navel, up my sternum, and then slowly circling my nipple without touching it.

I arched against him, but he just followed the same path back down.

"Elijah," I said on a sigh.

"You say my name much sweeter now," he said.

"Do I?" I asked, my eyes closing with pleasure as my nerve endings danced beneath his fingertips. And he hadn't even skimmed my most sensitive areas yet.

"You do." He placed a soft kiss on my lips. "I like it."

"Elijah," I said again, a small whine in my voice this time.

"Yes?" he asked.

"Touch me."

"I *am* touching you."

I shifted toward him, pressing my breasts to his chest to feel skin against mine. "You know what I mean," I said.

He rolled, shifting me onto my back before resuming his position. Then his mouth was on my breast, sucking my nipple into his mouth and then releasing it to circle it with his tongue. I let out a sharp moan of pleasure. His mouth left my breast and his hand went to my mouth, covering it like I had his earlier when he'd made too much noise.

I smiled but then opened my mouth and ran my tongue along his finger. He dipped his finger into my mouth and I sucked on the end. He watched me for a moment, his eyes intense. Then he took his finger back and pressed his mouth to mine instead, his tongue sliding past my lips. I took his now-free hand with mine and placed it back on my breast.

He smiled against my mouth but obliged, running a thumb over my peak before his hand moved down my body and stopped at the top of my underwear.

"Yes," I said urgently against his mouth when he paused.

His fingers inched ever so slowly into my panties. My breath was shallow and my body felt more alive than it had in a long time. His middle finger followed my slit easily, proving just how ready I was for him. I moved one leg over, opening myself up for him. My foot found nothing but air, and I kept going until my leg up to my knee was dangling off the side of the bed. The move gave him more freedom and he took it, his finger working me in just the right places. I arched against him.

And then there was a loud bang. At first, I thought his hand or back hit the wall, that's how small the bed was and how close we were to the wall. But then I heard a far-off cry and I sat up with a jolt.

"Shit," I said.

"What?" he asked, taking a second to catch up. "What was that?"

"My mom." I jumped out of bed and stepped into my shorts. Instead of pulling on my own button-up shirt though, I grabbed his T-shirt from my desk chair and tugged it on. "I'll be right back."

"Should I come w—"

"No, stay."

CHAPTER 26

I rushed out of the room and pulled the door shut behind me. In the hall, I could hear my mom's cries louder. I pushed open the door to her room. "Mom?"

She was on the floor, cradling her arm. I rushed to her side, turning on the small bedside lamp in the process. "Did you fall out of bed?"

"I needed to go to the bathroom. I thought I could do it myself."

"What hurts?"

"My arm." She held it to her chest.

"Did you land on your leg?"

"No. I just got dizzy. I'd made it off the bed to my good leg but hit the nightstand with my arm on my way down."

I squatted beside her. "Wrap your arm around my neck."

She did and I barely managed to get her all the way off the floor and then propped up against the bed. I was sure the adrenaline rushing through me had aided in the task.

"Let me get your wheelchair."

"Just brace me."

I knew what she was saying, but I wasn't sure she was strong enough to hop on one leg as I acted as a crutch for her other. And *I* definitely wasn't strong enough. "I can't, Mom. Your wheelchair is right there." I nodded toward the end of the bed.

She nodded, defeated.

Once she used the bathroom and was back in the wheelchair, I pushed her back toward the bed. I watched her shoulders shake from behind and small sobs sounded in the room.

"Are you in pain?" I asked. "Let me go get your meds." She'd stopped taking her middle-of-the-night dose, but if she was hurting, I didn't see the harm in adding it back.

"No," she said.

"No?" We were at the side of her bed now, and I moved around the front of her chair and squatted at her knees. "You don't want pain meds?"

She shook her head, trying to hide the tears I could see glistening in her eyes.

I wasn't sure what to do. I could feel sympathy tears pricking behind my own eyes, and I knew she'd hate that. I kept them at bay. "Do you want to get back in bed?"

She nodded and I leaned forward to have her wrap her arm around me again. This time she wrapped both. Maybe she hadn't hit her arm as hard as she thought. Maybe it was just an initial pain kind of thing, like when you stub your toe on the corner of furniture. But I made a mental note to call the doctor in the morning to let him know.

I hefted her up and out of the chair and shifted her toward the bed. But at the point she normally let go of me, when her full weight was on the edge of the bed, she didn't. She hung on. And then she was sobbing into my shoulder. I wrapped my arms around her, holding her tight. We didn't hug and this felt foreign to me.

"I'm so sorry, Mom," I said. "Things will be better soon."

"I wish you weren't here," she said, and my tight grip on her faltered. "If you weren't here, he would be. He would be taking care of me."

Hurt clogged up my throat, gagging me. I knew she meant that she wished he was here in this moment instead of me. But it felt like so much more than that. It felt like she meant that if I had never been here to begin with, then he would be. I wanted to tell her that he'd had every opportunity, every excuse, to come and he hadn't. That *I* had come. I had dropped everything, like I always did, and come. I didn't say that because I knew it wouldn't help anything in this moment. She was hurting in more ways than one.

"I know," I said instead. "It hurts."

After a few more minutes of clinging to me, she settled down and I helped her the rest of the way into bed, tucking her beneath the covers. "Your bell is right here, Mom. If you need to get up, ring it, or call me, your phone is also right here."

"I thought I could do it. I wanted to do it. You should've let me try." Her eyes were already closing, drifting back into sleep. I watched her for a moment as her breathing evened, as the worried, hard expression she always seemed to wear on her face relaxed into something almost soft. Then I turned off the light and walked back out. I paused in the hall to collect myself, breathing for several minutes. My chest hurt. If I had been seeing a therapist for my actual issues, I wondered what tools she would've given me for this moment. I wanted to call my dad and tell him off, but I didn't think that was the right tool. Maybe it was.

Or maybe I could let myself be ravaged by the really hot guy I'd left in my bedroom. Maybe that would take my mind off everything, make me feel anything but this. Was that a tool?

I walked quietly down the hall and back into my bedroom. After shutting the door behind me, I faced Elijah. He was on my bed, still shirtless, obviously, since I was wearing his shirt. But he was also still pants-less, just lying there in his underwear.

"Everything okay?" he asked. It had been at least twenty minutes, maybe thirty. He was on his back, my pillow tucked under his head, his phone in his hand like he had been using it to pass the time.

I nodded because I wasn't sure I could speak properly. He reached over, depositing his phone onto the nightstand. I sat on the bed next to him.

"You look adorable in my shirt," he said, pulling on the bottom of it. "You should wear it all the time."

I offered him a smile and then lay on my side next to him, my cheek on his chest.

He kissed the top of my head. "Talk to me, Sutton. What's going on?"

I shook my head, then stretched up and kissed him. He didn't resist, kissing me back. I deepened the kiss, slipping my tongue past his lips and tasting him. His hand gripped my upper arm, pulling me closer to his mouth for several blissful minutes. But he wasn't exploring my body like earlier, not even when I bent my knee so it was on his thigh, traveling the length of it and then higher.

That's when he stopped our kiss.

"What?" I asked.

"Something is wrong."

"This doesn't feel good for you?"

"That's not what I mean. It feels good. You feel good. But something happened. You look . . ." He didn't finish, just studied my eyes as I stared at him. I rolled onto my back, which was a mistake because I almost rolled right off the bed. He caught me around the waist, pulling me closer to him and shifting onto his side to make more room for me.

My palm went to my forehead, where I rubbed at the ache I could feel growing there. "I look what?" I asked.

"Haunted?" he said.

"This house is haunted," I said. "Ghosts of the past just walking around like they own the place."

"What does that mean?" he asked.

I sucked in a deep breath and counted to three before letting it out. I didn't talk about my mom. "She can't get over him. He left and she can't get over him. And she blames me." I choked on the last word, and the hot tears finally came, pouring out of my eyes and down my temples into my hair. My hand was still on my forehead, and I hoped that hid most of the evidence of my breakdown. This wasn't what he signed up for when I'd promised him excitement in a twin bed.

"She blames you? In what world is it your fault?"

"In the world where they were happily living a life without me, and my existence changed everything."

"Sutton," he said, in a deep, sympathetic voice. "Tell me they haven't said that to you."

"You know that we believe in actions around here and not words." I turned on my side, away from him. "But in this case, there have been both." I wiped at my eyes. "I don't know why I'm telling you all this. I don't tell people this. This is the kind of stuff people are supposed to bury deep down and only let out in long grocery store lines or LA traffic as bursts of unjustified anger."

He was quiet.

"You were supposed to laugh," I said.

"This isn't funny." He put his hand flat on my stomach and tucked my back tight against his front. Heat from his hand spread across my skin, like a balm. "You can talk to me."

"Can I just cry and then sleep instead?"

"Yes," he said. "As long as I can stay while you do both."

I nodded and he nestled me even more snugly against him, wrapping his leg around mine as well. Considering how much my mind was spinning, I was surprised how calm I felt. How safe. "Thank you," I said.

"Any time," his deep voice said in my ear.

I turned over in his arms and buried my face in his chest while hot tears continued to stream.

CHAPTER 27

I opened my eyes. I always seemed to wake up at the same time, no matter what hour I'd gone to bed. Six-thirty. I didn't need to look at my watch that was resting on its charger on the nightstand; the soft light filtering through the window told me that would be the time. Sometime during the night, I had turned over and my back was against Elijah's chest once again. His arm was draped over my waist, heavy, which told me he was still asleep. His deep breaths in my ear verified that fact. It had been a while since I'd woken with the weight of someone against me. I didn't hate it.

The night before had been a lot. For anybody. I knew this. So much for being fun. I'd turned the sext into a cryfest instead, at some point drifting off to sleep as he held me.

I carefully slid out from beneath his arm, not sure how deep of a sleeper he was.

My mom usually didn't wake up until seven-thirty or so, but with her late-night fall, I wondered if she'd sleep a little longer today.

I peeled off Elijah's T-shirt and draped it over the back of my desk chair. Then I pulled on my pajama shirt, buttoning it up as I headed for the door, phone in hand. I would let him sleep until I heard my mom, then I'd wake him and send him on his way before she realized he'd been here. Again, like a sneaky teenager.

It wasn't about that though—her scolding me. It was that I didn't want her to be embarrassed that someone else had been here last night when she'd fallen. Okay, maybe it was a little of both.

I shut the door quietly behind me and went to the bathroom, where I brushed my teeth and hair and used the toilet. Then I headed to the kitchen to start some coffee. I checked my phone for any messages. There was one from Mac, the food delivery guy.

Need to change to 6:45 in the am.

He'd sent that last night around nine. How had I missed it? I immediately called Raya. She answered with a sleep-deep voice.

"Emergency?"

"No, Mac changed the time to six forty-five for today."

"He did not. That's in like ten minutes."

"Can you get there?"

"No. I'll be there at seven, like every time he comes."

"Please, try. I'll call him."

"Ugh. He's doing this on purpose."

"Hurry," I said, then ended the call and dialed Mac.

"Hello," he answered, the engine noises in the background let me know he was already on the move.

"I just got your message. You know she has a hard enough time being there at seven."

"I do know, because she's late every time, Sutton. Every. Time."

"So are you just saying six forty-five so she'll be on time today, or do you really need her at six forty-five?"

He laughed.

"Gotcha," I said. "Probably a good strategy."

"Work smarter, not harder," he said.

I shook my head. "Next time, text her."

"Really?" he asked.

"What do you mean 'really'?" I said, confused.

"You told me to always text you. I don't even know if I have her number."

"Oh, right." Shit. I really was a control freak. A boring, predictable control freak. "I'll send it to you."

"Can't wait to start bugging her."

I laughed.

"FYI," he said, "you might want to do an inventory of the kitchen. Not sure if that's been done since you've been gone. I think you're ordering way too many potatoes."

"What makes you say that?"

"I carried a box inside Friday and added it to, like, four other unopened boxes."

"Yeah, take that off the list for your next delivery this week."

"Will do." I ended the call and forwarded Raya's contact info to Mac, then opened my email. Along with a whole lot of spam, a message from a call center company about reserving the patio for a team dinner waited. I leaned my butt against the edge of the counter. To my left, the coffeepot bubbled and hissed as I replied, offering available times. Next, I started an email to the team about inventory.

"It's too early to be working," a low voice to my right said.

I glanced over to see Elijah standing in the entryway to the kitchen, watching me. He was fully clothed and I was weirdly disappointed by that fact. I should've kept his shirt on.

"Yeah," I said. "Well, time stops for no one."

"Do I need to sneak out of here?" he asked, looking down the hall and then back at me.

"Soon," I said.

He walked closer until he stood in front of me, then braced his hands on the counter on either side of me. I still had my phone up, thumbs on the screen, email not quite composed.

"Personal space," I said with a smile.

He kissed me on the forehead. "Who's even awake at six thirty in the morning to be conducting business with?"

"Delivery drivers, food suppliers, restaurant owners."

He smirked.

"Is the boxing gym not open this early? People don't go before work?"

"It is. Our front desk person is there, opening. But I don't go in until eight."

"The perks of running the place."

"So many perks," he said sarcastically. He kissed me. His mouth tasted like toothpaste. He must've found my tube on the counter in the bathroom. Or maybe he carried a travel toothbrush on all his late-night booty calls.

"How are you feeling this morning?" he asked, straightening up, then turning in a circle.

"What are you looking for?"

"A mug."

I pointed to the cupboard above the coffee maker, and he pulled two out, pouring us each a cup.

I finished my email and hit send, then placed my phone on the counter. "I feel fine," I said. "I'm sorr—"

"Don't," he said, stopping my words short. "You have nothing to apologize for."

I sighed, not sure that was true but too tired to argue. "I need to call the doctor."

"The doctor?"

"About my mom's fall last night." I plucked a pen from the junk drawer and wrote a note on the pad I kept on the counter for when I had thoughts like that. "When the office opens. Ugh. I wish I could go down to LA for the weekend. I need to do inventory and analyze the space again." Maybe being there would inspire ways to give it more personality.

"Your mind never shuts off, does it?" he asked.

"It did for a little while last night."

"When?" he asked, pretending not to know what I meant. He lifted the mug of coffee. "Do you take cream or sugar?"

I nodded, opening the fridge and retrieving the vanilla creamer. I moved to his side and poured until the coffee was a light brown instead of black. I held out the bottle for him, and he did the same.

"How about a do-over?" he said. "My place? Tonight?"

"I . . ." I carried the mug to the table, sitting down there. "I can't leave her alone after what happened. I'll . . . I can't."

He joined me.

"I mean," I continued, "if I schedule Lucy from the home health facility or maybe during the day when she's . . ." I trailed off. I knew I wouldn't feel comfortable leaving again until she saw the doctor.

He put his hand over mine. "I get it. Don't worry. There will be time."

I nodded and pinched the bridge of my nose. Would there be time?

"Come here." He pulled me by the hand onto his lap. I wrapped my arms around his neck, resting my cheek against his head. The tension in my shoulders seemed to pour down my spine until I felt like a puddle in his arms.

I wiggled in his lap, rubbing my ass along his groin.

He chuckled and squeezed my sides. "Are you hungry?"

"Hungry?" I shifted, attempting to straddle him and doing a very poor job. He must've sensed my goal because he assisted me in the process, moving my leg into place.

"I can go pick up some food," he said while I kissed his neck and then cheek.

"Some food?" I asked, moving my mouth to his, running my tongue along his lips.

"Your attempts to make my questions euphemisms are not working."

"They feel like they're working," I said, pressing myself against his erection.

"Your body on me is definitely working, but my words are not sexy."

I laughed. It had been a while since I felt this light. The power of a good cry, probably. Or maybe this man. Yes, that was likely the reason, and I wasn't sure how to feel about that. I didn't like my emotions to be dependent on anyone, let alone a man. But that was a weakness, I reminded myself. One that needed to change.

"Are *you* hungry?" I asked, still kissing him.

"See, now I'm confused, because I don't know if you mean this"—he palmed my breast—"or actual food."

I smiled. "I think we have eggs. I can make eggs."

"Eggs?" he said suggestively, teasing me.

"I get it. It doesn't work."

He chuckled. "You are the cutest."

I gave him one last kiss, then climbed off his lap. "I'm going to make you eggs."

I opened the refrigerator and pulled out the carton of eggs, spinach, peppers, cheese, and some heavy whipping cream. From the cupboard I grabbed some spices. And just as I was about to get a pan, the bell sounded from down the hall.

I met Elijah's eyes.

His brows popped up in surprise. "She *rings* for you?"

"To avoid a repeat of last night, it's necessary."

"Do you want me to stay? I can help. Lift her out of bed, get her into the wheelchair."

I started shaking my head before he had even finished his thought. "No, I just need to . . . no . . . it's . . . no."

He stood from the table, put his mug in the sink, and then pulled me into a hug. "You need to take care of yourself." His hands went to my shoulders, where he rubbed at a knot with his thumb.

"She'll recover. It's not like this is my life," I said. "I can do anything for a short amount of time."

Her bell rang again.

"Coming, Mom!" I called out. "Give me a minute!"

"I'll get my shoes," he said.

"I'm sorry," I said.

"Don't be." He kissed me soundly, then we both went our separate ways. Him to leave, me to take care of my mom.

CHAPTER 28

I ran my finger over the Toyota emblem on the steering wheel of my car. It had a smudge on its otherwise shiny silver surface. My car wasn't new; in fact, it was the one I'd brought to college with me almost ten years ago, but I tried to keep it clean and well maintained so I could have it as long as possible. It was paid off, and I could not add another monthly payment to my life anytime soon. Plus, it was a hybrid and saved me tons on gas.

I looked around my car for a napkin or tissue to wipe the smudge. There was nothing.

Inside the house, my mom was probably still seething. We'd just gotten back from an appointment, where the doctor had sent us home with a rental scooter. I had thought she was excited about it since it would give her more independence, but when I'd wheeled her into the house and then brought the scooter inside, she'd just stared at it.

"It's easy, Mom, look." I'd kneeled on the raised pad and used my other foot to push off the ground. "It's so sleek and agile."

"You look ridiculous," she'd said.

"But I don't *feel* ridiculous," I said, even though I did. "I feel fast. Just try it."

"I don't want to. I'm dizzy."

"The doctor said you shouldn't be." It had been a couple of days since her fall, but she didn't seem much better.

"Does the doctor live inside my head?"

"Would he want to?" I'd muttered.

"Leave me alone," she'd said.

"Gladly," I'd shot back.

And that's why I was now sitting in my car. I'd just needed to get out of there. But I knew I couldn't go far.

There was a tap at my window and I jumped. I looked over to see Tara standing there.

I motioned for her to come sit inside, and she walked around the car and joined me.

"Mom issues?" she asked. I used to sit in my car a lot in high school when I needed space.

"All these years and nothing has changed." I nodded to the scrubs she still wore. "Did you just get off?"

"Yes, I saw you leaving but didn't catch you in time. Doctor Lewis said your mom is struggling mentally?"

"He did?"

She put her hand over her mouth. "He didn't tell you that?"

"Not in so many words."

"Shit. I shouldn't have. Sorry."

"No, tell me. He thinks it's all in her head?"

"I mean, obviously not *all* of it. She was in a serious car accident. But the measurable signs of the concussion are gone, and he thinks what's lingering has a lot to do with her mental health. Her will to get better. Or not to get better."

The words hit me in the chest as what they implied sank in. My mom was inside claiming dizziness she probably wasn't actually experiencing so that what? My dad might finally come running? On one side, it broke my heart. On another, I felt nothing. Like there was a brick wall between us and I didn't care enough to try to tear it down. Maybe I was the one who had built it in the first place. If I did, it was with the bricks she'd handed me.

"She wants my dad to come," I said.

"Your dad?" Tara said in a scoffing voice. "If he hasn't come in fifteen years, why would he come now?"

"Because she actually has a solid, measurable reason to need him this time."

She nodded, slowly understanding. "Well, shit. That's really sad."

"Seriously . . . but maybe I should call him." It was one o'clock in the afternoon now. That meant it was nine o'clock at night in London. I didn't talk to my dad a lot. Maybe once a year when he remembered he had a daughter. But I knew the time difference. And I knew my window was short right now, he'd be in bed soon.

"And tell him to come?"

I'd never asked my dad to come home, not once. I'd never asked him for anything. Maybe it was time. "Yes, actually. If for no other reason than to give them both closure."

"Good luck with that," she said.

"Yeah." I was going to need it. "How are you? Any more cake emergencies?" Was I asking this as a confirmation that it actually happened? Maybe. Did that make me a terrible person? Also maybe.

"Oh, you heard about the cake emergency? So annoying.

I think we got it resolved. Michael probably didn't tell you it was his fault though. He called and canceled the order as a joke, but the baker took him seriously . . . obviously."

"That's awful."

"Yeah . . . Your last therapy session is tomorrow, right?"

"Is it?" I had completely forgotten in the drama of the last couple days. Dr. Franklin had had to push our last one to later because she had taken time off, so it felt like forever since we'd been there.

"Do you think there is any hope in the world that this therapist will figure it out tomorrow?"

"Honestly?"

"Yes."

"No."

She sighed.

"But I still think you should insist that Michael go to therapy with you before you get married if it's important to you. Ask Elijah to help you convince him."

"Yeah . . . maybe."

• • •

When I pulled into the parking lot the next day, Elijah was leaning against the trunk of his car, hands crossed low in front of him, waiting for me. He smiled as I pulled in, and my heart picked up speed. When had just seeing someone ever lifted my mood so easily? I hadn't seen him in a few days, since the morning after my mom had fallen, and I'd missed him.

"Hello," he said, after opening the car door for me and helping me out. He immediately wrapped me up in a hug.

"You look handsome," I said, closing my eyes and breathing him in.

When we pulled apart, he looked down at his outfit. "You and your pretty words," he teased. He wore jeans and a collared green shirt that brought out the green in his eyes. He knew his color.

"You do," I insisted.

"How's Mom?"

"Are you calling her Mom now?"

"I'm not going to lie, I forgot her name."

I laughed. "Andrea."

"How is Andrea?"

"She ate this morning, took some new pills the doctor prescribed, and stared at the scooter while scowling but did not try it. So pretty much the same." I had called my dad yesterday, after my talk with Tara, for the first time in . . . a long time. He hadn't answered. I couldn't decide if I wanted to try again today.

"So not well," he said.

"Not great." I was trying not to think about the fact that my dad hadn't called me back in the last twenty-four hours. That didn't bode well for my campaign to get him here. For my mom.

Elijah took my hand in his and met my eyes. "Today . . . if you want to . . . if you need to . . ."

"What?" I asked. "What's wrong?"

"Lie," he said.

"What?"

"If you want to lie in session to get some good advice. Advice that will actually help you with your life instead of helping this fake engagement she thinks we have, you can. I can play the terrible fiancé."

"Are you saying I need therapy?"

"Don't we all? Isn't that your mantra?"

I smiled. "How dare you use my argument against me."

"I'm sorry. You don't have to, of course. Or if you want, you can go in without me even, I can make up an emergency work call or something." His offer and the way he offered it, knowing he was a people pleaser and liked everyone to see the best in him, expanded my chest with gratitude.

"You are so sweet. Don't let anyone tell you that you're just a pretty face." I tugged on his hand and walked toward the building, letting him know that no fake work emergency was in order.

"Nobody has ever said that."

"Really? Huh. Well, disclaimer, that's what I thought when I first met you."

"Wow." He squeezed my hand.

"And for the record," I said, "I won't need to lie."

"Okay," he said and pulled on the handle. The door didn't open, it rattled in its frame.

I stared at the door, confused. "Is it locked?"

"It's locked."

I tried the handle, like I could produce a different result. I did not.

"Is she sick or something?" I asked. "Did she call you?"

"I don't have her number. Michael is the one who forwards me messages. He did not forward me anything."

I turned at the sound of a car pulling into the parking lot. Dr. Franklin. She parked in the nearest spot and got out of her car. "Sorry! Sorry!" she called. Unlike her normal pantsuit, she was wearing jeans. Her hair was pulled back into a ponytail that made her look even younger. "I got held up across town. I'm so sorry." She fiddled with her keys as she approached and opened the door quickly.

"It's okay, we just got here," Elijah said.

"Give me one sec to get the office ready," she said, rushing through the door.

We stepped inside and stopped in the lobby. "Get the office ready?" I whispered with a smile. "What does she have in there?"

He laughed, then rested his arms on my shoulders and kissed my forehead.

I breathed in his scent and gripped the sides of his shirt. I nodded toward the small door to the right. When this office was an actual house, it was probably used for a coat closet. I wondered what was inside it now. "You're right. I think I could need someone so bad that I'd have the urgent desire to shove them into the nearest small, private space and have my way with them."

His eyebrows popped up nearly all the way to his floppy hair. "Really?"

"No," I said, straight-faced. "I could wait until at least the car."

He laughed. "You couldn't even do it in the car. Too many windows." He kissed me once, then twice.

"I could do it in a car," I said. "Probably," I added after analyzing it for a moment.

"God, you're adorable," he said.

"I am a strong, capable, intimidating woman."

"That too."

"Okay!" Dr. Franklin called from down the hall. "Come on in, guys. I'm ready for you."

CHAPTER 29

"You two seem . . . different."

Shit, we really were making it obvious that we had practically slept together a few nights ago. His arm was tight around me instead of on the back of the couch, where it usually was. My finger was drawing shapes on his leg. And we'd just barely sat down!

If anything, this would just cement the idea in her head that we were an engaged couple. Right? Or she'd think her premarriage program had done its job of bringing us closer together. I felt bad that I had done such a terrible job for Tara in this quest of ours. Maybe Elijah and I were never good candidates for the task. Our chemistry was too strong. I internally rolled my eyes at my silly schoolgirl romantic thoughts.

"Different how?" Elijah asked. His voice seemed sincere, but I could hear the humor behind it. Did I feel a little bad that we'd been tricking this poor therapist who was only trying to help us? Maybe. I knew I'd be embarrassed if I found out someone had fooled me for four weeks straight. Hopefully she'd never find out.

"You seem closer," she said. "Happier."

"It's all your killer homework and advice," Elijah said. I squeezed his knee. Now he was taking it too far. Although maybe, at the end of the day, her homework really was what brought us closer together. Forced us to get to know each other.

"Speaking of advice," I said, "I could use some."

"Oh?" she said, maybe surprised at my proactive question.

"Unrelated to this." I cocked my head toward Elijah.

"I'm a *this* now?"

I playfully patted his chest. "But you're *my* this." After I said it, my cheeks went hot because he actually wasn't *my* anything, but the words had come out as easily as if they were true. We hadn't really talked about what we were to each other. I was leaving, he knew that. And he was probably just having fun with me in the meantime, *I* knew that. *He* was fun.

I clasped my hands in my lap and took a breath.

"What happened there in your head?" Dr. Franklin asked.

"What? Nothing," I said.

"You pulled back after that statement."

"I did?" I asked, feigning ignorance.

"What did saying that Elijah is yours make you feel?"

"I just . . . he's not. He's his and we are two separate people who have our own identities."

I could feel Elijah's gaze on me and I didn't look over.

Dr. Franklin wrote something in her notebook, then said, "You wanted advice about something?"

"Right . . . um . . . my dad."

"Okay," she said, waiting.

"Well, let me backtrack. My mom got in a serious accident about six weeks ago, and mentally, she's not recovering well. Actually, let me backtrack even further. My dad left her about fifteen years ago and never came back. She still acts like they're married. I mean, they are still married. But they're not. She obviously still wants to be and it's sad . . ."

"Sad?" Dr. Franklin asked, like she knew that wasn't the word I wanted to use.

"Pathetic," I said.

"You think your mom is weak?"

"I don't know. We don't have a great relationship. We were average before my dad left and terrible after. She's hypercritical and distant and . . . mean." It was hard to talk bad about my mom out loud. I'd just barely started doing it with Elijah, whom I felt safe with. I was so used to protecting her.

"Have you ever told her how she acts?"

"Not when I was a teen. I was young and didn't understand. And now, it seems pointless. I moved away and we aren't in each other's day-to-day lives and it works."

"Does it? You don't think you should tell her how she makes you feel?"

I shrugged. "I guess I feel sorry for her. I understand why she might feel like that. She is the product of being left by someone she thought loved her."

"So are you," Dr. Franklin said.

My eyes pricked with tears, surprising me. "No, well, I mean, yeah. But he's her husband."

"He is your *dad*."

I looked to the right, trying to keep my tears at bay. Elijah's hand went to my back, just resting there, warm and firm.

"Do you want to leave?" she asked. "Is that why you're looking at the door?"

"What? No." I hadn't realized I *was* looking at the door, but I was. I gave a breathy laugh. "Yes."

She smiled at me in an understanding way, then turned her attention to Elijah. "How do you feel about all this?"

"This isn't about me," he said.

"It is, because it's her life and that affects you as well."

"I worry about her. A lot," Elijah said.

I tried to give him the *we aren't supposed to lie* look. But the sincere expression on his face caught me off guard.

"What advice about this situation were you hoping for, Sutton?"

"Oh, I think my mom, whether purposefully or subconsciously, is keeping herself sick in hopes my dad will come home and care for her. And I don't think manipulation is the answer on my mom's part, but I do think she deserves closure. What do you think I could say to him to get him to come?"

She drew in a breath. "That's a big question that I don't have an answer for. I don't know if there is anything you *could* say to make him come. That has to be his decision."

"So I shouldn't call him?"

"You should call him. Tell him what you just told me and then let him decide."

"And if he never answers the phone?"

"Then maybe you have his answer."

"Did you already try to call him?" Elijah asked softly next to me. "And he hasn't called you back?" How did he know that?

I nodded.

"I'm sorry," he said.

Maybe therapy wasn't for everyone, like I had originally thought, because this was too much. Too much pressure behind my eyes. Too much weight on my shoulders. Too many thoughts swirling in my head.

"It's okay to feel whatever you're feeling," Dr. Franklin said.

I gave a curt nod.

"It's also okay to say whatever you want to. This is a judgment-free zone," she said.

"I'm okay. I need it to be Elijah's turn."

Again, she gave me a soft smile. "Elijah, how did the homework go last week?"

"We didn't—"

"I scratched the first box," I said. "But then life got in the way of doing the rest."

"You did?" Elijah asked.

"Did you do what the first box revealed?" she asked.

"That sexy text," I said to him. "Asking you out."

"That was homework?" Why did he have to look so hurt? I didn't need more emotions right now.

"No . . . I mean, yes, but I wanted to. I really wanted to," I said.

I could see the Adam's apple bob in his throat, but he took my hand in his and smiled through whatever he was feeling. "It was a really fun text," he said.

Dr. Franklin beamed. "That's great. Finish the rest of the sheet, okay? It's a great exercise." She wrote something else in her notebook. "And Sutton, being a caretaker is hard. Taking a weekend away wouldn't be selfish. But I'm not going to assign that as homework, even though I want to, because I know the guilt that might cause. But if you decide to do that, I fully support you. I'm sure Elijah would as well."

"Yes," he said, "I would."

"Thank you."

She closed her notebook and leaned back in her chair. "You guys picked the four-week marriage prep course. And today was the last day. I would be happy to keep seeing you, as a couple, or individually. Talk about it and let me know."

"Oh," I said, having forgotten for a moment the whole timeline thing.

"I think we're good," Elijah said. "At least for now. Right, babe?"

"Yeah, right. For sure. This has been great. Thank you so much."

She stood and walked us out of her office to the lobby. As we reached the door, she said, "Sutton, hold on a minute."

Elijah nodded and walked out of the building. I turned back. "Did I fail?"

She laughed. "No, of course not. But . . . what you're dealing with, it's a lot. And remember what we talked about a couple sessions ago, it's okay to need help."

"Right, my hyper-independence." I gestured toward the front door where Elijah had just left. "I'm working on it."

"He's a good one," she said.

"He is."

"And it's okay to call him yours. Not everyone leaves."

I wanted to scream, *We were strangers and you couldn't see that so I'm not sure I should trust anything you say*. But I wanted to trust her, regardless of her lack of perception. "Bye," I said instead.

I joined Elijah outside, where he was once again waiting for me at the trunk of his car. "Did you get in trouble?"

"She just wanted to tell me that she knew we were strangers from day one."

"Really?" he said.

"And that I won the bet because this proves I know everything."

"Everything?"

"Yes."

He narrowed his eyes. "I was hoping she was telling you that you need to warn me when texts are the result of homework assignments."

"I'm sorry," I said, because even though he was joking, it had obviously bothered him. "I wish I was that fun and spontaneous, but I'm not. I think that's why she gave me the scratcher to begin with and not you."

"You are," he said.

"I'm not. But Elijah," I grabbed hold of his forearms that were crossed over his chest and looked him in the eyes. "The text, the words, were mine, not homework. And I meant what I sent. I wanted to. Bad."

"Do you still want to? Bad?"

I nodded.

"Will you come to my place for dinner this weekend?"

"Do you cook?"

"I do not. But I'm excellent at ordering food. Maybe even an expert."

I smiled.

"So will you?"

"Only if you send me a sexy text asking me," I said.

He whipped out his phone right that second and, unlike

me who had taken an entire day to compose the perfect thing, typed something without much thought and tucked his phone back in his pocket.

My phone chimed seconds later.

I checked the screen:

Are you huuungry? I can get you fooood. His text was followed by the winky-faced emoji and the eggplant one, then his address.

I laughed. "I like you so much."

He wrapped one arm around my waist and lifted me up, pressing his lips to mine as he did. "I like *you* so much."

He placed me back on the ground, my stomach all aflutter. But then I seemed to come to my senses. "But Elijah . . ."

"If you have to cancel at the last minute or leave because of your mom, I understand," he said, reading my mind.

"Thanks." My eyes stung again and I pointed to my car with the key fob I had dug out of my pocket. "I need to . . ."

He kissed my cheek. "See you later."

CHAPTER 30

There was an urgent pounding on the front door later that night, startling me.

"Who's that?" my mom asked, like I could see through walls. It was almost time for us to start her nighttime routine, which took at least an hour.

"I'm not sure." I got up and answered the door to see Tara on the porch.

"Hi," she said. "Can you come out tonight?"

"Um . . ."

She poked her head into the house. "Hi, Andrea!"

My mom's face lit up. "Hi, Tara. Come in."

Tara stepped inside and gave my mom a hug.

Mom immediately turned off the television. "How are you, dear?"

"I'm good. I want to steal your daughter tonight. Can I?"

"Of course."

"No," I said, confused at both Tara for asking and my mom for agreeing. "Not right now, Tara, we have a nighttime routine."

"You and your routines," Tara said.

"She lives and dies by them," Mom said.

I opened my mouth to object when Tara said, "Oh!" She pointed to the still-yet-to-be-used scooter in the corner. "These things are so cool." She put one knee on the raised pad and drove it around the living room. "Is it helping you a lot? Have you mastered it? I bet you have." She steered it to the couch and then stepped to the side.

"Tara, she . . ." I started to say she'd never used it, but my mom slid herself to the edge of the couch and then reached for the handles. And before I knew it, her casted leg was resting on the pad, supported by her knee, and her hands were gripping the handles.

"Why is this coffee table right here?" Tara asked. "It's a complete hazard." In several swift motions, she had the coffee table tucked into the far corner of the room, out of the way. "Better," she said. "Now, let's see your stuff, Andrea."

My mom tentatively pushed against the floor. I took a step forward to stand close in case she fell, but Tara grabbed me by the arm, stopping me. "She's fine," she mouthed to me.

My heart was racing as I watched, worried about her dizziness. I did not want to witness her crashing to the floor. But she didn't. She moved slowly at first but then with more confidence around the living room.

Tara clapped. "That's amazing! You're a natural."

"Good job, Mom," I said.

"So I can steal your daughter for the night?"

"Her left arm is still weak, so I don't know if she can . . ."

Tara walked forward and stepped in front of my mom. "Push against my hand." She held her right hand in front of my mom's left. Mom pushed against her hand. "How do you feel, Andrea? Do you think you can do your nighttime routine tonight without Ms. Helicopter Daughter over here?"

My mom let out a dry laugh. "I do."

"Great. But call us if you need us, okay?"

Tara dragged me toward the door.

"I'm not even properly dressed," I said.

"Okay, you have ten minutes. Hurry." She released me and I went to my bedroom. I felt uneasiness churning in my chest. I didn't want to leave. Sure, I had left her for several hours here and there, but not when she had to actually accomplish tasks. Tara hadn't been here to see how dizzy my mom got—even if it *was* in her head. She hadn't held her after she fell. She hadn't watched her suffer in pain, sometimes silently, sometimes not.

But if she thought my mom was ready and my mom thought she was ready, maybe I really was being overprotective, hovering. She was going to have to start taking care of herself again at some point, after all.

As I was leaving ten minutes later, I looked back over my shoulder at my mom, who was still standing there, gripping the handles of the scooter, watching us go, and my uneasiness grew.

• • •

"This isn't a karaoke restaurant," I said.

Tara had taken me to a restaurant to "celebrate" the completion of the therapy challenge. I thought it was a thank-you gesture, but when we arrived, Michael and Elijah were already there, and on the table in front of them was some sort of large speaker. It wasn't until my eyes followed the cord that was attached to a microphone at the end that I realized what it was.

"We talked to the manager," Michael said. "And it's all good."

Why didn't I believe him? Elijah was smiling beside him like this was an everyday occurrence.

"The other customers aren't going to be happy," I said.

"A bet is a bet, Sutton," Michael said. "Are you the type who follows through or aren't you?"

I groaned. "Fine, but can I get at least three alcoholic beverages in me before this goes down?"

Elijah laughed. "At least."

I sat down next to him. "I hate you."

He kissed me. "You can punish me later."

The waitress came by and we ordered drinks and some appetizers. It was past dinnertime, but we all agreed that we could eat.

It took me two drinks to feel any sort of loosening of my tight muscles, but that was about all I felt as I looked at the speaker that Michael had moved to the bench seat between him and Tara.

As our waitress walked by, I called out, "Excuse me!"

She turned.

"Can I get another margarita?" I held up my glass, which only had a few ice cubes in it.

"Sure thing," she said. "Anyone else?"

"I'm driving," Tara said.

"Me too, I'm good," Elijah said. They'd both had only one drink. Michael ordered another with me and added some shots for both of us as well.

I decided I was okay with that.

"And you're good on appetizers?" she asked, looking at the only half-eaten plates of coconut shrimp and chips and guac.

"We're good," Elijah said. "Thank you."

"Who thinks smashing cake in faces is a good wedding tradition?" Michael asked.

Tara rolled her eyes. "Do you know how much I'm spending on makeup? You will not smash cake in my face."

"Yes," I agreed, picking up a chip and holding it in the air. "I'm definitely team no-smash."

Elijah chuckled beside me.

"What about you, Eli?" Michael asked, grabbing him by the scruff of the neck in a playful gesture.

"I can see both sides. People can get so uptight at weddings."

"Exactly," Michael said.

I looked at Elijah. "Seriously?"

"I mean, I get not wanting to ruin your makeup too. Especially after all that work."

"So diplomatic," I said, squeezing his side.

The waitress came back with our drinks, and Michael grabbed his shot right away and held it out for me to tap with my glass. I did and we both downed them. I cringed with the burn but then laughed.

Tara, still obviously hung up on our conversation, said, "You will not smash cake in my face. It's humiliating."

He raised his hands in the air. "Fine. Fine. I won't. But speaking of humiliating . . ." He placed the speaker on the edge of the table and held out the microphone to me.

"What are my song choices?" I asked, hoping to stall for just a little bit longer. I took two more big mouthfuls of my drink.

"We just hook up a phone," he said, "so you can really pick whatever."

That almost made it harder. My phone was already on the table, face up. I'd been checking it regularly in case my mom called or messaged. I picked it up and searched for popular karaoke songs.

"Just think of something you know well," Elijah said. "Something you sing in the car or shower, maybe?"

"I do neither."

"Really?" he asked. "Never?"

"Are you surprised?" Tara said with a laugh.

"It's not a bad or good thing," he said to Tara, most likely feeling the need to defend me. "Just a neutral."

"That sounds like therapy talk," she said. "Did you learn that in therapy?"

"Maybe I did," he said.

"With the therapist who couldn't even tell you were strangers?" Michael said. "Might not want to take anything you learned there too seriously."

"It was good," Elijah said.

"You're a therapy convert now?" Michael asked.

"Possibly," he said. "It wasn't that bad. Helpful even."

I smiled, glad he was trying to convince Michael now too. I squeezed his knee under the table, and he pressed his thigh against mine.

"See, Michael," Tara said. "It's not so bad. And four short weeks. Four!"

"Pass," Michael said.

"Ugh," she said. "You're so maddening sometimes."

"*All* the time," I said, then realized I'd said that out loud. I was more intoxicated than I realized. "Just kidding," I added quickly. "I'm just annoyed you're making me sing."

He laughed.

I continued scrolling through the song list on my phone.

"How about 'Mamma Mia'?" I said. I'd watched that movie a dozen times and loved ABBA. Maybe I could hold the tune or, at the very least, the beat. I took another swig of my drink.

And then it was happening. Michael was standing up and turning some knobs and speaking into the microphone. "Attention, restaurant-goers. My poor friend here was on the losing end of a very important bet, and her punishment is to sing for a restaurant full of people who were not expecting to hear singing tonight."

That last bit was completely untrue. I was always under the impression we were going to an actual venue for this kind of thing. That other people would also be participating. But Michael was Michael, and it was more than obvious he was well versed in doling out humiliation. It was his specialty.

"So give it up for the songstress herself—Sutton."

There was some light clapping and a small "woot!" from the other tables.

I stood, breathing deeply, trying to remind myself that I could have fun. These people would never see me again. This was happening. I could do this.

Elijah plugged his phone into the speaker and pushed play. The intro to the song started playing.

"Forgive me," I said into the mic. "For ruining your dinner."

The good news was that the actual vocals started as I did. They were light in the background, but they helped a lot. What didn't help was how the whole restaurant just stared, blank-faced. The words were coming out of my mouth, I was stepping back and forth to the beat, my free hand moving through the air like I had done this before, but dead eyes stared back at me.

When I got to the chorus, I held the mic toward the restaurant. Nothing.

Elijah chimed in loudly with the chorus to my right. I smiled gratefully over at him. Tara was just staring at me. Her eyes narrowed a bit. Like she couldn't believe I was doing this. It made me stutter a few lines. I averted my gaze and looked back at the restaurant patrons who, in comparison, seemed less judgmental.

"Nothing?" I said into the microphone as the prelude to the next verse played.

"Are you done yet?" someone called from across the room.

Maybe it was some sort of rebellion that kicked in with those words, but I said, "I might do two songs now!" and then launched into the verse.

"Please, no!" someone else said.

I sang louder, adding more steps to my dance.

"Yes!" Elijah called.

This time, when I got to the chorus, I walked to the next table and held the microphone out for the closest guy. To my surprise, he actually sang a line. And then the next person did as well.

"Thank you!" I said into the mic, continuing the chorus myself. "Mamma Mia, I will never make a bet with Michael again," I sang into the microphone.

"You made this one with Elijah!" Michael called.

That's right, I had. I lowered the mic and said to Elijah, "Same sentiment applies to you."

He just smiled.

"Thank god for alcohol," I said back into the mic, trying to figure out where I was in the song.

Someone across the room cheered, "Yay, alcohol!" And finally,

finally, the song came to an end. I gave a dramatic bow and handed the mic back to Michael before I collapsed into my seat.

"That was awesome," Elijah said, draping his arm over my shoulder. "You are full of surprises."

"You really are," Tara said, throwing a wadded napkin at me. She was trying to joke, but it seemed half-hearted. Had I done something wrong?

"Do you still hate me?" Elijah whispered in my ear.

"Ask me when I'm sober." I looked at my phone screen, double-checking for messages and missed calls.

"She's fine," he said.

"I hope so."

CHAPTER 31

"See, she's fine," Elijah said.

My mom was fine. Her scooter was by her bed. In her bathroom, her toothbrush was out and resting on the side of the sink. The only thing it looked like she wasn't able to do was change out of her pants, but that wasn't the end of the world; she'd been wearing comfortable, elastic-waisted pants to make both our lives easier anyway. I nodded and quietly left the room.

"You seem almost disappointed," he said in the hall.

I wasn't disappointed that she was fine, just disappointed in myself for making us leave the restaurant. Earlier, I'd had another drink, definitely one too many, probably two too many, and then became preoccupied with the fact that this was her first time using the scooter. How her muscles had been underutilized lately and this was a lot to expect of her.

"I left her," I'd said, brushing the chip crumbs on the table in front of me into an orderly pile. "On her very first try. She hadn't even wheeled it down the hall. What if it doesn't fit through her bedroom door?"

"The wheelchair fits through the door, the scooter will," Elijah had said quietly beside me, rubbing my back.

"But what if it doesn't?"

"She would've called you."

"True. But what if she fell? And hit her head and can't call me?"

"Do you want to leave? I can take you home. I drove."

"No," I'd said. "She's fine." But five minutes later I was repeating the same statements over again.

"I'm taking you home," Elijah had said. He stood and helped me up. "I'm taking Sutton home," he'd announced to Michael and Tara, who were having a private conversation of their own. It looked kind of heated, but I was trying not to eavesdrop. He'd led me outside to his car, where he'd helped me sit down and even buckled my seat belt.

"I can do it." But I hadn't moved to take over the task.

Now, we were standing in the hall of my house. "No, I'm not disappointed. I'm glad she doesn't need me as much anymore. It's nice."

"It is."

"Maybe I can even go check on the restaurant this weekend. Ease my mind there as well." I moved toward the kitchen, suddenly feeling a strong urge for a glass of water.

"That's a good idea. I know how worried you've been about it."

I took a cup down from the cupboard and filled it with tap water, not willing to wait for the slower-flowing fridge-dispensed water. I downed it in several big gulps, then let out a loud sigh. "Oh, but you were going to feed me this weekend at your house."

He smiled. "That's okay, we can do it another time." He took the glass out of my hand and put it on the counter. I wasn't sure why. I wasn't going to drop it.

"Do you want to come?" I said, spitting out the words without thinking too much.

"To LA?" he asked.

"I mean, I know you're busy, but if you want to I—"

"I'd love to come," he said.

"Do you think Tara would check on my mom? Or maybe she wouldn't. She seemed upset with me tonight. Was she upset with me?"

"For what?" he asked.

"I don't know."

"She wasn't upset with you. She owes you. She absolutely would look in on your mom."

I leaned against the counter, feeling tired or dizzy or something. "And maybe I can hire Lucy for Saturday just so Mom's not alone *all* weekend."

"Good idea."

I gripped the edges of the counter and stared at the wall in front of me. The room was dim, lit only from the hallway. I hadn't flipped on the light when coming in here, and the room was spinning. "I'm still very drunk."

He laughed. "You are. You did good tonight, by the way."

"I'm sure I will regret it in the morning."

"Which part? The singing or the excessive drinking?"

"All."

He pulled me close. "You keep surprising me."

"I'm not actually full of surprises, I'm actually pretty predictable, so don't expect much more than what you've seen."

He pressed his lips to mine several times, lingering close to my mouth between each kiss. "What I've seen is what I need."

My chest expanded with his words, and my arms snaked around his waist. "Don't make me take you right here," I said.

"You're still very drunk," he reminded me.

"Oh, right." I grabbed a handful of his ass. "Later."

He let out a quiet laugh, then gave me a slow, passionate kiss that set my insides on fire.

"Maybe I'm not that drunk," I said.

"I should go. Do you need help getting to bed?"

"No, I'm good." I walked him to the door.

"I'll see you soon, Sutton." He placed one more kiss on my lips and then left.

I leaned my back against the door, then sighed like a lovesick teenager.

• • •

"Okay, so here are her meds. She doesn't take these anymore, but she does take these three, and she can take this one if she's in pain. It's all written down here."

"You know I'm a nurse, right?" Tara asked, standing in the kitchen with me Friday morning as I was spelling everything out for her. Along with the chart I'd made weeks ago for her medication schedule, I'd made another one for where things were kept in the house and a list of emergency contacts.

"I know," I said.

"She seems to forget I have a brain as well," my mom called from the other room.

"I haven't," I said. "I just want to make sure more than one person knows."

Tara put her hand on my arm. "She'll be fine. You've done good."

"Thanks for doing this," I said.

"Of course. I'm happy to. Thanks for the four weeks of therapy you did for me."

"It didn't help you," I said.

"But you tried and that's what matters. Plus, you got a new toy out of it." She wiggled her brows at me.

I let out a single loud laugh, then sucked in my lips.

"What's so funny?" Mom asked from the other room.

"We're just talking about Sutton's new boy toy," Tara called.

"He's not younger than me," I said.

"Does *boy toy* only work if the person is younger?" she asked.

"I think that's what the saying means."

"Well, I've decided it could also work if the person is more fun," she said. "Younger at heart."

"Thanks a lot," I said.

"Oh, come on, you know you're an old woman living in a twenty-eight-year-old's body." She lifted up the charts I had painstakingly made for her and Lucy.

"I guess I do know that."

"Who's her new boy toy?" Mom asked.

"Elijah," Tara said. "You've met him."

"Oh, yes. I don't like that boy."

"He's fun, Andrea."

My mom grumbled something that resembled *fun, my ass.*

"Your mom still doesn't like him?" she asked me quietly.

"Apparently, he reminds her of my dad. But honestly, I think everyone reminds her of my dad."

Tara considered this for a moment. "I guess I could see why he does."

"You remember my dad?"

"I do! He was outgoing and friendly."

"Elijah is not my dad," I said. Maybe Dad was outgoing and friendly, but he was also private and sneaky.

"No," Tara backtracked. "Of course not, I just meant I can see why your mom might find a few tiny commonalities."

"Everyone has a few tiny commonalities."

"Probably true."

"Are we okay?" I suddenly asked.

"What?" she said in confusion. "Of course."

"Just, when I sang karaoke the other night . . ."

"It just surprised me. I didn't think you liked performing in front of a crowd."

"I don't," I assured her. "That's why I got very drunk."

She nodded and then laughed. "You really did."

I took a relieved breath. We were fine.

She tapped the edges of the papers she still held on the counter, then set them down next to the collection of things I'd compiled to properly care for my mom. "What time are you leaving?"

I looked at my smartwatch. "In like thirty minutes. We're hoping to beat rush hour traffic. But seriously, Tara, please call me if I need to come back. I can always jump on a flight in an emergency."

"You won't need to," she said. "Just have fun. You deserve a break."

I wasn't sure this weekend was going to be much of a break. It would just be a different kind of work. But at least it was work I chose and with people who appreciated all I did.

CHAPTER 32

I drove, since it was my trip and I had a hybrid car, making it the cheaper option. Elijah was easy to road-trip with, I decided, as we approached three hours in the car together. He selected good music. Only playing "Mamma Mia" once and mimicking some of my dance moves from the karaoke experience. But when I backhanded him playfully on the arm, he laughed and changed the song.

"How long has it been since you've been home?" he asked now, as the traffic slowed in front of us.

"Six weeks? Seven?"

"What are you looking forward to the most?"

"My bed," I said.

"Really?" His voice went low and throaty with the word.

I reached over and squeezed his leg. "Not like that." Well, that too, if I was being honest. "My childhood mattress is shit, and I'm ready for my actual mattress."

"Your childhood mattress is shit? It seemed fine to me. Comfortable, roomy."

I laughed. "Room to spare even."

"Exactly. We could've invited another guest."

"Is that what you wanted? Another guest?" I asked, my brows going down.

"No," he said quickly. "It was just a joke. A bad one."

"It was funny," I said. What I really wanted to say was *What are we doing? What* do *you want from this? From us?* But I didn't because I wasn't even sure I could answer those questions. Or maybe I was scared of his answers. For now, even though it was completely against my nature, I could live in the moment. Let whatever was supposed to happen, happen. And have fun while it was happening. Because he was making everything better right now. And seeing as how *everything* was a lot, I needed this. Him. Even if only for a little while.

• • •

I held my key tightly in my fist as we walked down the hall of my apartment complex on the way to my fourth-floor apartment, nervous. We'd parked in the covered parking garage after a longer-than-average trip. We had not, in fact, beaten traffic. Or maybe I had forgotten how bad traffic was here.

"I didn't expect to be gone this long. And I was supposed to have someone checking on my place while I was gone but . . ."

"He broke up with you instead?" Elijah guessed when I didn't finish my sentence.

"Yes."

"Were you two living together?" he asked.

"No, but I didn't prep for a completely abandoned house." Was it going to stink of rotting food? Was there going to be a moldy sink and a black-rimmed toilet? Why had I invited Elijah along on my first trip home?

I slid the key into the lock and turned. No smell greeted me when I opened the door, which was a relief. The only thing I'd packed when leaving my mom's house earlier was a tote bag with my toiletries, knowing I had an apartment full of clothes I hadn't worn in weeks. I swung that bag onto the entryway table and made my way into the main living area, a small room with big windows and a brick fireplace. It was attached to a decently sized kitchen with stainless steel appliances and granite countertops.

I opened the long curtains on the windows to let in the last light of the day. The sun was going down fast. A plant sitting on a table between the windows was completely dead. Its soil cracked and dry, its leaves brown and crispy. I picked up the pot and brought it to the kitchen, where I set it in the sink and turned on the faucet.

Elijah had wheeled his suitcase inside and shut the door behind us. He now stood watching me.

"I think it's dead," he said.

"But can it be revived?"

He tilted his head as if he didn't think it could but was going to let me try.

"I feel bad." I picked up another dead plant off the counter in the kitchen and added it to the sink.

"For the plants?"

I let out a breathy chuckle. "Yes. There are at least two more that I'm sure have met the same fate. Including my shower fern."

"Shower fern?"

"You've never heard of a shower fern? Don't act like it's not a thing."

"It's not."

"Well, I like to shower with living things."

His eyebrows popped up.

"Plants, I mean. Greenery." I gestured toward the very-much-not-green plants in my sink.

"Well, if you ever mean anything else, I'm here to help."

I laughed and turned off the water. "Um . . . you can put your suitcase . . ." I pointed while moving toward my bedroom.

He wanted to stay in my bedroom, right? God, it had been too long since I'd started a relationship. I didn't remember what the beginning phases consisted of. But we weren't starting a relationship . . . were we? Why hadn't we talked about this? And why was it on *me* to bring it up? *He* could ask me. He could say, *Do you want to date me? Are we exclusive? I'll move to Los Angeles for you.*

No, not that last one. He didn't need to say that last one. Shouldn't. Why would he? He was in a hole with his dad that I knew he needed to climb out of. And even once he was out of the hole, he'd already failed at what he had wanted to do—photography. Why did I think he was suddenly going to try it again just because I was in the picture telling him he could? He would probably stay at that boxing gym forever.

"This is the famous bed?" he asked, coming through the door behind me.

I took a happy breath. I'd missed my apartment, my bedroom, my life. "This is it."

"Which side do you sleep on?" he asked.

"The right." I pointed to the side farthest from the door and closest to the windows.

"Uh-oh."

"Is that your side too?"

"It is. But I will concede since it is your bed."

We slept on the same side of the bed. Was that a sign from the universe that this relationship was not meant to be? Stop. *That* was nothing to read into.

My eyes caught on a piece of paper on the nightstand on the other side of the bed. I walked over to it. A key sat on top of the paper with handwritten words that read: *Got my stuff, here's the only thing of yours that was at my place.*

I stared at the key. Was that really the only thing? The key that I had given him before I left so he could water my plants and keep an eye on my stuff. I hadn't left a T-shirt or a toothbrush or even a hair tie?

I looked at the backside of the paper. It was empty. I crumpled up the note and balled it in my fist, then tossed it in the trash can in the bathroom. "I . . . uh . . . this is the full bath," I said, continuing to give him a tour of the place.

"Is this the one with the shower fern?" He poked his head inside. "Yes, it's very dead."

"That's what happens," I said, looking at the poor fern. "When it doesn't get watered."

"Maybe that's what happens when it's deprived of seeing you naked for so long."

I laughed. "Could be."

"We could solve that problem. Work on reviving that one, as well."

"We could," I said, exiting the bathroom.

He stepped in front of me, his brows drawing down. "What's wrong?"

"I don't know," I said.

"Is it being back? Is it whatever your ex wrote on that note?

Or *didn't* write? Your dead plants? Your restaurant? What do you need?"

I shook my head because I really couldn't pinpoint what it was at all, but he was right that it *was* something. I felt out of sorts.

I wrapped my arms around his middle and immediately relaxed a bit. I relaxed even more when he held me tight and rested his cheek against my head.

"You're not worried about your mom, are you?" he asked.

"No," I said. "I think I just need to see the restaurant and then I'll feel better."

"Do you want to go now?"

"Can we?"

"Of course. You're the boss this weekend. I do whatever you say."

"*Whatever* I say?"

"Yes, *whatever* you say." He kissed my temple, then my neck, and ended on my lips.

I kissed him back, wishing I was the kind of person who could completely relax right now, let him throw me on the bed and forget everything for an hour.

Maybe I could be.

My hands went to the bottom of his T-shirt and snuck their way inside, brushing along the smooth skin of his back. He let out a low hum and my insides set fire, my body melting against his.

His hands brushed along my ass, then down to the back of my thighs, where he lifted me up and walked several steps until my back was pressed up against the nearest wall. I sucked in a surprised gasp of air but then wrapped my legs around his waist. I could feel him hard against me through my jeans. I dug my fingers into his hair, and his tongue thrust deeper into my mouth, eliciting a moan from me.

Then he was kissing my neck, and his hand slid up my side until it was cupping my breast in a firm grip. His mouth went back to mine, almost desperate. Or maybe that's how I felt. Desperate for him to feel every inch of me. For this fire inside me to combust.

With that word, my mind suddenly imagined a cell phone falling into a fryer. And potatoes. Boxes of potatoes. And really cheap art and how everyone must've hated our really cheap art.

"Where'd you go?" he asked.

I unhooked my legs from his waist and he slid me down the wall.

"I'm just worried about the restaurant and . . ."

"It's okay. You're not a machine. You're allowed to worry. Let's go." He nodded toward the door.

"Are you sure?"

"Of course I'm sure."

I pointed to the bathroom. "Give me a minute."

He pulled at his jeans. "A minute will be good for me too."

• • •

"What were you more nervous about me seeing? Your apartment or the restaurant?"

"The restaurant," I said as I pulled into the lot next to our building and parked, shutting off the car.

"Why?"

"Because I've put a lot of work into it and you're an artist and you're going to tell me it's boring."

He laughed. "First, I am not an artist."

"You are."

He unbuckled his seat belt. "Disagree. But second, I would never tell you it's boring."

"But will you?" I turned in my seat to face him.

"What?"

"Will you say it if it's true?" I grabbed hold of his hand with both of mine.

"No."

My brows shot down. The fact that he'd lie to me to save my feelings actually wasn't a good thought, even though he probably thought that's what I wanted to hear. "No, I'm making a request. Will you please tell me if it's boring?"

"Oh. You want me to."

"And how to fix it?"

He smiled. "Not sure I'll know how to fix it."

"If you have any thoughts." I put his hand on my cheek and let his warmth sink into my skin for a moment.

"Okay," he said carefully. "I'll tell you."

"Thank you."

"For the love of god, I hope it's not boring."

CHAPTER 33

"What?" Raya yelled when I walked in the front doors of the restaurant. I hadn't told her I was coming. I wanted it to be a surprise. "Whaaattt?!"

Several customers looked her way, and she lowered her voice. "What are you doing here?" She was running to greet me.

Her arms wrapped around my stomach, and her cheek went to my chest. "I missed you so, so, so much. Tell me you're back."

"Just for the weekend," I said, hugging her.

Presley was working tonight, and from across the room I saw her mouth, "Thank god." There were a few other servers as well since it was a Friday night. I only didn't recognize one of them.

Raya groaned. "Just the weekend?"

"I thought you said it wasn't that bad without me."

"But everything is better with you."

Warmth spread through my chest at her words. I'd missed

her too, and hearing I was missed and my absence made a difference was nice.

She straightened up and her eyes immediately went to Elijah. He was by my side but taking in the restaurant. I looked around too. Having been away for a while made me see it more objectively now. The wall that housed the windows was red brick, and the other walls we'd painted a clean ivory. Those walls were where the generic art was hung—large pictures of food displayed in a fancy way. The bar was the coolest thing in the room. A beautiful stained wood with a copper bar top. We'd commissioned it and thought it would carry the room. It was the most interesting thing in the room, but it didn't carry it.

"Cool bar," Elijah said now, obviously studying it at the same time I was.

"Who is that?" Raya mouthed to me.

"Raya, this is Elijah," I said. "Elijah, Raya."

"Oh!" he said, thrusting out his hand. "Hi. So nice to meet you. I've heard so much about you."

So much was a bit of an exaggeration, but he was nothing if not polite.

"Um . . . who are you?" she asked, obviously confused.

"I'm . . ." He must've been as lost about our status as I was.

"He's a friend," I said, since he obviously didn't want to put a label on us.

"That she kisses," he added.

I laughed.

"Oh, really?" Raya said.

"Let's move this reunion to the back," I said, realizing how unprofessional we were being with tables of customers so close.

"You guys haven't talked much in the last several weeks,

have you?" Elijah asked as we walked toward the back of the restaurant.

"Only every single morning," Raya said.

I cringed. This wasn't going well. Should I have mentioned Elijah to Raya? We'd just barely started kissing . . . like two weeks ago.

"You talk to her every morning and she's never mentioned me?" he asked, more surprised than hurt, it seemed.

"What you need to learn about Sutton, if you haven't already, is that she's very much a down-to-business type of woman."

"I *do* know that about her," he said.

"Hello," I said. "I'm right here." They had both started talking about me in the third person, so I felt like the reminder was necessary.

"And she's pretty private," Raya said, like I hadn't spoken.

"This is the back hallway," I said, trying to change the subject.

"Oh, you need to meet Lucas," Raya said to me. "Our new server." Then to Elijah she said, "Sutton hired two new servers from three hundred miles away."

"*You* hired them," I said.

"Sure I did." She winked. "Oh, and thanks for taking care of the potato issue. And the inventory we did the other day helped a lot."

"Good," I said, pushing through the swinging doors into the kitchen.

Chef was standing over some steaming pans at the stove, and he looked up as we entered. A smile broke out on his face. "Sutton? You're back?"

"Just for the weekend."

He moved the chicken he was searing onto a paddle and slid it into the brick oven.

"And this pretty boy right here," Raya said, nodding with her head, "is Elijah."

"Hello," Chef said. "Welcome."

"I used to call him Pretty Boy," I said. "Well, Villain Pretty Boy."

"*Villain* Pretty Boy?" Elijah asked.

"You have a devilish look about you," I said.

He chuckled.

Raya nodded. "I can see it."

"There's a botched order on the warming counter if anyone wants it," Chef said.

"Botched how?" I asked.

"Overcooked . . . according to the customer."

"Annoying," I said, but collected the plate—a filet. I added some mashed potatoes and seared veggies and passed it off to Elijah.

"This looks amazing," he said, and I directed him out of the kitchen and to the bar out front where he could eat. "Take care of this man," I said to our bartender, Angel.

She smiled at me. "Welcome back, boss."

"Only visiting."

I started to walk away, and Elijah grabbed me by the hand and pulled me against his side. "Have I been put in a time-out?" he asked in a low voice that made my insides flip. Angel raised her eyebrows at me. People at the restaurant weren't used to seeing me with anyone. Nate came by occasionally, but we kept it professional.

"No," I said. "You haven't. I thought you might be hungry."

I reached over the bar and retrieved a set of utensils wrapped in a cloth napkin. "Come to the back when you're done."

"I like seeing you in all your boss glory," he said, again in a low, quiet voice. With those words, he released his hold on my waist and I rejoined Raya in the back just as a younger guy came to collect a plate from the kitchen.

"Lucas," Raya said, "this is Sutton. You talked to her on the phone."

"Hi," he said. "Thanks for hiring me. I really like it."

"Good to hear."

He picked up his orders, balancing them expertly on his arms, and was gone again.

Raya smiled. "It really is good to see you." She studied my face for a moment. "You look . . ."

"Tired?" I filled in for her.

"No, I was going to say happy. Light."

"Do I?"

"Do we have that very pretty man eating food out there to thank for this? Or have you made peace with your mom?"

I gave a fake laugh. "Yeah, me and my mom are magically besties now."

"Oh, I need your signature on a couple things in the office."

I nodded and we made our way through the hallway stacked with miscellaneous boxes to the office at the back. It had a single window to the outside, but other than that it was small and depressing, and I forgot how much time I used to spend in here going over numbers and rearranging schedules.

The desk was stacked with papers, and there was another stack on top of the file cabinet. I didn't want to think about how much work was waiting for me when I came back. I hoped none of it was urgent. No, it wasn't. The urgent stuff Raya had dealt with, I was sure. It was probably spam mail from suppliers and vendors.

Raya retrieved a clipboard that held a few pages. "This is our contract with Mac. It's time to re-sign. Did you want to look over the terms again?"

"It's been a year," I said quietly.

"Happy year to us."

"I'm sorry I wasn't here to make a big deal about it with you." I hadn't even thought about it. But the year mark was last week. April 21.

"It's okay," she said. "But let's throw a party when you get back. Have Chef make some fancy appetizers, charge by the head, it will be fun."

"That does sound fun," I said, reading through the points on the contract. They seemed the same as last year.

She narrowed her eyes at me. "Are you mocking me?"

"What? No! Did it sound like I was?"

"That just normally wouldn't be your thing."

"Well, it's my thing now."

"I think I love Elijah."

I rolled my eyes but then smiled. "He's actually so great and fun and funny, and I really like him." I signed on the line at the end, next to her signature.

"I'm happy for you."

"But . . ." I said, trying not to get ahead of myself. "He doesn't live here, so this is just . . ." I waved my hand toward the door, indicating where he sat beyond it.

"Sutton is letting herself have a fling?" Raya practically screamed.

"Shhhh!" I hissed. "No . . . I mean, yes? I don't know what it is."

She laughed. "You don't need to. It's good for you not to constantly have everything about your life planned."

"I guess," I said, putting the clipboard on the desk.

She took me by the shoulders and shook me back and forth. "It's a good thing."

I laughed. "Okay, okay. It is."

"Is his body as nice as his face?" she asked.

"Raya!"

"What? I'm gay, I can ask questions like that. It's for scientific purposes only. So . . . is it?"

"Yes, it is. But we haven't . . ."

"You haven't what? You haven't slept with him yet?" Her eyes went wide with her second question.

"No, it's been complicated. I've been with my mom and sleeping in a twin bed."

"Okay, that makes sense. No wonder you brought him this weekend."

I gasped. "It had nothing to do with that."

"Sure it didn't."

"Oh my god, pull yourself together," I said.

"I'm not the one having a fling."

"You said it was good for me!"

She laughed as she left the office. "So good."

CHAPTER 34

After leafing through a couple stacks of mail on the desk, throwing some out and tucking some others into my purse to look at later, I went to find Elijah.

He wasn't at the bar where I'd left him. His plate was still there, not a single piece of food left on it, along with an empty glass of what was probably our draft beer. A twenty sat on the counter, tucked under the knife.

Presley stopped on her way to the kitchen, stacked Elijah's dirty dishes on top of the ones she already held, and said, "You are a saint for hiring Lucas. I love him."

I could feel my brows go down, which must've been why she quickly added, "Not *love*, love. Just in the sense that he has helped a lot."

"That's great, Presley. Thanks for hanging in there. You are excellent at your job, and we need you here."

She smiled, said, "I know," then opened the door to the back with her butt.

I really did miss it here—the moving parts, the constant

work, the hum of voices and clinking of dishes, the smell of delicious food.

Out the glass door to the patio, I saw Elijah standing there, chatting with some customers. They were laughing at whatever he was saying. Damn if he didn't look good standing in my restaurant.

I pushed open the door. The patio was at only about half capacity with guests. I looked at my watch. Seven PM on a Friday. It should've been busier than this. This was obviously what Raya had meant when she said business was down after that review. The thought tugged at my chest.

I smiled at tables as I walked by, then stood shoulder to shoulder with Elijah. He had moved on from the customers and was now studying the fruitless olive tree we had planted in the center of the patio. It wasn't very tall, but its knobby branches and pale green leaves spread out wide. "Hey."

"Hey," he said.

"You didn't need to leave a tip."

"Of course I did," he said.

I slipped my hand into his and squeezed.

"Your restaurant is really nice."

"But not cool," I said.

He smiled. "It could be cooler."

"You have ideas?" I asked.

"Maybe a few." He reached out with his free hand and pinched a leaf between his thumb and forefinger. "This tree is nice. This patio has a lot of potential."

It was a large, covered patio. The tree was literally the only thing we had done to bring any sort of atmosphere out here. Aside from the tables and chairs, there were also a few potted plants at the corners of the short gate that enclosed the area.

"Yes, you let your big, beautiful, artistic brain think of how we can turn this place into a must-visit destination."

He dropped my hand and put his arm around me. "I'd like to show you a must-visit destination," he said in a low, suggestive tone.

"That didn't work."

"But I used the voice."

I laughed. I felt like I could float out of here, not touching the ground. I took him by the hand and led him back inside. "I have a must-visit destination for you."

I pushed through the doors to the back hall again, then past the kitchen. I pulled him into my office, shutting and locking the door behind us.

He was turning in a circle when I faced him, as if I really was showing him a special place. "I don't think—" he started to say, but I tugged him closer by the waistband of his jeans.

"Here?" he asked, a smile sneaking onto his lips.

"Are you objecting?"

"I thought you could control yourself," he teased. "That you would never feel an urgent enough desire to take someone in a back office."

"You worried you can't perform with all the people just outside this door?"

He took my hand in his and placed it on his very hard groin. "What do you think?" he growled.

"Oh, guess not," I said, my cheeks heating up as though flustered. Was I flustered?

He kissed me while guiding me toward the desk. He pulled away, assessing our options, and I could tell he was about to make a dramatic move to swipe all the papers to the floor.

I pulled him to the couch instead. It was about the same

size as the one in Dr. Franklin's office, shoved in the corner, and stacked with boxes of cloth napkins and aprons. I yanked one box to the floor, and it landed on its side, the contents spilling out. He lifted the other two, carefully stacking them against the wall.

The task was taking too long, so I shimmied out of my blazer in the meantime. He turned and, when he saw me, pulled his T-shirt over his head.

"People won't bother you back here?" he asked.

I smiled at his worry. It was a complete one-eighty from the normal roles we played.

I raised my eyebrows. "Isn't that part of the fun?"

His smile widened as though impressed.

I pushed him back toward the couch. He got the hint and sat with his back against the armrest and his legs across the cushions. Then I climbed onto his lap, straddling him.

"Hmmm," I hummed, rocking against his erection.

"You're determined to always give us the least possible space to work with," he said.

"You're the one who started the small-space brag list."

He gave me a wicked smile and somehow managed to completely reverse our positions by wrapping an arm around my waist, pushing off the armrest, and depositing me onto my back against the opposite one. He slid me down until my head was flat on the cushion. He kneeled between my legs and undid the button on my pants, his eyes on mine while he did. He slid them down my legs and deposited them on the floor along with himself. He now kneeled on the carpet beside the couch. His mouth went to my stomach, and my eyes fluttered closed, feeling every nerve ending in my body buzz to life.

His mouth moved down, gliding along my underwear

where his teeth scraped the material covering me. *Oh, god.* A zing of pleasure shot through me. It had been too long since I'd had an orgasm. I should've taken care of myself a few times in anticipation of this because I was going to climax embarrassingly fast. In the back, dingy office of my restaurant with all my friends on the other side of the door.

There. That did the trick. I was not on the edge anymore.

Well, I wasn't.

Until his mouth was moving up to my breast and his hand was slipping into my underwear, easily finding its way inside me.

I gasped.

"Bad or good?" he said in a low, throaty voice.

"Good," I said through a moan.

His free hand moved aside my bra, exposing my nipple to be gently caressed by his tongue. His finger inside me curved just right, hitting a spot that made me see stars.

I groped around for any piece of him to return the favor, but he was outside my reach. He gathered my hands in one of his and trapped them against the armrest while he continued to work me.

"I'm out of practice," I said.

He abandoned my breast and covered my mouth with his in the softest, most intimate kiss I had ever felt. It made me want to weep or scream *I love you* or never let him go.

"Just relax," he said. "Let it happen and then I can get you there all over again."

"I . . ." I arched against him as he slipped another finger inside me. "I want *you* inside me."

"First this," he said. "You feel so good. Warm. Soft." He released my hands to brush his fingers lightly through my hair. Both his hands knew exactly what they were doing, and tingles spread from both ends of my body until they met in the middle.

I was trying to keep quiet, but moans escaped, one right after the other as the joy in my body climbed to barely containable. His fingers worked me just right, bringing me to my peak. Then waves of pleasure exploded through me, my back arched, my mouth open, my breath gone.

"You're beautiful," he said in my ear.

My eyes shot to the door, wondering if anyone had heard me.

He smiled, freeing his hand from my underwear and moving the edges back into place. "You did that," he said. "In public," he added in a whisper.

I gave a breathy laugh. "We're not done."

"Wasn't sure your nerves could handle more than that."

"I'm not a taker," I said, sitting up. "I believe in fair play."

"Do you?"

"Now sit down so I can give you a hand job."

He laughed. "Yes, ma'am."

CHAPTER 35

I patted my hair and straightened my clothes again. Elijah was dressed and picking up the cloth napkins that had fallen out of the box, putting them back in. He'd used one of those napkins to clean himself up. That one was tucked in my purse to wash later. There was hand sanitizer on the corner of the desk, and we'd both used that as well.

"Is everyone going to be able to tell?" I asked. "Like when you come out of the plane bathroom, does the whole plane look at you knowingly?"

He laughed. "I've never actually done it on an airplane before, Sutton. You know that, right?"

"I thought you were the expert here. One of us needs to be."

He plopped the box back on the couch and stood in front of me, running his hands along my shoulders a few times. "You look good. Maybe a little flushed, but gorgeous. What about me? Do I look like I just got taken care of?"

My cheeks heated with the reminder of feeling him in my grip, of watching him groan with pleasure.

I straightened his shirt and then pushed onto my toes for a kiss. "You look perfect." On the way out the door, I grabbed an apron off a hook on the wall. "Would you hate me if I worked for a bit?"

"I figured you would."

"Do you want to go back to the apartment? I can get a ride home with Raya."

"Are you sure?"

"I'm sure." I dug my keys out of my purse and handed them to him.

He took them. "Okay. I'll see you in a while then."

"I'm sorry if my fridge has moldy food."

He smiled. "You think I'm going to go rummaging through your fridge?"

"And my drawers and my couch cushions."

"I'm not."

I kissed him again. "You won't find anything."

"Except moldy food?"

"And dead plants."

"The poor plants."

"I know."

He left out the front while I headed to the bathroom to wash my hands for real. I came out and tied the apron around my waist.

Raya, who was entering something into the ordering screen, narrowed her eyes at me. I probably had a goofy smile on my face.

When I reached her side she said, "Did you just have sex in the office?"

I nearly choked on my inhale. "I, I—no, I mean, sort of."

"Holy hell, what spell does that man have you under?"

"I'm sorry, that was super inconsiderate of me. I'll have the couch cleaned."

She laughed. "Sutton, I'm shocked, not disgusted."

"Oh, okay." I picked up a pen and ordering pad from beside the computer.

She paused for a moment and said, "I already broke in the office like ten months ago."

I let out a surprised little yelp.

She nodded to my apron. "Are you staying? Working?"

"Of course. I'm here. I've abandoned you for seven weeks. I'm going to work this weekend."

"You know you don't have to."

"I want to. And can you give me a ride home later?"

"You're closing?"

"Yes!"

"It's good to have you back."

• • •

I closed the lid on the container of lettuce and stacked it on top of the bin of cucumbers, then carried them both to the walk-in fridge. Raya was already inside, sliding containers back into place as well. I'd easily fallen back into the routine of closing up for the night. Like my body knew exactly what to do, muscle memory.

"It wasn't that busy tonight," I said.

"I know," she responded. "It's usually better."

"How much better?"

"Not much."

"I need to get that viral review guy back in here."

"Not if nothing has changed," she said.

"Yeah . . ." I took the spray bottle off the wall and doused the counters, wiping them up. "Elijah might have some good ideas."

"Oh, really? He's more than just a pretty face then?"

"He's a photographer."

"A professional photographer? Nice."

"No. He runs a boxing gym that his dad opened for him." I sprayed another working surface with the cleaning spray.

"What does boxing have to do with photography?"

"Nothing. But he *should* be a professional photographer. So maybe this project will help convince him to try again or to try differently or something."

"Our restaurant project?"

"I don't know. Maybe I'm putting too much faith in his ideas, but I have zero. What about you? Have you thought of how we can bring in more atmosphere?"

"I'm barely keeping my head above water with just running the place and the additional social media posts."

"I know," I said. "Thank you."

"A four-week honeymoon is sounding nice this summer."

"Take eight weeks," I said.

She latched the handle on the fridge, and we left the kitchen and headed for the dining room. Presley and Lucas were there, wiping down tables and sweeping. Angel passed Raya the zippered pouch from her register.

"Did you already tip yourself out?" Raya asked.

Angel patted her pocket as her answer. "See you all tomorrow."

I let her out the front door and relocked it while Raya went to the main register that we'd closed out earlier to combine the funds.

It was late. We closed at eleven on the weekends, but people always stayed past closing, even when we shut down the kitchen and bar at ten forty-five. And as a newish restaurant, we were not trying to make enemies. The customer was doubly right in the first couple years of business. At least, that had been our motto. Word of mouth was one of the best marketing tools for good . . . or bad (we were learning).

"Was that your boyfriend earlier, Sutton?" Presley asked.

"No, just a friend."

"That she kisses," Raya added.

Presley raised her eyebrows. "What happened to Nate?"

"Nosy," Raya said with a laugh.

"He broke up with me a couple months ago."

"Ouch," Presley said.

"I think I came out ahead."

Raya laughed.

"What about you?" I asked. "How's school?"

"Hard," she said. "And busy."

"What are you going to school for?" Lucas asked.

"Teaching," she said.

"That's cool," he said. "My major is nursing."

"My mom would love you," I said. "She wishes I would've become a nurse."

"She does not," Raya said. "You're a business owner."

"No, really. My high school best friend became a nurse, and my mom adores her." Maybe it wasn't the nurse thing she adored, maybe it was just everything about Tara. She was pretty lovable.

"Well, I adore *you*," Raya said, smacking me on the butt as she walked toward the door. "You guys ready to get out of here?"

"Yes, please," Presley said. She collected Lucas's broom and went to the back where the supply closet was to put the things away. Raya unlocked the door, and we waited outside for Presley to come back. Even Lucas waited. Then we locked up, and Lucas walked Presley to her car while Raya and I went to hers.

"Is something going on with them?" I asked quietly, nodding my head in their direction.

"I don't think so, but I guess we'll see. We haven't really talked about workplace romance. Do we forbid that?"

I laughed. "Let the children love."

"They are only like seven years younger than us," she said.

"Babies," I said.

"And really? No rules about workplace love? Not a single policy? You really are lovesick right now, aren't you?"

"No, I'm not . . . probably just love starved and being fed my first meal in a long time."

"And he's a *whole* meal."

"I've missed you," I said.

"Let's get you to your dessert."

CHAPTER 36

I knocked softly on the door because I'd given my keys to Elijah earlier. There was no answer. I texted him: *Hey, I'm at the door.* Again, no answer. I tried the handle. It was unlocked.

I let myself in and locked it behind me. "Hello!" I called out. "I'm home."

On the entryway table were my keys and, beneath it, his shoes. At the table in the breakfast nook was an open notebook with some notes about lighting and paint color next to an empty water glass. I wondered if he was writing down ideas for the restaurant or something else completely. The curtains over the windows had been pulled closed, but my eyes immediately caught on the plant sitting on the table between them.

It was very much alive. Green and healthy and the exact plant I'd had there before.

A warmth spread through my chest. He'd replaced my dead plant. And his things were around my apartment and I loved it. I'd never lived with a man, not once. Had never wanted to. Nate stayed over a few times, but not very often because I got home so late most nights that it seemed pointless. So most of the time I'd go to his place after work, which was the reason he wanted me to move in. I was glad I hadn't now. Glad I hadn't given up my apartment.

I retrieved a cup from the cupboard and filled it with water. That's when I noticed another one of my plants on the counter that used to be dead, now alive.

I made my way down the hall, same thing for the plant in the hall. The light was on in my room, and I started to say, "You are the sweet—" when I walked inside and saw him asleep on the bed. On my side of the bed—well, his side too. I smiled. Habits die hard.

He'd changed his jeans for a pair of green athletic shorts, and he wore a black T-shirt. His phone rested on his chest, face down. I wanted to climb on top of him and kiss him awake, but a shower was calling to me. I was sure I smelled of food and sweat. I turned on the light in the bathroom and off the light in the bedroom so he could sleep better.

A damp bath towel hung on a hook, he'd obviously showered as well. I quietly closed the door behind me and turned on the shower. That's when I saw the last plant, my shower fern, alive and well. Green and beautiful. Its leaves were still beaded with water from the shower Elijah had taken earlier. That made me happy.

I stripped myself of my clothes, depositing them into the empty hamper. I may not have cleaned out the fridge before I left, but I had done all my laundry. The thought of laundry reminded me of the used cloth napkin in my purse I needed to wash, filling my mind with thoughts of the office and Elijah. His body against mine, his groans of pleasure.

I stepped into the already-steaming shower. The heat felt

good against my tense muscles. I wondered if there would ever be a time when my muscles weren't tense. I reached for my shampoo from the corner shelf when I realized it wasn't there. Only a single bar of soap.

"I knew seeing you naked would revive that plant," the deep voice of Elijah said from the doorway.

I hadn't heard the door open, but I startled a little at his voice. "You scared me," I said.

"Sorry."

"I was just thinking about you and our office activities," I said.

"Those are very good thoughts."

"Sorry I got home so late. Thanks for the plants."

"It's fine. I entertained myself by digging through your couch cushions."

"I knew it." I stepped to the sliding glass door of the shower and slid it open, poking my head out for a moment. "Can you hand me my shampoo and conditioner from my toiletries bag? I forgot to grab them."

His eyes went to my boob that was now pressed against the glass. He reached out and ran his hand along the glass on his way to the counter where I'd moved my bag earlier.

I laughed. "I think you missed."

He freed my hair products and walked them back over to me. I took them and stood for a moment in the open doorway, wanting him to not miss this time.

His eyes went to mine and he took a step closer. His fingers lightly brushed over my damp skin, starting at my stomach and ending on my breasts, cupping them in his hands and rubbing his thumbs over my nipples. Then, slowly, lowering his head to draw one into his mouth. I'd made the mistake of not putting the shampoo and conditioner down right away, and now they were like cuffs, keeping me from grabbing hold of his hair.

A shiver went through me and he pulled back. "Get back under the warm water. I'll let the fern enjoy you for now, but you're mine when you get out."

The shiver hadn't been from the cold. "You don't want to come in?"

He smiled and looked at the shower. "I've only had you in small places. I'm ready for more room to work."

I swallowed and nodded.

"Can I stay, though? Watch? Is that creepy? That's creepy, isn't it? I'll . . ." He backed toward the door.

"No! You can stay. It's not like I don't know you're here. *That* would be creepy."

He stopped right as he hit the threshold of the door and leaned against the frame with a nod.

I poured some shampoo into my palm, rubbed my hands together, then began massaging it into my scalp. After rinsing, I repeated the process. This time, I let the shampoo sit for a while and took the bar of soap to my skin, rubbing it all over. Was I doing it differently because Elijah was watching? Absolutely. I was lingering, touching myself in different ways than I normally did. My skin tingled under his gaze, under my touch.

I rinsed out my hair like I was some sort of swimsuit model, looking up at the ceiling, flaring my elbows, and pushing out my chest. I couldn't even decide if I was being sexy. I probably looked ridiculous. But when I reached for my conditioner and poured it into my hand, Elijah ran a hand through his hair. "How many steps are there?"

"This is the last one," I said with a smirk. "I'm almost done." I let my conditioner sit as I turned to face the showerhead, rinsing off the front of my body. Then I turned again and repeated the hair rinsing I'd done earlier. I knew I was taking longer than I needed to with my thorough rinse, teasing him. I wasn't a teaser, but he brought out a different side of me. A side I liked.

"Get your ass out here, Sutton," Elijah growled after another full minute of me rinsing my hair.

I chuckled and turned off the water. "Where is your patience?" I brought my hair around to the side and twisted it, wringing out the water. Maybe I was taking too long to complete that task as well because Elijah slid open the shower door, stepped inside, and picked me up into his arms. He carried me out of the shower, depositing me onto the bath mat. I laughed while he took a dry towel and placed it around my shoulders. He used the ends to run along my face and neck, drying me.

I wasn't sure why the act of being dried off by someone made me feel so cared for, but a warmth spread through my body, and I wrapped my arms around him. I was still dripping, which soaked the front of him even more. He continued drying me, taking the towel to my hair, where he ran it up and down a few times and then to my back. After that, he was squatting down and drying my legs. Then the towel was back around my shoulders.

"Do you want to blow-dry your hair or anything before I . . . what was that word you used in the parking lot of therapy that first day? Pound?"

I laughed. "Yes."

"Would you like to dry more before I pound you?"

I probably should've at least run a brush through my hair,

but his thumbs were digging into my hips and his erection was pressed against my stomach and my nipples were hard and I didn't want to wait. "No, I think you did good."

He threw the towel to the floor and lifted me back into his arms, not needing to be told twice. Then we were in my room, and he was lowering me to the bed and pulling the covers up to my chin. Then he tore off his shirt.

"Have I told you how sexy you are yet?" he asked.

I nodded, watching him undress. Maybe I was biased, but he seemed to do it better than most people. Undressing, that was. I lifted the blanket when he was done, and he crawled under it with me. My hands immediately went to his smooth skin, and I turned on my side to press my body against his. He met me halfway, turning to face me as well. Then he was brushing my wet hair back from my face and kissing my forehead.

"God, Sutton . . ." he said on an exhale. "You make me feel things."

I pressed my hips against his. "I can tell."

"No, not that," he said, softly kissing my temple.

"I know," I responded, feeling things way beyond physical as well. I hadn't felt this way in a long time. Maybe ever. And that scared me. It was too soon. Too much. Too complicated. Our hands explored each other as our lips softly met again and again. It was so tender that I felt tears stinging behind my eyes.

I cleared my throat. "I was promised a pounding, not a sweet session with feelings involved," I teased.

He laughed, then moved to his knees, grabbed hold of my thighs, and twisted me onto my back. Then he yanked me toward him, my ass sliding along his thighs. His hands gathered mine and pushed them up over my head, where he directed them each onto one of the metal bars that made up the headboard. I held on. Then his hands slid down my arms, over my breasts and to my hips, where he pulled me even tighter against him. His thumb traveled to the bundle of nerves between my legs and worked me until I was gasping for breath. I planted my feet on the bed and pressed even harder against his touch.

And then, while staring intensely into my eyes, he rolled on a condom and slowly pushed himself inside me. He went still, filling me up, savoring the moment. I rocked forward, pushing myself onto him even more. He moaned and that made me tighten around him. He grabbed onto my hips and slowly pulled out, holding me in place so I couldn't resist the movement. I closed my eyes and whimpered, and then he thrust back inside me. He repeated this several times, this slow, torturous movement, and then he picked up speed, slamming into a spot inside me that sent waves of pleasure through my body.

I cried out as the waves reached a crescendo. And when I did, he doubled his speed until he reached a peak as well, moaning my name. He collapsed on top of me, his face burrowing into my neck. I released the metal bars of the headboard and wrapped my arms around him.

"Can I keep you?" he asked, his voice muffled by my skin.

I kissed the side of his head, hugging him tighter against me.

CHAPTER 37

I woke up and it seemed too bright outside. "Shit."

I was in the middle of the bed, Elijah on *my* side. That little thief. There was no frustration behind my thoughts though, only fondness. It helped that my leg was draped over his and my arm across his stomach. I grabbed my phone, which said six forty. Not too late, but I meant to wake up at six fifteen. I'd told Raya when she'd dropped me off the night before that I'd take care of the delivery this morning. My hair, which I'd put in a French braid last night after our activities, was still slightly damp. I pulled it out of the braid as I walked toward the bathroom.

"Where are you going?" Elijah mumbled from his half-asleep state. "Come back to bed."

"I'm going in to work."

"So early?"

"Delivery. I shouldn't be long, and then I'll come back home for a couple hours."

"Home?" he asked.

"I mean here. My home."

"Okay," he said, rolling over and closing his eyes.

• • •

"Well, well, well," Mac said, walking up with a box of produce. Mac was a large man—tall and wide with a friendly face. "If it isn't the prodigal daughter returned home from her life of debauchery in the real world." He shoved the box he held into my arms and walked back to the open back of his box truck.

"No debauchery," I said. "Just an ill mother." I set the box just inside the door I'd propped open.

"I should've known it was you when the door was actually open when I pulled up."

It was five to seven. I'd gotten ready in record time—no makeup, just throwing on clothes and brushing my teeth.

"What's going on with your hair?" he asked.

I'd taken it out of the braid, and it was very wavy. Probably bordering on too wavy. I normally wore my hair in a tight ponytail or bun at work. Occasionally loose beachy waves after work. But never this. "Was that meant to be a compliment?" I asked.

"It wasn't meant to be an insult," he returned.

I laughed. "What's going on with your jeans?" I asked, pointing at the several stains on his knees.

"I'm at work," he said.

"So am I," I said.

He passed me another box. "You look nice, Sutton. Happy."

"Thanks, I am." I placed the box on top of the last one. "Thanks for keeping an eye on things here."

"You back then?"

"No. Hopefully soon." It all depended on how well my mom did this weekend. If she thrived on her scooter and if her dizziness subsided, maybe I could be home in a couple of weeks. That thought twisted my insides, and I tried to ignore it. I *wanted* to be home in a couple of weeks. I wanted to get back to my life.

"I didn't realize you were taking care of your mom. You didn't say."

"That's because I'm a super private shit," I said.

"Your words, not mine," he returned.

I helped Mac with the rest of the boxes, and as he was about to leave, I said, "Oh, I have our contract for you. Let me get it."

I retrieved it from the office and handed it over.

"I was wondering if I was ever going to get this back."

"Our year mark was only last week," I said.

"But I gave that to Raya three weeks ago."

"Oh, sorry."

"No problem."

He left and I pulled out my phone. At first, I was going to call Raya, ask her if there were other things that she'd forgotten about but realized my whole point in taking over delivery this morning was so she could sleep in. Plus, she'd had a lot on her plate. I was sure she'd remembered the most important things. Instead of calling her, I spent some time unloading boxes and cleaning areas we never got to, like the supply closet. Things that might help her after I left.

When I was done, I realized a couple of hours had passed. Chef would be in soon, and I needed to get home to change. I headed for my car and dialed my mom while I did.

"I'm fine," was how she answered. "Lucy said she doesn't even need to be here."

"I didn't say that," I heard Lucy call out.

"How did yesterday go?"

"Tara took me on a walk. How come you haven't taken me on a walk in seven weeks?"

"I have asked you a dozen times to go on a walk. You always say no."

"I don't remember that."

Did she think I was lying? "But I take you to doctors' appointments where we walk."

"I don't like doctors' appointments," she said.

That makes two of us, I thought, but kept to myself. "Did you like those cupcakes I sent you last Christmas? I could pick you up some more to bring home tomorrow."

"No thanks," she said. "I'm supposed to watch what I eat. Tara made me healthy granola bites."

"Sounds delicious," I said. "I'll see you tomorrow."

• • •

I turned the handle and shoved open the door with my shoulder, my hands full of bags from the grocery store. If Elijah was stuck at my house today and tomorrow, I figured I'd better feed him.

"I'm sorry," I said, seeing Elijah sitting on the couch, his notebook on his knees.

"Your hair."

I pushed the door shut with my butt. "I know, it's insane."

"No, it's big, but not insane. I dig it."

I shook my head, causing it to dance around me. Then I sighed. "I trapped you here without a car."

"It's okay."

"I shouldn't have brought you," I said, swinging the bags onto the counter.

"Well, I missed you too."

"No, I just mean I wasn't thinking. I was being selfish. I wanted you to come, and in my brain, it was going to be like a vacation, but once I got here I realized I needed to work. I still need to work."

"I'm a grown man, Sutton. I don't need to be entertained or babysat. And I was pretty sure you were happy I was here last night."

I joined him on the couch, first next to him and then working my way onto his lap around the notebook he held. He laughed and tossed the notebook onto the coffee table, followed by the pen. Then he wrapped me up in his arms, and I decided this was my new favorite place. The warm skin of his neck against my nose, his strong grip holding me, his heart beating against mine.

"I was very happy you were here last night," I said into his skin. "I'm happy you're here now."

"But?"

"But I need to go back in an hour. Do you want to drop me off so you can have the car? You could go to . . . I don't know, the observatory? The Hollywood sign? The Walk of Fame?"

"Can I not go to work with you?"

"You *want* to go to work with me?"

"I want to be where you are."

The words seemed to inflate my heart, but I had to remind myself that he wasn't making a declaration. He just meant today. He didn't mean forever. "You can come to work with me."

"Good, because I hear they give out hand jobs in the back room."

"Only to our favorite customers."

He laughed and flipped me onto my back on the couch,

lowering himself on top of me. My hand immediately went down the back of his shorts, and I grabbed a handful of his ass, pushing him against me.

"You feel good," I said.

"Do we have time for a quickie?" he asked.

"We have time for more than that."

"Thank god." He practically ripped the jeans off my body, followed by my underwear. "I want to taste you."

I swallowed, then nodded, dropping my knees open. He placed a hand flat on my stomach and let it drift down until his palm rested against me, his eyes following the movement. I was on my back, watching him, aching with desire. He traced a path between my legs, both his hands wedging themselves beneath me, cupping my ass and lifting me slightly. And then his mouth was on me, his tongue moving in just the right way, slow and sensual. I gripped the edge of the couch with one hand and the back of the couch with the other, squeezing the material in my fists. An embarrassingly loud moan escaped my mouth as he explored me.

I grabbed onto his shirt at his shoulders and tugged. He got the hint, his mouth trailing hot kisses up my body to my breasts. Then to my neck.

I moved up to my elbows, then my palms, and he followed suit. I peeled off his shirt, then pushed him onto his back, lying on top of him, letting my body move along his erection. He undid the latch on my bra, and I wiggled out of it and my shirt at the same time. Then I laid my bare chest against his, and we explored one another for the next hour.

CHAPTER 38

I was behind the bar, helping Angel restock drinks after our lunch rush, and in anticipation of the dinner one to follow, when I looked up as someone walked in the front door. It took me a moment to register who it was: Nate.

My eyes immediately shot around the restaurant in search of Elijah. The last time I'd seen him, he was on the patio, talking to guests and helping the busser clean off tables. But he wasn't out there. Maybe he was in the kitchen.

I quickly walked around the bar and met Nate in the middle of the dining area. But I kept walking, out the front door, hoping he'd follow. He did.

"You're back?" he asked, when I stopped halfway down the sidewalk, hopefully out of view of the windows.

"No," I said. "Just for the weekend. How did you know I was here?"

"Mac told me. He didn't know we'd . . ."

Mac, a food delivery guy and a tattletale, apparently. "You corrected him, hopefully."

"You're wearing your hair down," he said, instead of responding to my statement. The waves had settled a little from that morning, but they still flowed over my shoulders free, unlike normal.

"Yes." I patted my hair. "What do you need, Nate? Why are you here?"

"I miss you, Sutton. I made a mistake. I was being selfish and needy."

I shook my head. "No, you weren't. You're allowed to want someone who's invested in the relationship."

His expression softened, and I realized he probably thought I had done some reflecting as well. That I was telling him I would be different or something. "Not me," I blurted, then tried to smooth it over by adding, "I mean, I wasn't invested and there was obviously a reason and you need someone better than me."

"The reason was that you had just had the busiest year of your life opening this place and I wasn't very understanding. And then your mom had her accident."

"I think that's only part of it," I said. Because now I had experienced what it was like to be truly invested in someone and have someone be truly invested in me. It was an all-consuming feeling. And maybe time would take away the all-consuming nature of it, but I'd never felt this at any stage with anyone else. That had to mean something. It was new, but it was something. I could feel it.

As if I conjured him with my thoughts, the deep voice of Elijah, from behind me, said, "Are you okay out here?"

I turned to see him as he stepped outside, lingering by the door but ready to jump into action if I asked it of him.

"Who the hell is that?" Nate asked.

"Who the hell are you?" Elijah returned, walking several menacing steps forward. I was beginning to see why he might've been intimidating in a boxing ring.

I put one hand on Elijah's chest as he approached, keeping him back. "I'm fine. Will you just go inside?" I asked. "Please." I gave him my best pleading eyes, and he nodded and only hesitated a few beats before he left.

"Seriously, Sutton?" Nate said. "It's been two months."

"It's been longer than that and you know it."

"Maybe for you," he muttered.

"I'm sorry," I said, because I really was. I didn't want him to feel however he was feeling. But I also knew how I felt.

"This guy is from your childhood farm town? He's moving here for you?"

"No. Don't. Just let it go."

"I thought you said you'd never do long distance."

I rubbed my arms, goose bumps suddenly forming along the length of them.

"Wait, were you cheating on me with him?"

"What? No!" A wave of anger rushed through me, and I took a deep breath. It didn't matter what he thought, I knew the truth. "Bye, Nate."

"Whatever," he said. "I don't know why I came." He stormed off, practically stomping his way to his car in the parking lot.

I watched him leave, hoping he got whatever closure he needed. I was surprised to realize that I hadn't needed closure. I'd felt nothing but worry when I saw his face. Worry that he'd make Elijah feel insecure or unsure of us. I hoped it hadn't.

I walked inside and straight to the back. It was like I instinctually knew that Elijah would be in the office, waiting for me.

He was pacing when I walked in. I paused by the door.

He stopped moving and asked, "You okay?"

"I'm okay."

"Was that Nate?"

I nodded.

"He came to see what he was missing?"

"Something like that."

"And did it make you see what you'd been missing?"

I shook my head. He took one step forward and I rushed toward him, folding myself into his open arms. "No. Not at all. It made me see that he and I may have had a long relationship, but it wasn't very rooted. You know?"

"I'm sorry."

I looked up at him. "Why are you sorry?"

"I don't know why I said that."

I laughed and wrapped my arms around him again. "Because you care about everyone and don't want to hurt anyone's feelings."

"You make it sound noble. Really, it's about me. How I want to be regarded by everyone."

"That sounds like something to bring up in therapy."

He laughed. "I guess I should've. Should we go back? Have a couple more sessions?"

"You know that therapy exists without me, right?"

"Things exist without you? This is new information to me."

I shoved him, but he just pulled me closer with a low laugh. I took a deep breath and smiled. I was happy. Like completely, to my bones, happy. It had been a while since I could say that.

"Is it going to be hard for you to go back to Clovis tomorrow after spending time here? Do you wish you could just stay? Are you sad?"

His words, after my thoughts had been the exact opposite, sent a jolt of awareness through me. I was going back with him, but our days together were numbered. Then we'd be separated. His ability to move here hadn't magically changed, and my ability to stay there hadn't either. *Could* I do long distance?

I straightened up and scratched at an itch that tickled the back of my neck. "I'm . . ." I looked up into his gorgeous eyes. "I'm not sad. I'm trying not to think about everything too much or analyze things."

He raised one eyebrow because, even though we hadn't known each other very long, he obviously understood some core things about me. "Really? And here I assumed you'd looked at everything from a million angles."

"Nope," I said. "Living in the moment."

"I mean, a little thinking about the future wouldn't be the end of the world," he said, giving me some hope that he'd been thinking. That he had figured something out for us.

• • •

The city lights twinkled in the distance and a breeze picked up, making the flames in the firepit dance. Elijah carried a glass of wine across the rooftop to me. Selma, Raya's fiancée, had put together an impromptu get-together since I was back in town, and even though it was after midnight, a handful of our friends showed up. We were eating finger foods and drinking wine and enjoying the view.

"Thanks," I said, taking the glass as he sat down in the chair next to me.

"Tell us how you two met," Selma asked, also sitting near the fire.

Elijah smiled. "We met because my brother was trying to

get out of going to therapy and made a ridiculous bet in order to do so."

"He bet that a therapist wouldn't be able to tell if two strangers were sitting in front of her for couples therapy," I clarified.

"Seriously?" Raya asked. "A therapist would be able to tell if two people claiming to be together were actually strangers."

"Right?" I said. "That's what I thought too."

"You're telling me she couldn't?" Selma asked.

"Apparently our chemistry is so strong it can fool even a professional."

Elijah chuckled beside me.

I raised my eyebrows at him. "Do you disagree?"

"Not at all." He had that teasing glint in his eye. He was probably thinking about our chemistry.

"Wait, wait, wait, *you* actually went to this therapist as one of the strangers?" Raya asked.

I gestured between Elijah and me with my wineglass. "We were the strangers."

"Oh my god," she said. "That doesn't seem like something you would do."

"Wait, start over," our friend Russel said, joining us at the firepit. "I only caught the end."

I told the story again and he laughed. "Surprising."

Raya was studying Elijah as she sipped her wine, like she was trying to figure him out, then her gaze shifted to me. "I don't want you to leave tomorrow."

I scrunched my nose. "I know. I don't want to either. But I don't think I'll be there much longer. My mom is finally more mobile. She'll probably kick me out soon. She's barely tolerating me as it is."

"How soon?" Elijah asked softly from next to me.

"I don't know," I said just as quietly back. But in that moment, staring at his vulnerable expression, I knew no matter how far away from him I was, I wanted to make it work. We could figure something out. A visiting schedule, a way for him to pay his dad back and stop working at the boxing gym sooner, a way for him to monetize what he really loved. We could do that. I knew we could.

Maybe he felt the same, because he reached out for my hand and pulled me over onto his lap. I willingly went.

CHAPTER 39

It wasn't a delivery morning, so I didn't have to wake up early, but my eyes popped open anyway at six thirty. Elijah's arm rested heavily across my stomach. I smiled at the weight of it, and then the smile slipped off my face. We were leaving today. I didn't want to. He looked peaceful next to me. I wanted him to be a regular in my bed.

"Are you watching me sleep?" he asked, his voice scratchy.

"Maybe," I said, tracing his jaw with my finger. His scruff had grown longer than he normally let it, and it scratched me.

We could do long distance for a little while. He could come on the weekends. I could go to him sometimes, maybe on the slow days during the week.

"Do you always wake up this early?" he asked. "You never sleep in?"

"My body hates me."

"Your body is perfect," he said.

"You're right, it's my brain that actually hates me."

He placed a kiss on my forehead. His lips were sleep-warm

and soft. His arm moved from my waist to my head, where he cocooned me against his chest. I nuzzled into him.

"You can just stay in my bed forever," I said. "Be here when I need you."

He chuckled. "You want me to live in your bed?"

"I'll feed you," I said. "And I'll allow you to get up and use the bathroom when you need to and bathe."

"How gracious of you," he said, a smile in his voice.

"It really is."

He squeezed my side. I grabbed his ass.

He ran a hand down my face in a joking manner. "Shhh. Go back to sleep. It's too early to be awake."

I laughed but closed my eyes and pressed my body as close to his as I possibly could. Between us, there was some very hard evidence that he didn't actually want me to go back to sleep. Now his hand was on my ass, and he was pulling me tightly against him.

I hummed out a happy noise. I loved this. I loved being held and waking up to someone. I loved his warm body against mine and the way it relaxed me. I loved that I could feel his smile against my cheek.

I was almost certain that I loved all this because I loved him.

• • •

We sat in my car in front of my mom's house, both unwilling to admit that the weekend was over and we had to get back to our separate lives. At least I was unwilling to admit that. I wasn't sure why he wasn't getting out of my car. His car sat on the curb, ready to take him away. One of the plants from my apartment sat in my cupholder, the others in the back seat. I wasn't going to let them wither away this time.

"I've never been to your place," I said after a few minutes of silence.

"No, you haven't," he responded quickly. "You should come over. Tonight?"

I reached over and squeezed his hand. "How about tomorrow night? I don't want my mom to think I'm ditching her again so soon."

He nodded. "Tomorrow night." He brought my hand to his lips and kissed my knuckles. "I had a good time this weekend."

"Which part did you like better? The working in my restaurant or the sex? Be honest." I smiled at him.

He pretended to think. "So hard to choose." He turned in his seat to face me more fully. "No, but really, I enjoyed working with you at the restaurant. You probably think it was a chore for me, but it wasn't. It reminded me of college."

"Did you wait tables in college?"

"I did."

"I bet you got so many tips."

"Is this a commentary on my prettiness again?"

"It is."

"Did you work in college?"

"I did. At a photo-processing place."

"Really?"

"No, I just thought it would be funny if you were a server and I did something related to photography. But I really didn't."

"Smartass."

"Are you stealing my insults?"

"I am." He still held my hand in his and was running his thumb over my knuckles. "Where did you really work?"

"I worked at this juice place, selling super-expensive juice to people who ate very little else," I said.

"How very Los Angeles of you."

"Are we stalling?" I asked.

"I don't know what you're talking about," he said with a smirk.

I sighed and looked at the house. I really needed to get in there. It was already four in the afternoon. Tara had checked on my mom this morning, but she hadn't had anyone with her for any amount of consecutive hours since the day before with Lucy.

I must've stared at the house too long because Elijah said, "My house is still on the table for tonight."

I scrunched my nose and then grabbed the plant from the cupholder and pulled on the door handle. Elijah followed me to the trunk, where he lifted out his suitcase. I took my toiletries bag, then collected the box of plants from the back seat, wedging the cupholder one in between the others.

"Let me carry that for you," he said as I shut the trunk.

"I think I've got it," I said.

"Will you give me an excuse to walk you to the door, please?" he said.

"You need an excuse?"

He left his suitcase by the back wheel of my car and took the box from me. I tucked my hand into the crook of his elbow.

"My hero."

We walked to the porch and then faced each other. I reclaimed the box with a smile, moving it to my hip. I pushed onto my toes to touch my lips to his.

"See you tomorrow," he said.

"Thanks for coming with me this weekend."

"I'll put together some design ideas for the restaurant tonight. I don't know if they'll be any good. I'm pretty rusty."

"I'm sure they'll be great. Thank you."

"Of course."

I kissed him again, and as I did, the front door swung open. It surprised me so much that I gasped. I wasn't used to my mom being mobile enough to open the door on her own. But she stood there, scooter under her knee, hand on the knob.

"You're home," she said.

"I am."

"And with your boy toy."

"Mom," I chastised. "You know Elijah's name."

"I got the check from the insurance company for my new car."

"That's great," I said. "We'll have to start looking."

"Also, I don't feel good." She did look a little pale.

"Okay, I'll be right in."

She shut the door without another word.

"Sorry," I said. "She heard it once and now won't forget it." Why had Tara called him *boy toy*, and in front of my mother, of all people?

"It's fine," he said, his tone different, but not one I could read. It was probably the *I don't like this woman's mother and I'm not sure what to do about that* tone. "I'll see you tomorrow?"

"Okay."

I watched him retrieve his suitcase, put it into the trunk, and get in his car. Then he drove away without another acknowledgment.

"What did you want, Sutton? A fireworks show?" I muttered. The man had sat in my parked car with me for close to thirty minutes. We didn't need to also have a thirty-minute porch goodbye. Especially not after my mother's appearance.

My phone buzzed in my purse, and I dug it out, for a split second thinking it was going to be Elijah saying goodbye again, in a normal tone. One that didn't make me analyze things. It wasn't. It was Raya.

I swiped to answer. "Hi."

"Hey," she said. "Did you take some mail that was on the desk?"

"Oh, shit. I did. I wanted to take some things off your plate." But I had forgotten to look at them again.

"Things you had absolutely no idea what they were?"

"They seemed more important than junk mail but less important than bills."

"Well, one of those things was tickets to an invite-only vendors' market I was going to tomorrow."

"I'm so sorry," I said. "I'll overnight them."

"You thought I was neglecting the tasks on the desk, didn't you?"

"I mean . . ." That was what I'd thought, wasn't it? Why else would I take the mail without properly looking at it? The mail had been my chore in the past, and I obviously thought she wasn't handling it right. "I just thought maybe you were overwhelmed."

"I *am* overwhelmed, Sutton, but I'm doing a damn good job."

"I agree."

"But you think *you'd* be doing it better."

"Where is this coming from?"

"From you. I spent two hours reorganizing the desk. I had a system, and you just sweep in here and don't even bother to ask me what it is? Just assumed nothing in the office had been touched since you left? Way to trust me."

"I'm sorry, Raya. You're right, I'm a shit business partner and I've been a shit friend."

"Ugh," she said. "Don't. Just, just send the tickets. I'll talk to you later." With those words, she disconnected the call.

I stood there for several minutes, composing myself, then opened the door and walked inside. My mom had wheeled herself back to the couch.

"Hey, Mom, I have to run to the shipping store real fast."

"Seriously?" she said. "I just told you I'm not feeling well."

"I know. What can I do for you? And can I do it when I get back?"

"I need a refill on a medication and some good food in this house."

"Great, I can do both of those things while I'm out." I tossed my toiletries bag onto the bed in my room, put the box of plants on the chair, and went to the kitchen. "Which med, Mom?"

"The empty one, obviously."

I picked up each bottle and shook. "They all have pills in them."

"By the toaster," she called.

I raised the empty bottle in the air to show her I had found it, shoved it in my purse, and left.

• • •

Only two people stood in line at the shipping place in front of me. I studied the wall organizer of envelope options to my right until I found the flat-rate express one. I dug a pen out of my purse and filled out the front of the envelope with the shipping and return addresses.

"You ready?" I heard and looked up. I had been so focused on my task that I hadn't realized it was my turn.

"That was fast," I said, stepping up to the counter.

"She was a drop-off only." The woman nodded toward the lady leaving the shop.

"Right. I need to send this." I placed the envelope in front of her.

She picked it up and turned it over, noting that it wasn't sealed.

"Oh! With something in it, of course." I opened my purse, which suddenly felt too big. And too full of stuff. I knew I had shoved those envelopes in here from the office. My purse was normally very clean and organized. But after the weekend away and . . . I stopped. The cloth napkin from the back office, the one Elijah had used to clean himself up with after we'd fooled around, was still in there. And just past that, the envelope from the vendor's market. I pulled it out, and smeared across the side was . . .

My cheeks went hot.

"What is that?" the lady asked.

"Um . . . just some primer. Makeup primer. For my face," I clarified unnecessarily. "It must've spilled."

"Must've," she replied.

I opened the envelope, dug out the tickets, which thankfully seemed unscathed, and tucked them into their new home.

"Do you have a trash?" I asked, holding up the cum-smeared envelope.

The lady reached for it.

"No," I said, yanking it back. "I'll just take care of it when I get home." I shoved it back into my purse. This was why organization was good for everyone.

"O-kay," the lady said. "Just this then? Anything else for the envelope?"

"Nope, just that. Can you guarantee delivery tomorrow?"

"Yes." She entered some things into her computer while I got out my credit card and tried to get my face back to its normal temperature.

After that humiliating experience, I sat in my car and sent a text: You must dispose of your own cum in the future.

My phone buzzed in my hands with an incoming call, and I laughed and answered, "You don't want to know about the most embarrassing experience I just had with the evidence of our office hookup."

"Honey bunny," the voice on the other end said, and my chest went cold.

"Dad."

CHAPTER 40

My fingers felt numb as I held the phone to my ear.

"How are you, love?" my dad sang in his charming British accent. "You sound happy, which makes me happy." Words. Empty words. He was good at them. Good at saying things and making it sound like he meant them. But I knew better.

I swallowed, my eyes darting to the clock in the car. Five. I did some quick mental math. One o'clock in the morning London time. "It's late. How are you calling so late?"

"It's seven PM. I'm not that much of an old man yet."

"Seven PM?" I didn't understand. My brain and all the thoughts in it seemed to freeze. "Seven PM?" I repeated.

"How is your mother?" he asked.

"Not well," I said.

"Recovery from an accident takes time. She's a fighter though. She'll be back at it again in no time."

"No, I'm not sure that she . . . Dad, how is it seven PM? Are you not in London?"

He laughed. "Of course not. I'm at home. In New Orleans."

"Home?"

"I play the fiddle in a band here. You know this."

I did not, in fact, know this. "No . . . I . . . for how long? Does Mom know?"

"Yes, dear, she knows." He didn't answer my "how long" question, but I wasn't sure I wanted to know. I wasn't even sure if the answer he'd provided about my mom knowing his location was an honest one. How could my mom know that? And if she did, I could see why she'd be more hurt that he hadn't come after her accident.

"Then why aren't you here?" I asked. "Helping?"

"I have commitments, love."

"Stop," I snapped. "Stop with the endearments, please. We're not . . . you're not . . . you should be here."

"You need to have more faith in her. Your mother is a strong woman, she'll pull through."

"She's really not. You don't know her at all. She still wants you here, needs you here." I wasn't sure why I was even asking him to come. He hadn't come in years and years. Why would any of that change now?

"Oh, I don't know about all that, but I do know she has you and that's the greatest thing for her right now. I'm so happy you're with her. I'm sure it's aiding in her recovery more than you know."

"Dad, I've never asked you for anything. Anything at all." I hadn't asked him to come to my high school or college graduation (my mom had), I hadn't asked him for help opening the restaurant, I hadn't even asked him to call me on my birthdays. "But I'm asking you now, please, can you come home and give Mom some closure at the very least? Please. I'm begging you."

"Well . . ." He paused for a moment, probably trying to

put together whatever sweet-talking excuse he could come up with. "I'll see. I'll look at my schedule and maybe . . ." As he was saying it, I realized he was only saying what I wanted to hear. He had never come before. He was not coming now. He would *never* come in the future.

"Okay, you do that. And while you're at it, don't ever call me again." With those words, I disconnected the call and threw the phone onto the passenger seat next to me. I immediately pushed my forehead to the steering wheel, tears burning behind my eyes. I took a deep breath in through my nose.

No. He did not get to have this kind of emotional power over me. I knew who he was. I always had. He meant nothing to me.

I pushed myself away from the steering wheel and started the car, driving to fulfill my next task, shutting off all emotions.

• • •

"That will be about fifteen minutes," the pharmacy tech said.

"Okay, sounds good. I'm just going to do some shopping."

"Yes, of course. We'll call your name when it's ready."

I nodded and went to the front of the store to collect a shopping cart. I still felt numb from the phone call with my dad. I had always thought that if I just asked him, really asked him, to come visit or come home, he would. Maybe that's why I never had, because I wanted to keep that little speck of hope alive that he cared at all. If I never gave him the opportunity to say no, he would never actually say no.

I guess technically he still hadn't said no, but my heart knew a no when I heard it.

I picked up a box of spaghetti noodles and placed it in my

cart along with a jar of sauce. That's when I heard voices, floating over the shelves from the next aisle. They were loud, and the man's I recognized right away as Michael. He was laughing and saying, "So many issues."

"Daddy issues," the other voice said. At first, I figured it was Tara, but it didn't sound like Tara. The voice did sound familiar though. "The worst kind."

Michael laughed again. "It doesn't matter. Eli said it's temporary. He's just having fun, so stop analyzing."

Temporary. The word seemed to hit me between the eyes but also right in the gut. I braced myself on the cart.

"Oh, excuse me, I wouldn't want to interrupt his *fun*," the woman said. "Or yours."

Who was that? I recognized her voice but couldn't place it. I finally got my legs to work and pushed the cart down the aisle and rounded the corner. I stopped just before clearing the shelves. Did I want to know? Of course I did. I quietly pushed the cart forward and saw someone worse than I was imagining.

The couples therapist. *Our* couples therapist. Dr. Sara Franklin. Michael was with Dr. Franklin. Was something going on between them? At the very least they were friends, and that meant Michael picked his friend to be our therapist so he could win a bet.

That little shithead! *Big* shithead.

Then something else hit me. Did *Elijah* know? This whole time?

He had to know, right? If this woman was Michael's friend, Elijah probably knew her too. I thought back to our sessions. Had they acted familiar? I remembered a pointed look or two. And there was that time I'd come after Elijah and found them chatting it up in her office.

Shit. Elijah knew too. *I* was the one who got played. Me and Tara.

I backed up quickly but obviously wasn't looking because I ran into a display of Sponge Daddys. The cardboard stand fell, and packages of sponges, with their little smiling faces, scattered across the floor. Dr. Franklin and I locked eyes.

I saw her mouth the word "Fuck."

Michael looked at her in confusion, and then he was also mouthing an expletive as his gaze landed on me. Then they were both rushing toward me, and I was trapped by a floor full of sponges. I dropped down, gathering them up.

The loudspeaker above us crackled to life: "Sutton, your pharmacy pickup is ready."

"Sutton," Michael said, "this isn't what it looks like."

"I don't want to hear your terrible excuses," I said. Then I looked at Dr. Franklin, remembering what she'd said about my daddy issues minutes ago. She was *telling* people that? What else had she told everyone? "You don't practice patient-therapist confidentiality?"

"No . . . I mean, yes. I mean, this isn't what it looks like."

"You can lose your license over something like this." I deposited my armful of sponges onto the nearest shelf and righted the cardboard display.

"Please don't turn her in," she said.

"*Her*? What does that mean?"

"Sara . . . Dr. Franklin. That's my sister."

"What?"

"I was just borrowing her office after hours. She didn't know. It was supposed to be funny."

"Funny?" I asked in disgust. "You're not even a therapist?"

"I will be, I mean, I'm studying to be. I'm sorry."

My face must've displayed how I felt about those statements because she shook her head and added, "I screwed up."

"You knew? The whole time you knew we weren't a couple?" I asked. Here I'd been spouting off about how mine and Elijah's *chemistry* was so strong that she couldn't guess we were strangers. Really, it was because she knew all along. "This was some sick prank?"

Her mouth opened, then closed.

"Don't tell Tara," Michael said. "Please. I will. I'll tell her."

"You have twenty-four hours," I said, and now that my path was clear of sponges, I wheeled away.

"I'm so sorry!" Fake Dr. Franklin called after me.

I held up my hand. "Save it." Because I didn't want to hear anything else she had to say. I couldn't, not right now. Not with anger bubbling in my chest and tears pooling behind my eyes. They didn't get to see me like this.

CHAPTER 41

Even though I'd overheard Michael say that me and my daddy issues were temporary in Elijah's life, I still found myself at his door an hour after dropping off the meds and groceries back at home. I still wasn't sure if he knew that Dr. Franklin was a fake, but the longer he had to prepare a lie, the better that lie would be. Maybe my mom had always been right, Elijah and Michael were just like my father.

Michael had probably immediately warned Elijah. I should've instantly told Tara too. Giving Michael twenty-four hours to perfect his story wasn't a good idea. But I was still reeling.

I took a deep breath and knocked on his door.

Elijah opened the door with a smile, shirtless and wearing a pair of athletic shorts. "You changed your mind." I could feel every emotion—anger, shock, sadness, fury—written on my face and his smile disappeared. "What's wrong? Is your mom okay?"

"She's fine. Can I come in?"

He held open the door. "Of course, come in. I wasn't expecting you, so don't judge me." He picked up a few cups from the coffee table and a shirt from the back of the couch and walked to the connecting kitchen. The room was dim, the paused television providing a hazy glow. He flipped on a few lights as he walked back toward me, pulling on his shirt. "Do you want to sit?"

The room was nice, cozy—a large couch and an oversized chair in warm colors. Big, beautiful nature photographs hung on the walls. Unlike the black-and-white at his parents' house, these were in vibrant color.

"Yes," I said, sinking into the couch. He sat next to me, but then I popped right back up, unable to sit. My chest hurt, and it felt like I needed to keep moving or I would implode.

"Talk to me," he said. "Does this have to do with your text? I responded. You never wrote back."

He'd responded? I hadn't even looked at my phone since hanging up with my dad. Where was my phone? Still in the car?

I shook my head. "I saw Michael at the store. Did he tell you?"

"No," Elijah said, a wariness in his voice. "Was he being stupid?"

I thought about the things he and Fake Dr. Franklin were talking about. How I was temporary. That's what Elijah had told him, obviously, if Michael was repeating it. I was temporary. He didn't want a long-distance, scheduled relationship with me. What was I even doing here? "He was with Dr. Franklin."

Elijah's brows went down, his eyes squinting in thought. "What do you mean? He decided to do therapy?"

Was he trying to come up with an excuse? I wouldn't let him think about it any longer. "No, he didn't. She wasn't actually Dr. Franklin."

"What?" He was confused.

"Dr. Franklin, the person we know as Dr. Franklin, isn't actually a doctor. She was posing as her sister and Michael was hanging out with her, talking about us."

He was silent for a moment, maybe trying to piece together what I had just said.

"Did you know all this? Did you know she wasn't a therapist?"

"What? No."

"Did you know Michael knew her?"

"Michael knew her?"

"Yes," I said. "They were hanging out like friends. Just now."

"I didn't know. I swear."

"He wanted to win the bet. He knew her sister was a therapist. He somehow convinced this woman to impersonate her own sister." At least that was my theory. It was a damn good one. Really the only possible one.

He shook his head. "That competitive asshole."

"I find it hard to believe that you two don't know the same people."

"It's probably one of his college friends. We didn't go to the same one." A smirk was coming onto his face as if he found this all funny as well.

"She lied to us," I said.

"We were lying to her too."

"I told Michael I'd give him twenty-four hours to tell Tara he lied, but I'm going to tell her now."

"Wait, what?"

"So he doesn't have time to spin this."

"Spin it?"

"Use his pretty words and his charm to make it seem less serious than it is."

Elijah stood up and walked to where I was pacing on the far side of the coffee table. He grabbed my arm as I passed him and pulled me against his chest. "I thought we were going to stay out of their relationship from now on."

I narrowed my eyes at him. "You don't want to tell Tara at all? You want to let your brother get away with this?"

"Get away with what exactly?"

"Making us go to therapy so he could get out of it. He obviously needs some serious therapy. Why aren't you mad about this?"

"His prank is what brought us together, so it's hard for me to be mad."

"I talked about some really personal things there. To someone not even qualified to hear them. And now she's telling Michael about them."

He smoothed some hair away from my face. "What makes you think she's telling other people?"

"I overheard her."

He kissed my cheek. "I'm sure she didn't mean to."

I pulled back, creating space between us. "Why would you be sure about that?"

"I guess I just like to think the best of people."

"Even when they've done something completely wrong?"

"Babe, babe, babe." He widened his stance so he could be closer to my level and looked me in the eyes. He ran his hands over my shoulders. His charming smile was on his face as though trying to appease me. "You're taking this so seriously."

God, those words felt so patronizing.

"You're right, why would I take anything about us seriously? We're just short term, right? I can't believe I let myself fall for a sweet talker." I whirled around and marched for the door. "I'm telling Tara."

"Fine, tell her," he snapped. "Because why not destroy everything in your wake on your way out of town?"

I grabbed the door handle but didn't open the door. "It's important to go into a relationship with your eyes wide open. She deserves that."

"Maybe she's not constantly looking for reasons not to trust people, like you are. She probably won't even care about this as much as you do."

"If she doesn't, it's only because she didn't just waste a month of her life!" Something feral came over me, and I reached into my purse, fished out the dirty napkin, and flung it at him. Then I threw open the door and left.

• • •

I felt crazy, mad with rage or grief or something, as I pulled back into the driveway at home. When I walked in the front door, the first thing I saw was my mom slumped over on the couch. As if she'd been sitting, but now her head was at an uncomfortable angle on the armrest.

"Mom," I said. "Are you okay?"

There was no response. I rushed forward and shook her shoulder. "Mom."

She moaned. "Cold."

"You're cold?" I pulled the blanket off the back of the couch and wrapped it around her shoulders. As I did, my hand brushed the back of her neck, which was burning hot. I felt her forehead. Also hot.

"Hold on to me. I'm going to make you more comfortable, then call the doctor."

"You shouldn't have left me," she said. "I wouldn't be sick if you hadn't left me for so long with nobody."

"I'm sorry," I said, guilt pouring through me.

• • •

I'd placed a cold compress on my mom's head and given her some ibuprofen per the doctor's instructions. If the fever didn't break by the morning or rose over one hundred three, I was supposed to take her to the hospital. Right now, several hours later, it was still hanging steady at one hundred two.

"Does anything specific hurt?" I asked her now as she blinked awake from a short nap.

"My leg," she said.

I inspected her leg, which was still in a cast, but her foot and the skin around her knee all seemed to be the right color. No signs of an infection or anything. I took the cloth off her forehead to rewet it. I brought it back and draped it onto her hot skin. Her hand reached up and grabbed hold of my wrist. I sat down on the floor next to the couch, allowing her to hold my wrist in her grip. "Do you need water? Or some food?"

"No," she said. "Your father called yesterday."

I took in a shallow breath. I wasn't going to tell her Dad called. Not after our conversation that went nowhere. I hadn't realized he'd called her too, however. "Oh, yeah?" I asked.

"He said he might come," she said.

I closed my eyes. I wanted to kill him. "And . . . do you think he will?" I asked softly.

"No," she said. A tear escaped from the corner of her eye and ran down her temple.

"I think you were right about Elijah," I said in response. "He says whatever it takes to make everyone happy, even if he doesn't mean it." Like Dad, I didn't add. I still wondered how much of what Elijah had said was a lie. Had he known the woman pretending to be Dr. Franklin before our sessions? Had he known Michael knew her?

"I told you," Mom said.

I laid my head on a small patch of cushion next to her arm. "You did."

I'd dimmed the lights during her nap, and an overhead fan spun on its lowest setting above us. The breeze tickled the small hairs on the back of my neck that had escaped the ponytail I'd pulled my hair into earlier. The cushion smelled of the lavender laundry detergent we used.

After several moments of silence, Mom drew in a breath. "I'm angry all the time."

"I know," I said. Maybe it was taking until now to realize that's exactly what it was, this distance between my mom and me. She'd been angry for fifteen years, and I'd been the nearest target. I wondered if this was the closest thing I'd ever get to an apology from her. "I'm mad at him too." And by *him*, in this instance, I meant my father.

She gently patted my head. "You'll be okay."

"So will you."

CHAPTER 42

"Knock, knock," Tara said, poking her head into our hospital room. "I heard you were here."

I'd taken my mom to the hospital early that morning because nothing had changed overnight. The rotating Tylenol and ibuprofen schedule and cold compresses throughout the night had done nothing to shake her fever.

"Hi," I whispered, getting up from where I'd been attempting to sleep in a chair. It wasn't working. My mom was on fluids and antibiotics and was very much asleep. They still weren't sure why she had a fever, but they were running tests and treating it like an infection in the meantime.

I joined Tara at the door. She opened it wider and I stepped out.

She immediately pulled me into a hug. "Are you okay?"

"I'm tired," I said. "Wait, why wouldn't I be okay? Is this more serious than the doctor made it seem?"

"No," she said, walking toward a row of chairs across the

hall. "No. It's just a lot. You went away for a weekend and you came back to this."

"Yeah," I said. I came back to a lot more than this, but I couldn't think about that right now. With everything that had happened with my mom, I hadn't followed through with my threat to Michael about telling Tara. And I was honestly too emotionally and physically exhausted to want to tell her now, even though I knew I should.

"She was fine when I hung out with her Friday. Maybe she just caught a bug or something," Tara said.

"That's what the doctor said."

She sat down. "I broke up with Michael, ended our engagement."

"Whoa, what?"

"You know why."

So he *actually* told her on his own. I nodded slowly while I sank into the chair beside her. "Are *you* okay?"

"No," she said, her flat expression unchanging. "But it was my only choice, right? He lied to me and jumped through a million hoops for what? To get out of a few weeks of therapy? How stupid is that?"

"It's pretty stupid."

She sighed. "If he can't even do this one little thing for me, how is he going to be as a husband? A father?"

"I'm sorry."

She blinked rapidly, obviously trying to hold back some emotions.

"I'm sorry," I said again. "About not going to the piano recital with you."

Her head whipped over to me. "What?"

I took a deep breath. Why did I shut people out so much?

I needed to be more open. Talk. Let her in. She'd long since proven she belonged in my life.

"My dad played the violin. Plays. Of course, you know that," I said, shaking my head.

"Yes."

"I had watched so many concerts. He had left out of nowhere . . . I was devastated. I didn't know if I could go watch another concert. Be there on that stage with you when the last stage I'd been on was his. I know I blamed it on my mom, and she *had* recruited me in her angry cleaning. She was on one that day." I let out a breathy laugh. "Every day. But I could've left. I mean, I should've left, gone with you."

"I thought you were embarrassed, didn't like all the attention on you."

"I didn't. I don't. But it was about my dad."

"I didn't know that."

"I know. I don't know that I fully knew that either at the time. I was always pretty private, suppressed a lot of things. Especially about my parents. But you were always a good friend. Made me feel light. Made me feel better. I'm sorry I couldn't do that for you that day."

She pulled me into a hug. "Thanks for saying that. It means a lot."

I nodded against her cheek. "I'm sorry you gave up piano because of me."

She wiped at her eyes as she pulled away. "No, Sutton, what? I didn't. It wasn't because of you. That was just the last straw. I'd never wanted to do it. I hope you haven't been feeling guilty about that all this time."

"Guilt is one of my main food groups."

She smiled. "I fear it's one of mine too."

"We need to work on that."

"I agree." She sighed. "Enough about that. How was your weekend with Elijah?"

"Good. Really good. Then we came home and it blew up."

"It did?"

"He didn't want to tell you about how Michael lied and I did. It was a whole thing."

"Don't call it off over our problems."

"It's more than that. I overheard Michael say that Elijah thinks I was just a short-term thing and that I have daddy issues."

"Elijah thinks *you* have daddy issues? That's pretty ironic coming from him, the *king* of daddy issues."

"Yeah. I mean, he's not wrong. I do. But still, he didn't need to tell the world."

She laughed.

"And he was defending everyone else in this situation except me. Michael, Fake Dr. Franklin." I sighed and slumped against the back of the chair.

She did the same. Our hands were linked. "That sucks."

"Yeah," I said.

"Out of curiosity," she said, "before all this, did *you* see Elijah as more than a short-term thing? I figured since he was here and can't really leave anytime soon and you're nearly out the door, that it would be over."

"I wasn't sure *how* I was going to keep Elijah in my life. But I wanted to. I'd decided that on our trip."

"And now you don't?"

I thought about her question. "It was already complicated. I guess this made it easy."

"To let go?"

I nodded. "Why do I feel like you're team Elijah here? You think I should give him another chance?"

She let out a tired laugh. "Do you think I should give Michael another chance?"

"I think you've given Michael a lot of chances."

She squeezed my hand. "They're both stupid."

"Agreed."

• • •

"Her leg appears to be healing properly. In fact, we're going to take off her cast while she's here. She'll have to be gentle with it, but she should be able to put some weight on it. Start using it. Her other injuries on her head and abdomen aren't infected. I think she just caught a virus," the doctor said.

I stood at the foot of her bed, watching her sleeping form. "But she'll be okay?"

"Her fever is really high and not budging, so we'd like to keep her here until that shows signs of improvement. But I believe she'll be fine," he said.

I rubbed my arms. "Okay."

"We'll call you if anything changes," he said.

"I can't stay?"

He shook his head. "No, we can't accommodate overnight visitors."

"But you'll definitely call me if something changes and I'll come right away."

"We will."

"I'm first on her call list, right? The first person you'll call."

He lifted her chart from a hook on the wall beside the door. "Sutton . . ."

"Yes."

"You are . . . the second."

I sighed and nodded toward the hall. My mom appeared to be asleep, but she also could've been listening. We stepped out of the room.

"Is Charles Scott the first on her emergency contacts?" I asked.

"Yes," he said.

"That's my dad and he hasn't been back here in fifteen years. And he's not coming back. Can you call me first? And second and third? Can you take him off the list?"

"That part is up to your mother."

Wasn't that the truth? It was always up to my mother, and she always seemed to make the wrong choice. I wondered if, after our talk last night, that would change.

"But I will make a note to call you first," he said.

"Thank you."

• • •

I didn't know what to do with myself back at the house. I'd already cleaned and organized and done several loads of laundry, full of all my mom's blankets from her bed and coverings from the couch. My phone had been in my pocket the entire time, in case I got any calls. I hadn't. I was exhausted, but also, I couldn't sleep.

I pulled my phone out and dialed a number.

"Hi," Raya answered in a soft voice.

"Did you get the tickets? I sent them yesterday."

"I got them. Thank you."

"I'm sorry," I said, tears immediately springing to my eyes. "I trust you. You're doing an amazing job, and I couldn't do any of this without you. I want to be different. I feel like I've learned so much in the last couple months here about myself and my past and my issues, and I can't change overnight, but I am aware that I need to. That I need to let go of the tight grip I like to have on everything. But also, I do have problems with trust, and it doesn't help that half the time they are unfounded and half the time they are completely right. But not with you. Never with you. You've been perfect."

"I have not been perfect," she said. "And I'm not mad anymore. I get it, Sutton. And it's not fair of me to appreciate your nature when it benefits me and our business and not appreciate it when it doesn't."

"But I understand. I don't have to be so controlling all the time."

"No, you don't. I bet you'd feel much better if you weren't as well."

I chuckled. "I'm sure I would."

"Did something happen?"

I sat down on the couch, the blankets I had just taken out of the dryer were in a pile next to me, and I pulled one over, its warmth seeping into my legs. "What do you mean?"

"You said half the time your trust issues are justified. Did something happen?"

I told her about therapy and Michael and Fake Dr. Franklin and Elijah and finished with, "So yeah . . . justified."

"Wow," she said. "What a bunch of assholes."

"Yeah."

"You should definitely tell her sister. The real doctor. She'd be horrified."

"Maybe," I said. "Maybe she'd think this was funny too. And what would I say to her? So yeah, we were lying to your sister about needing therapy, and she was lying back to us about being a therapist. You might want to talk to her about that."

"Yeah, I guess this is messy and all morally gray."

"I don't think I'm mad at Fake Dr. Franklin anymore. She probably has a crush on Michael or something, wanted to do it for him. Thought we'd all think it was funny. I'm mad at . . ."

"Elijah? He was more than just a fling, wasn't he?"

I took a deep breath and hugged the blanket to my chest. It was no longer dryer-warm. "I really liked him. Probably loved him. More than I have anyone in a while. But I don't trust him now."

"Even though he's not the one who lied?"

"But I don't know that. At the very least, he was completely ready to lie to Tara for his brother. If he could lie so easily, what else is he lying about? Maybe nothing. But maybe everything."

"What would he have to do to make you believe him?"

"He's done nothing. He told me I was taking this all too seriously, that I was looking for a reason not to trust him, and let me walk away. I don't think I have to worry too much about what it would take for me to believe him. He doesn't care enough to try to make me."

"Oh, babe, I'm sorry."

I shook my head, even though she couldn't see me. "It's fine. Don't be sorry."

"It's not fine. You're sad."

I sucked in some air at her words, and my chest expanded with an intense ache. Tears filled my eyes and streamed down my face. "I'm sad."

CHAPTER 43

I woke up with a start, as if someone had yanked me out of sleep. I didn't like that feeling. It was disorienting and something I wasn't used to. My body normally woke up gently, at the same time every day. But I knew it wasn't six thirty in the morning. It was pitch black. I'd fallen asleep sometime in the early evening, on the couch, on top of the unfolded pile of cold blankets. My eyes hurt from crying so much. Raya had comforted me the best she could. But after we'd hung up, I couldn't stop crying. I'd cried myself to sleep.

I checked my phone, there were zero messages. I was right, it wasn't my normal wake-up time. It was three AM. I sat up and a stab of pain in the side of my neck made me wince. I must've slept at a weird angle.

I rubbed at it and looked around. The small light over the stove was on, but other than that, I could barely see. The sink was dripping, I'd never called a plumber, and the fridge was humming.

I'd never felt so alone.

I lived by myself in Los Angeles. Most mornings I woke up alone. But this felt different. Maybe because when I woke up at home, I immediately started moving, getting ready for the day. I hardly had a spare second to think. Or maybe it was because I hadn't woken up alone for the last three days and the contrast was stark.

I pressed my palms to my eyes. I hadn't gotten ready for bed the night before, and the mascara on my lashes felt crusty and stiff. I made my way into the bathroom to shower. I had put the shower fern I'd brought from home inside. Even that didn't help me feel less lonely. I absentmindedly performed the routines of washing my hair and body, then got out, dried off, and dressed myself.

Then I was staring at my phone again. It was too early to go back to the hospital. It was way too early to call Raya for our daily business talk.

I pulled up Elijah's number in my text app. I'm sad and I miss you. I typed those words, then immediately erased them.

I don't know how you can convince me that you didn't know about Fake Dr. Franklin when you were so willing to lie for Michael about the whole thing, but I need you to try.

I thought about actually sending that one, but instead, I slowly erased it as well.

You don't want to talk about it? Change my mind? Nothing?

That one I sent.

I immediately thought about unsending it, but then I saw the three dots light up on my phone indicating he was typing back. It was three forty-five in the morning, and he was texting back. He must not have been able to sleep either.

I've been called a fling, a boy toy, and a liar all in one weekend.

I didn't think you wanted to hear anything I had to say. I didn't think you'd *believe* anything I had to say.

I blinked. He wasn't wrong. I knew he'd heard my mom call him a boy toy. I didn't think he'd heard Raya call him a fling, but he must've. And I had definitely implied he was a liar.

Shit.

Was *I* the one in the wrong here?

No. He told his brother I had daddy issues and was temporary. He defended his brother when he lied and used us and then acted like I was the one overreacting, the one *taking this all too seriously*. And now, instead of fighting for me, for us, he was just abandoning me. I was not going to repeat history. I could not become my mother.

For the record, I typed. I did not call you a fling or a boy toy, but I'm sorry other people did. As for the liar part, we're obviously both liars. And the biggest lie of all was thinking this could work.

You knew this could never work, he replied.

I sucked in some air, the words stabbing me in the gut. That hurt. More than any breakup before ever had. But was it even a breakup when we were never really together? I couldn't refer to it as a breakup. Not even to myself.

I lay back down on the couch and stared at the dark ceiling until I fell asleep.

• • •

"Are you feeling better?" I asked on the drive home from the hospital. My emotions hovered just below the surface, the sadness, and I was trying my best to keep them at bay. Mom's fever had broken overnight, and the doctor said she was eating and drinking like normal and seemed to be on the mend. He discharged her with instructions to bring her back if she got worse.

"Much," she said. "He said I could start driving soon."

"Are you not dizzy anymore?"

"That cleared up a few days ago."

"That's good."

When we got to the house, she asked for her scooter instead of her wheelchair, and I thought that was a good sign as well.

Once I had her settled onto the couch with some water and the remote, I said, "I'm going to take a nap."

Her head whipped in my direction, concern on her face. "You don't nap." She wasn't wrong, I couldn't remember the last time I took a nap.

"I'm tired. I haven't slept well." After finally falling asleep the night before, I'd woken up several times before giving up around six o'clock in the morning.

"Yes, go nap. You *look* like you haven't slept well."

"Thanks, Mom. Appreciate it."

"I'm just agreeing with you," she said as I made my way down the hall.

I slept like the dead, without thoughts or dreams, and woke up disoriented, not sure what time it was or where I was for several long moments. The sadness was still there though. I rolled onto my back and stared at the ceiling. The blinds on my window were framed by light, so I knew it was still daytime. I draped my arm over my eyes, not sure why that thought made me even sadder.

Maybe it was because I knew I had to get up and check on my mother, cook her something for dinner that wouldn't be good enough.

I crawled my way out of bed and to the bathroom, where I brushed my teeth for the second time that day and used the toilet.

My mom was where I had left her.

She gave me a single glance when I walked in, then was back to watching her show, some law drama.

I sighed. "Are you hungry?"

"For what?" she asked, because that might change her answer.

"I don't know. Whatever I can find in the kitchen."

"Okay," she said.

I went there, opening the fridge and surveying our options. But then I shut the fridge with a sigh and turned to face her. "Mom."

She glanced my way. "Yeah?"

I walked closer. "Will you turn off the TV?"

She looked around for the remote and eventually found it and clicked off the television. "What?"

I stopped myself from blurting out what I wanted to say and instead sat down and took a calming breath before I said, "I think you need to go to therapy. I think it would help."

She gave me a look I'd seen on her face a lot in my life, disappointment combined with incredulity. "When I can get back to work in a couple weeks, I'll be fine."

"I don't think you've been fine for a long time."

"And you're the picture of perfection?"

"No," I said quickly. "God, no. I was actually seeing a therapist for a little while." Sure, it was a fake therapist, but even that had been helpful. "Not for my things, but . . . long story. Anyway, it made me realize that I need to go back for real. I have a lot to work on. This being one of those things." I pointed between the two of us.

"I've screwed you up? Is that what you're saying?"

"Yes. But we all screw each other up. Dad and you and me and life and friendships and relationships. We all get dragged around, and we all have damage from it. Some of us worse than others."

"I just need to get back to work," Mom said, her hand gripping the remote like she wanted to forget what I was saying and watch her show.

"Okay." I stood. At least I'd said something. I couldn't choose for her, but I could choose for myself, and I was done having a toxic, guilt-ridden relationship with my mother. I would come when I wanted to and leave when I wanted to from now on. No more set schedules that I felt I had to stick to in order to prove to her I wasn't going to abandon her. I had proven that to her time and again. Now it was her turn to put some work into this relationship. "I'm going back home after we get you a car," I said.

"When can we do that?" she asked, the first excitement I'd heard in her voice in a while.

I looked at her cast-free leg. The doctor said it would be a little while before it was fully functional. "A week," I decided.

CHAPTER 44

My suitcase was packed, all my clothes clean and rolled into perfect little rows. It was the only thing in my life that felt anywhere close to perfect right now. I shut and zipped it, then gave my room a once-over, to make sure I hadn't forgotten anything.

It had been ten days since I told my mom I was going to leave. One week ago, I'd helped her pick out a car. But it wasn't until yesterday that her doctor finally cleared her to drive it. Which was why I stayed three days past when I said I would. I may have declared new boundaries, but I wasn't going to leave her stuck at home. Yes, old habits were hard to break. Starting today, I would only visit when I wanted and leave when I wanted.

I paused at the desk in my room. Two things remained on top. One was the flyer for Elijah's boxing tournament that was happening this Saturday. I wondered if he would keep working there forever, or if he'd tell his dad that he didn't want to run the gym anymore. He wanted to fail or thrive on his own terms.

An ache still throbbed in my chest when I thought about him. I wasn't used to those kinds of things lingering. I usually did such a good job of shutting off my emotions, packing any negative feelings into a box and not thinking about them ever again. But the box I'd tried to put all my sad feelings into kept bursting open, kept making me reach for the phone but never call him, pick up my car keys but never drive to him. His box with any feelings about me in it was obviously sealed tight and thrown off a cliff.

I sighed as my eyes lingered on the second thing on my desk: the scratch-off that Fake Dr. Franklin had given me. Was this scratch-off part of *real* Dr. Franklin's marriage tools? Her sister had taken it out of a drawer in the office. I had only revealed the one square that had prompted me to write the sexy text. My finger ran slowly over the other boxes. The penny I'd used to scratch off the filmy top layer still sat next to the paper on the desktop. I sank into my chair and, slowly at first and then almost frantically, scratched off the remaining four boxes. When I was done, I brushed off the debris and leaned back in my chair to read.

Appetizer: Before dinner, go to a park or hiking trail or beach. Take your shoes off and feel the earth as you tell each other something that you loved about your childhood.

I blinked at the prompt. She went from *send a sexy text* to *feel the earth under your feet as you talk about your childhood*? After the sexy text, this would feel like false advertising.

I read on.

Main course: Order food for each other without showing the other person what you ordered. Share one of your favorite things about each other.

Letting someone order for me would've been hard for me to do. I flipped the page over—was this numbered? Did she know she had given me this specific sheet? Sexy text, talk about childhood, and let someone else pick my dinner felt tailor-made to my specific issues. There was no number on the back. Maybe they were all the same. I kept reading.

Dessert: Take an after-dinner walk in your dream neighborhood. Talk about something that scares you about the future.

Nightcap: Stay fully clothed while you touch and describe each body part of the other person, out loud.

I let out a single laugh. That escalated quickly. Elijah and I had mostly done the first and the last prompts of this exercise. I hadn't described his body parts out loud, but I sure had touched them. The memory made my cheeks go pink. Why did she want us to describe body parts? So we got more comfortable with each other? So we started asking for what we wanted in bed? So that we got extra horny? I flipped the page over again—had I missed a square? The square that said, *Now make passionate love.* Maybe that was just the natural outcome of the last prompt. I quickly folded the page and shoved it into my shoulder bag along with the tournament flyer.

Then I strapped my bag across my body and wheeled my suitcase out of the bedroom.

Mom was standing in the kitchen, meal prepping. She was going back to work the next day. I hadn't seen her this happy in a long time. All day she'd been humming in the kitchen, staring out the window at her car, glaring at the scooter I still hadn't taken back to the hospital. I needed to do that on my way out of town.

"I'm going to load my car," I said.

"Okay, sounds good."

I stepped outside, it was a beautiful day. The sun was shining, big puffy clouds exploded across the blue backdrop of the sky, and the trees seemed a brighter green than normal. I was happy to be going home, I told myself. So happy. And I was . . . I should be. I wanted to be . . . needed to be.

I put my things in the back seat and then popped the trunk in preparation for the scooter. I headed back inside.

Mom had her Tupperware containers out and was filling them with chicken and rice. She looked up when I walked in. "You should never wear cream," she said. "It's not the right color for you."

"Not nice, Mom," I said.

"How is that not nice? I'm giving you tips about your complexion."

"Okay, thanks for the tip I didn't ask for." I walked to her side, leaned forward, and kissed her cheek. "I'm glad you're doing better."

"Me too," she said.

"We'll talk soon?"

"Okay, hon, bye."

I cried on the way to the hospital. I'd never cried this much in my life. Maybe my body was trying to release all the negative energy it had stored over the past fifteen years. I was able to pull myself together by the time I made it inside and returned the scooter. I had texted Tara on the way over, and she met me in the cafeteria.

"How are you?" I asked her. I'd seen her twice in the last ten days. One time she had been happy that she had *dodged a bullet*; the next time she'd claimed her life was over.

"Meh," she said. "How are you?"

"Same," I agreed. "Will you come visit me in Los Angeles sometime?"

"Yes!" she said. "Please." She gave me a tight hug. "I don't believe you're leaving."

"I know," I said, hugging her back.

"Any word from Elijah?"

I shook my head, barely managing to hold back another wave of tears.

"Then let him go. This can be the first day of the rest of your life," she said.

I forced out a laugh. "Here I come."

The four-hour car ride home was brutal. What started out as me repeating the mantra—*the first day of the rest of my life*—turned into me wondering if I'd made a mistake. That then turned into me realizing that maybe I was wrong. My trust issues had turned him into a liar, not his lies. What if he hadn't lied? And if he hadn't lied, he had every right to be angry at my accusations. Especially after being called a boy toy and a fling.

"Shit," I said, as I pulled into my parking garage. "I'm the problem."

CHAPTER 45

"Don't get me wrong, I'm glad to have you back," Raya said as I wiped down the counters in the kitchen after a slow Friday night. "But you've been mopey all week."

"Do you know how many places in my apartment we had sex?" I scrubbed at a spot of barbecue sauce on the edge of the stove.

"Um . . . no? And I'm scared you're about to tell me."

"Pretty much all of them. Every single place. My bedroom, the couch, the shower. Everywhere except the kitchen. I can't go anywhere in my apartment without thinking about him. He's so lucky we never did it in his apartment!" I raised the rag in the air to emphasize my point. "Oh, and the wall. I can't even look at the wall he pushed me up against."

"Don't forget the office," Raya said in an even voice.

"How could I forget the office? See, I can't come to work either. Sex is everywhere I look."

"I really don't want to hear this," Raya said.

"You think *I* want to hear this? See it in my head?"

"No?" she guessed.

"I shouldn't be thinking about it at all. I need to be here, figuring out how to get that asshole of a reviewer to make another viral review that hopefully will be glowing this time." Because business was struggling. I'd gone over the books when I got back, and we were barely breaking even.

"But we can't have him back until we do something cool."

"Exactly! But my brain won't even let me think of something cool because it's too busy thinking of . . ."

"Awesome sex?" she guessed.

I let out an ironic laugh. "Yes . . . and the fact that he has this big tournament tomorrow where he's going to miserably fill out score sheets and manually add numbers. I told him I'd help. I thought maybe after the tournament he'd talk to his dad. Tell him he was unhappy there. But maybe he only said he was unhappy there to make me happy."

"Why would that make *you* happy?" she asked.

"Because if he didn't like his job, then he would have an excuse to leave Clovis. He could come here. But coming here was never his plan. And even if it was, he still had to climb out of the hole, pay his dad back. He was never going to leave until he did that. And I just ran away. Left him there. Shit, Raya, I ran away."

"You did."

"Maybe I should go back?" I said. "At least to talk to him face-to-face. Help him with this tournament. Do you think he'd want me there? Do you think he'd take me back? I don't deserve to be taken back."

"Sutton," Raya chastised. "It's been a couple weeks since your fight, not fifteen years. You didn't abandon him. You were scared and you left. Now you're seeing you were wrong."

"I was wrong."

"Then go get your man."

"I'm still scared."

"I know. Do it anyway."

• • •

The gym was full. Fuller than I'd ever seen it. Tables were set up and people were checking in. On the walls, schedules were posted. I'd left my house at four AM to make it for the eight o'clock start time. I'd made it with fifteen minutes to spare.

Right away I saw Michael in the boxing ring, talking to some fighters. Elijah's dad was walking the perimeter, directing people. But I didn't see Elijah anywhere.

It was loud, with both music being piped through speakers and voices and people warming up on punching bags along the wall. I headed for the back office, but he wasn't there either. The window was dark and the door was locked. I turned away from the door just in time to see Michael ducking through the ropes of the ring and hopping to the floor.

His expression immediately went dark upon seeing me. "What are you doing here?"

"Where is Elijah?"

He shrugged. "Sent a text that he wasn't coming."

I blinked in surprise. "Wasn't coming? Is he okay? Hurt? Did he say why?"

"No, he didn't and why would I tell you if he did?"

I wanted to shake him but instead just clenched my fists. "Your anger is misplaced, Michael. You should be looking in the mirror."

"Whatever," he said, and brushed by me, heading for the front tables.

"And you should have to shave your head," I mumbled to his back.

Elijah wasn't here. Did that mean he talked to his dad? Told him he didn't want to do this? And if he had, then what? Where would he go instead?

Speaking of his dad, he gave me a double take. "Have you spoken to Elijah?" he asked.

I shook my head.

He grumbled under his breath something that sounded like, *What am I going to do with him?* Then he kept walking.

People were moving and talking and laughing and punching all around me, and I just stood there, not sure what to do next. I hadn't thought beyond this moment. I was going to come and talk to Elijah. I was going to help with the tournament. Show him the app I had found for events like these. I was supposed to help, to be here for him. Prove that I was sorry through my actions. But how could I be here for him when he wasn't even here?

I knew how much he loved his family and his brother, even if his brother didn't deserve it half the time. I could still help. I wasn't about to take over with my unwanted app ideas though. Especially because it looked like they had everything under control. But I could check people in or hand out wraps. So I did. I stayed there all day, being extra hands wherever I was needed. I even went on an ice run once. But Elijah never showed up, even though I'd been secretly hoping all day that he would.

The tournament ended at seven, and I left without saying goodbye to anyone. I drove to Elijah's house and stood on his dark porch for several minutes. The inside showed no signs of life either, but finally I knocked. I wasn't surprised when nobody answered, and yet I stayed for five more minutes, just in case.

I released a breath of air and sank down, sitting on the porch steps. Then I pulled out my phone and texted Tara.

Can I crash at your place tonight?

You're in town?!

Yes.

But you're not crashing at Elijah's? I'm sorry. Yes, come over.

She'd obviously put two and two together and figured out I'd come running back for him. And that it hadn't gone well.

She pulled me into a tight hug when I got to her apartment. "Tell me everything."

So I did. We sat on her oversized couch with throw blankets and glasses of wine, and I told her about my week and my decision to drive here and about Elijah being MIA. It was nice to be more open with my friends. I finished with, "Where do you think he is?"

"I don't know," she said. "Maybe he took his camera to the mountains or the beach. He does that sometimes."

To feel the earth under his feet, my mind said, thinking about Dr. Franklin's prompt.

"He does?" I didn't know why I asked. His pictures were proof that he did that sometimes. I just didn't know that he still did that. That he'd done that recently.

As if reading my mind, she said, "Not so much recently. But before he got busy with the gym, before you came into town, he would."

It made sense. That's probably exactly where he was. But how long would he need to commune with nature? Would nature tell him that we were supposed to be together? When would he be back?

"Are you irritated?" I asked.

"Irritated?"

"That I'm trying to make up with Elijah? Despite what he did to you."

She blew air out of her nose. "He didn't do anything to me. Michael did. Elijah was only ever trying to help. You are definitely picking the better brother."

I set my glass of wine, still half full, onto the end table and pulled one knee to my chest. "I might be picking him, but I'm not sure he'll pick me back. I don't know that he wants anything to do with me."

"I've never seen him like anyone as much as he liked you. The way he looked at you, the way he held your hand, or touched your back. He'll pick you, Sutton. I know it."

"I hope you're right."

CHAPTER 46

I should text him. Tell him I am here. For him. Maybe he'd come back. For me.

These thoughts circled my brain as I lay on Tara's couch later that night. Much like my apartment, hers was only a one-bedroom. She'd brought me sheets and blankets and a pillow when I'd insisted I sleep on the couch instead of sharing her bed like she'd offered. I knew I'd toss and turn tonight. She had to work in the morning. I wanted her to get sleep.

I lowered my phone without sending a message. Texting seemed so anticlimactic. How could I dramatically announce my presence if I texted him a warning first? But if he didn't know I was here, I wouldn't be able to announce my presence at all. Things didn't always go exactly like I planned or imagined them, and I was learning to be okay with that.

I huffed out some air and raised my phone again, trying to think of the perfect text. It could not involve the word *tongue*, I knew that much.

Elijah . . . I'm here. You're not. If you'll hear me out, I have things to say. But I'd love to do it in person. Are you coming home anytime soon?

I read the text at least ten times before I let myself hit send. When I finally did, my heart began beating a million miles per minute. Then I bit my lip and waited. Last time I'd sent him a late-night text, he responded almost immediately. This time there were no little blinking dots indicating he was writing back. There was only silence. And it stayed that way for however long it took me to accept that he wasn't writing me back, at least not tonight. I rolled onto my side, set my phone on the carpet, and tried to sleep.

• • •

"Sorry, sorry," Tara whispered as something in the adjoining kitchen clattered on the counter.

I cracked my eyes open. She stood, fitting a lid onto her travel coffee cup. "It's okay," I croaked. "Are you heading to work?" She wore her scrubs, and her purse was already strapped across her body. I sat up, adjusting the T-shirt I wore and running my fingers through my hair.

"I am, but you can stay as long as you need. I'll leave you a key here, and if you'll just put it in the plant outside my door when you leave . . . or maybe you're staying longer? You're welcome to stay as long as you want," she rambled this out in one continuous stream of thought.

"No, I'm leaving. Probably. I need to if . . ." My eyes drifted down to my phone on the floor. It sat face up and no notifications were waiting for me. "Yeah, I'm leaving," I finished through a tight throat.

"I'm sorry," she said, scrunching her nose in sympathy.

"No, it's fine. Grand gestures are kind of pointless when the other person isn't around to see them."

"You going to see your mom while you're here?"

I thought about that question. "I don't think so. I'm already in a terrible mood."

She laughed.

I'd set a boundary with my mom, and I wasn't going to feel guilty about it. I'd talked to her once this week, and she told me all about how happy she was to be back at work. I was glad for her. She had sounded happier.

After Tara left, I got up and brushed my teeth and got dressed. Then I cleaned Tara's kitchen. It was already pretty clean, but I scrubbed out the microwave and wiped down the fronts of all the appliances. I was lingering. Waiting for a response to my text. It took way too long for me to admit I wasn't getting one.

• • •

The Los Angeles traffic seemed insufferable at the end of my already-long drive. How did people live with this many humans and cars around them? How did I? I was suddenly dreaming of long stretches of empty roads bordered by orchids as far as the eye could see.

My phone rang through the car speakers, too loud, making me jump. I answered it with a tap on my steering wheel. "Raya, hi. Is everything okay?"

"No," she said. "Where are you?"

"I'm about twenty minutes from you."

"You're almost home?" she asked. "I thought you would still be in Clovis."

"Nope," I said, popping the *p* on the word.

"Oh," she said, her voice indicating she knew what that meant. "That sucks."

"It's . . ." I almost said it was okay. But I couldn't. "Yeah, it does," I finished with instead.

"Would you hate me if I sent you on some work errands? We're busier than normal tonight and completely out of potatoes. Can you grab some at the store?"

"Seriously? We can't seem to get the quantity right on those."

"I know."

"Yes, of course I'll grab some. I'll be there in thirty."

"Thanks, you're a lifesaver."

While I was at the store, she texted me several more things they needed, and I ended up taking longer than I anticipated. It was close to eight o'clock by the time I got there, and the windows looked dark as I walked up. Did the potato shortage force them to close early? I couldn't imagine that would be the case, but my mind wasn't supplying any other explanation for what my eyes were seeing. I pulled out my keys, expecting the door to be locked, but when I turned the key in the lock, it met zero resistance. I opened the door. The lights suddenly flipped on, and a restaurant full of people yelled, "Surprise!"

The tables had been moved into a big line in the center of the room, the chairs missing, most likely stacked out back to provide more floor space. I recognized some of the people in the room, but most I didn't.

Raya walked forward.

"Our one-year anniversary celebration?" I asked, remembering this was what she wanted to do to commemorate it. But then I noticed something—painted branches climbing up the walls and onto the now sky-blue ceiling. And leaves. But the leaves weren't painted. They seemed three-dimensional. Photographs. They were pictures forming the shape of leaves. As my eyes followed the branches, looking for a trunk, I saw that they all led to the back patio door.

"Good surprise or bad surprise?" Raya asked, hooking her arm into mine. "I would normally run big decisions like this by you but . . . do you like it?"

I nodded, slowly realizing what this meant. "It's amazing."

I walked toward the back door, wanting to see the rest of the design. Knowing there was more. I was right. The ceiling of the covered patio was dark, like a night sky dotted with lights that made it seem like stars were shining through. And the painted branches continued all the way to the actual tree in the center. Hanging from that tree were more photos. But these photos were of people, customers sitting at our tables, enjoying our food. A centerpiece that would draw people to it. A water feature now bubbled to the right of the tree. And down the walls of the restaurant were more photos that looked like leaves.

"I was here two days ago . . . how?" I asked.

"It's impressive, right?" Raya said.

"Where is he?" Everything in me needed to know this. I wanted to be in his arms, against his skin, in his life. I hoped this meant I could do all three of these things. I hoped this was some grand gesture and not some guilt-induced goodbye.

"Now this is something to brag about," a man stepped in front of me whom I immediately recognized as the viral reviewer of the restaurant.

"Oh, right," Raya said. "I invited Samuel back."

"I'm glad she did," he said.

My brain was slow, taking moments to process everything,

still searching out the patio for Elijah. But I had enough sense to put my hand out. "Thank you for coming. For giving us another chance."

"Second chances are my favorite," he said.

"I hope they're about to be mine too," I said. "Please excuse me." I rushed back toward the door leading inside when I realized that Elijah was there, standing in front of it. He had an uncertain look on his face. I came to a halt five feet before reaching him, also uncertain. Not about how I felt but about why he had done all this.

"Hi," I said. "You're here."

"I'm here."

"This is amazing. I can't believe you did this in two days."

"I had a lot of help. You like it?"

"I love it."

His shoulders relaxed, dropping a couple inches. "I'm sorry I didn't answer your text. I was trying to surprise you, and it's not as impactful if I tell you over text."

"How did you know I wouldn't be here?"

"I didn't know you wouldn't be here. I just showed up. But then when you weren't here, I thought bigger."

"It's . . . beautiful. Thank you." All around us people were chatting and laughing and looking at the pictures. Inside, through the window, I saw Presley refilling trays of finger food. Behind me, Raya was still chatting with the reviewer. Over Elijah's right shoulder there were more leaves made out of photos. "Did you take all these pictures . . . recently?"

"Some," he said. "But I borrowed a lot from my childhood bedroom as well."

"You did? Your mom hates me," I said. She loved that setup. Had left it up for all these years.

"She doesn't. She really likes you," Elijah said, then he sighed. "I didn't know about Dr. Franklin. That she wasn't real. That she was a friend. She was *his* friend, not mine."

"I know."

"You know?"

"I mean, I believe you. I was in Clovis, at a boxing tournament yesterday, helping."

"You went to the boxing tournament?"

"I did."

"Why?"

"Because it was important to you, and I knew you were stressed about it. And I found an app that I didn't end up using because I didn't want to be controlling, but it ran just fine anyway. And I'm pretty sure I love you."

A smile spread across his face. "*Pretty* sure?"

"All the way sure."

He nodded and again a breath of doubt whispered into my ear. Why was he still five feet away? Why wasn't he saying it back? Why hadn't he kissed me yet?

I swallowed.

"Can I just . . . can we just . . . ?" He took my hand and led me inside, then around the tables and groups of people. He pushed through the doors to the back, continued down the hall and into the office. "It was loud out there," he said, facing me. "Say it again."

"I believe you. I know you weren't lying about Dr. Franklin."

"No, not that part."

"The tournament? It went really well. I'm guessing you did a lot of that setup work. I'm sure that's why it ran so well."

"Sutton. Not that part either."

"Which part?" I asked with a smile.

"You know which part."

I took a step toward him, put a hand on his chest, and said, "I love you, Elijah."

He pulled me into a tight hug. His lips brushed along my temple, and he said, "They weren't talking about you. My brother and Fake Dr. Franklin. They were talking about *me*. The daddy issues thing. That was me. *I* have those issues. My brother was telling her about those issues, apparently. And the boxing gym, *that* was temporary, at least me working there was. I'd told my brother the gym was temporary, that I wasn't having fun anymore. It was never about you."

"Are you not going to say it back?" I asked. I'd heard what he said, and that all helped me feel even better about everything, but I was hung up on what he *wasn't* saying.

"What?" he asked.

"Do you not feel the same?" I'd put some space between us so I could look him in the eyes with the question.

He only seemed confused.

"I mean, if you're not there yet, I get it, but . . . are you not there yet?"

"Where yet?"

"In love. With me."

His eyes went wide. "Fuck. Yes! I'm sorry, I thought I said it. I've been thinking it since I saw you tonight. Since way before that. Since you punched me in the face. Since you sat on my lap and asked me if I wanted eggs. Since you showered with a fern. Since you ordered limes in your sleep. Since you threw a dirty napkin at my head. I love you, Sutton." He took my face in his hands and brought my lips to his. He kissed me softly, lingering there. "I love you."

My whole body melted into his, and my eyes stung with

happy tears. I smiled against his mouth. "I don't order limes in my sleep."

"You do. And it's the cutest thing ever."

"Sit down. I need to tell you the story about that napkin I threw at your head, and then maybe we should use another one."

He laughed. "I can't wait to hear it."

I kissed him before he sat down and then again when he sat down, and we didn't get to the story until much later.

EPILOGUE

Six Months Later

"I've never lived with a man," I said as I carried a box full of Elijah's stuff toward my . . . our . . . apartment.

He was also carrying a box and he laughed. "So I've heard."

"And I'm working on it, but you know I'm particular."

"I hadn't noticed."

I smiled his way. His laid-back nature had actually helped me relax as well, not need to control every little thing. Maybe that's what trust did for a relationship. I hadn't been able to depend on most people in my life until now. But I could depend on him. For the last six months we'd gone back and forth between Los Angeles and Clovis. He was winding down his role in the boxing gym when in Clovis and picking up his camera when in Los Angeles. Mine wasn't the only restaurant now that he'd helped find a style through photography. His specialty was bringing nature indoors in unique ways, and he was building a name for himself. I was so proud of him.

In Clovis, I would visit Tara and sometimes my mom. My dad never showed up. That wasn't a surprise. The surprise came when something clicked inside my mom and she stopped calling him, stopped making excuses for him. She wasn't perfect, she was still overly critical and negative, but she was thinking about going to therapy and I could tell she was trying.

And now, Elijah was moving here, and our lives were going to involve much less driving and much more time together. I wasn't nervous at all. I was only excited.

"I still want the right side of the bed," I said, unlocking the front door. A package sat on my doormat, and I kicked it inside as I walked in after it.

"You've *had* the right side of the bed. I gave it to you six months ago."

"I just wanted to make sure you weren't taking it back."

He smacked my butt as he followed me inside and I laughed.

Just as I slid the box I held onto the table in the breakfast nook, my phone rang. "Raya, hey."

"We need to hire another server." Ever since our restaurant makeover and new viral review six months ago, we'd been busy. More than busy, waiting list busy. I'd already hired another server.

"Did you have someone in mind?" I asked.

"Yes," she said. "Already did the preliminary interviews. Do you want to meet her first?"

"No, I trust you." Raya and I were rarely both at the restaurant at the same time anymore, like we'd been that first year. Looking back, I realized it was because I'd had to be involved in every minuscule decision. I hadn't trusted her. But she'd more than earned my trust, and I was finally giving it to her.

Because I didn't spend fourteen-hour days there anymore, I'd had more time. More time to go on nature hikes and walk on the beach and watch Elijah take pictures. I was happy. So happy. And I only thought about the fact that it could all be snatched away from me about once a month now. That was progress.

I pulled the tape off the box I'd just set down and opened one of the flaps. The leaf of a plant poked out. It took me a second to realize it was fake.

"Thanks," Raya said on the phone. "You're in tomorrow, right?"

"Yes," I said. "You're not."

"I miss you," she said. "Can we do a double date soon or at least a shift together?"

I laughed. "Absolutely."

We hung up the phone, and I lifted the plant out of the box and turned toward Elijah, who was sitting on the couch unloading the box he'd brought in. "What is this atrocity?" I asked.

"Not all of us can keep real plants alive," he said.

I set the plastic plant on the table and walked over to him. He seemed to know what was coming because he shifted to the back of the cushion. I sat on his lap, straddling him, his hands immediately cupping my ass, a smile on his face.

"You can't take care of live plants? But you're so attentive and thoughtful and nurturing." I rocked against him.

"Don't use the word *nurturing* when you're straddling me."

"Is that a bad word? I thought it was a compliment."

"It makes me think of motherhood."

"Yeah, don't think of mothers right now. Unless you want to. How are your parents?" His dad had been disappointed in Elijah's decision to walk away from the gym, but his mom had been more than supportive for both of them. And his dad seemed to be coming around. The more photos he saw and the more time we spent with them, the better he seemed. Plus, Elijah was still paying him back.

"How are my *parents*?" he asked with a laugh.

"Yeah, have they said anything else about your move here?" They were sad he was leaving but said they'd visit us soon. Maybe we really would have to move into a two bedroom eventually so we could have more guests.

He took me by the waist and flipped me onto my back, lowering himself onto me. "I'm about to nurture the shit out of you."

I wrapped my legs around him. "Yeah, you're right, not a sexy word."

He laughed and kissed me.

"I'm going to love living with you," I said against his mouth.

ACKNOWLEDGMENTS

I loved writing this book! I hope you loved reading it. I hope you could tell from the contents that I am a pro-therapy person. And maybe I'll start by thanking all the hardworking therapists of the world. Mental health is so important and I hope it can become more accessible to all.

Thanks to my agent, Michelle Wolfson. I know this book is one of your favorites, and I appreciate you loving it so much. I think this is book twenty for us. That's so wild! What an amazing journey we've had together. I wouldn't have wanted to do it with anyone else.

Thank you, Sara Goodman, for your smart suggestions and helping me shape this book into something I am so proud of. I appreciate the support you've given me as I've made this transition into the adult genre. You've been so easy to work with and so fun to have in my corner. And also, thanks to the rest of the team at Saturday books: Zoë Miller, Marissa Sangiacomo, Lexi Neuville, Brant Janeway, and Sarah Pazen. And to my production editor, Cassie Gutman, and my copyeditor,

Naomi Burns. You've all been so kind and lovely and excellent at what you do.

I appreciate my family so much. My husband, Jared, who doesn't bat an eye when reading the sex scenes in my books. Who only says, you're really good at this. He's seriously the best. To my kids, Skyler, Autumn, Abby, and Donavan (who are now adults), thanks for being such great people. I'm so proud of all the things you have done and are doing with your lives. You inspire me every day.

Thanks to the best writing friends a person can have: Bree Despain and Renee Collins. I would not write as much as I do without you both. And also to my amazing friends who get me out from behind my writing screen and help me fill the creative well: Jenn Johansson, Stephanie Ryan, Brittany Swift, Mandy Hillman, Emily Freeman, Megan Grant, and Misti Hamel. Love you all.

And finally, to my super supportive extended family—I have the best—Chris Thompson, Mark Thompson, Heather Garza, Jared DeWoody, Spencer DeWoody, Stephanie Ryan, Dave Garza, Rachel DeWoody, Zita Konik, Kevin Ryan, Vance West, Karen West, Eric West, Michelle West, Sharlynn West, Rachel Braithwaite, Brian Braithwaite, Angie Stettler, Jim Stettler, Emily Hill, Rick Hill, and the twenty-five children and numerous children of children that exist between all these people. I love you all so much.

About the Author

Stephanie Ryan Photography

Kasie West is the author of more than fifteen (and counting) young adult novels. Her books have been named ALA-YALSA Quick Picks, Junior Library Guild Selections, and ALA-YALSA Top Ten Best Books for Young Adults. Her books have been translated into more than twenty languages. Kasie is also the author of *We Met Like This*, her debut adult rom-com. When she's not writing, she's binge-watching television, devouring books, or taking care of her growing collection of houseplants. Kasie lives with her family in central California.